SECOND DAUGHTER

Royals of Dharia 2

SUSAN KAYE QUINN

www.SusanKayeQuinn.com

Cover by Steven Novak

ISBN: 9798330589012

Second Daughter
(Royals of Dharia, Book Two)
fantasy steampunk romance

Chapter One

THE LOVE of the Jungali people washed over Aniri in waves of sound and color.

She stood on the palace balcony, one hand raised, welcoming the applause, the other held gently by Ashoka, the handsome young prince she was supposed to marry within the week. They had returned the night before in Ash's skyship, the *Prosperity*. Now, the morning sun had barely peeked over the white granite walls of his capital city, and they were already addressing his people. He had insisted they make an appearance as soon as possible—to announce their return and to reassure the people that all was well.

Even if that was far from true.

The crowd couldn't all squeeze into the street

below, so the people climbed rooftops and threw open windows, all craning to see the dashing hero who brought home not only their skyship, but a Queen-to-be and a shiny new treaty with the powerful country of Dharia, her home. The mountain air was thin, the sun was warm on her face, and the buildings were painted with brilliant reds, sharp yellows, and blues as deep as the infinite sky above them. The lack of proper air and the too-dazzling colors no longer left her dizzy, even with the tightly bound corset of her royal attire. What lay like a hundred pound weight on her chest was the secret she and Ash were keeping from everyone, one they had discovered on the flight back to Jungali: that the *Prosperity* might not be the only skyship that had been built, and that the Samirians may yet be planning war.

Ash tugged her forward to the silver orb that wired the balcony for transmission throughout his capital city of Bhakti. The warm welcome showed no sign of stopping, so he smiled wide and raised their clasped hands in triumph and celebration. The snapping of fingers and cheerful hollering swelled.

Ash leaned close to whisper, "They love you, Third Daughter of Dharia." His lips brushed her ear lightly as he spoke, sending a delightful shiver across her sun-warmed skin. She ached for a moment alone with him. Not to chase after that shiver with a kiss, but to steal a chance to talk about the possibility of war and what that meant for all three Queendoms. Given that Aniri's sister, the Second Daughter of Dharia, was married to the First Son of Samir, the specter of war between their countries felt like a secret dagger poised over Aniri's heart.

The crowd's approval settled to a low rumble. Ash leaned toward the transmitter. "I've returned to my beloved Jungali with not only a skyship and a treaty, but with a new day ahead of us. The traitors who would drag our mountain provinces back into the days of anarchy have been found and dealt with."

The crowd finally hushed. The rogue Jungali general responsible for kidnapping Aniri and using the skyship to attack her homeland was already dead, but his men still lived. When Ash and Aniri had returned with the skyship, they had also brought her handmaiden Priya, Master Tinker Karan, the skeleton Jungali crew, and a brig full of the general's men. Ash had locked the traitors in the palace dungeon, making clear his intention to use the fearful new technology of the skyship as an instrument of peace, not war.

"There is no room for returning to the ways of the past," Ash said into the transmitter. "The skyship will carry our country into the future with new trade opportunities, a more rapid form of transport, and enhanced security for all our provinces. The time has come to move forward into that new era for Jungali, one filled with peace and prosperity." He smiled at Aniri and raised their clasped hands again. "And a wedding."

The crowd leapt with those words, small children dancing circles in the street below, and women pressing hands to their mouths to hide their glee. He was telling them exactly what they wanted to hear. But a royal wedding seemed like a fanciful dream with the possibility of war on the horizon... and the lie of peace weighed heavier the more the people cheered for it.

Ash urged her away from the transmitter. He released her hand, but drew her close, one hand at the small of her back, the other slipping into her hair. He hesitated from the kiss to look into her eyes, his pale amber ones intense with excitement of the speech, his people, and his triumphant return home. He wasn't pausing to ask for permission this time—there was no need—but whereas before he had been eager to show his people a love that didn't exist, now he seemed almost shy about kissing her in front of them. Aniri closed the last space between them and pressed her lips to his. His hesitation fell away, and she tried to push back thoughts of skyships and war to meet the eager demands of his lips with an equal measure in return.

The noise of the crowd grew to a frenzy, and Ash pulled back, ducking his head and fighting a smile. A cool breeze rose up and caressed them. She waved again to Ash's people—the lie still weighing down her smile—but Ash turned from them and tugged her back through the crystal doors to his receiving room.

Aniri's handmaiden, Priya, awaited them with an unquenchable smile shining from her delicate face. Next to her was the prince's sister-in-law, Nisha, who was likewise beaming, although more of a knowing kind of smile. She was the wife of Ash's murdered brother, Tosh, but she seemed more sister than sister-in-law to Ash. Both Nisha and Priya wore full courtly attire that was properly colorful to match the Jungali sense of these things. Their bronzed skin was radiant against the brilliant blue silks, as if the Jungali sky had splashed down to embrace them in the form of corsets and skirts. The room was likewise well-appointed, lush with silk drapings on the walls and embroidered furniture for guests. Two guards kept watch by the door, and several more attendants waited near the crackling fireplace that kept the cool mountain air at bay.

"Well done." Nisha's smile grew. "I think you could say anything out there and the people would approve."

Priya nearly bounced with happiness. "Especially when you end it with that sort of kiss."

Ash grinned. "I think they mostly approve of my future bride."

Their words just clamped the vise on Aniri's chest tighter. They should be speaking of wars, not weddings.

She turned to Ash, looking up into his face. "Could I have a word alone with you, Prince Malik?" She hoped the formal tone would transmit her seriousness, but instead his eyes grew wide and sparkled with mischief.

He turned back to Nisha and Priya, both of whose eyebrows had risen high on their foreheads. "Please excuse us."

Without waiting for a response, he pulled Aniri away from them, past the fireplace, and toward a small alcove at the end of the room. Curious looks followed them, and Aniri wondered if there were a secret passageway between the potted, leafy plant and the painting of the Jungali mountainscape that he intended to escape through. But she was glad for the chance to finally discuss in private their plans about the possibility of war, even if they had to leave a scattering of amusement in their wake.

The drawings Aniri had discovered aboard the *Prosperity* clearly showed that a second skyship, the *Dagger*, had at least been conceived, if not already built. The question remained by whom and where and for what purpose. And Aniri was afraid all three could be found in the half-truths whispered by her ex-lover: Samirian diplomat, courtesan, and ultimately spy, Devesh. But Devesh was gone, slipping away with the Samirian ambassador. To where, and whether they would find sanctuary in Samir, was still unknown. But the possibility of a second skyship increased the chances that they may yet have war as their aim.

Ash found a door tucked at the very end of the alcove. He quickly swung it open, pulled her inside, and closed it behind them. It was more a very large closet than a room. Shelves lined the walls, stuffed with boxes and crates that overflowed with all manner of decorative items. The room was a relentless storm of white: dozens of spools of snowy lace stacked high, yards of sheer white fabric spilling to the floor, a flurry of white paper lamps strung along the ceiling, and at the far wall, a bleached-wood arch taller than Aniri immersed in a blizzard of beads, ribbons, and gossamer white fabric.

Aniri turned to Ash, a thousand questions on her lips, but he met her by sliding his arms around her waist, then devouring her with a kiss.

She was shocked… then consumed. He spun her around and pressed her to the door, crushing his body against hers as if he couldn't get enough contact between them. Her corset was an effective barrier, and his glittering black formal wear was similarly constraining, but that didn't stop his hands from roaming or his kiss from deepening. Aniri's fingers wound into his hair, then clutched at his shoulders, taking the stolen moment for all it was worth. Ash slid his kisses to her jawline and edged toward her neck. The room turned as hot as if the fire had spilled from its place and ignited the walls around them. Aniri gently pushed him away, urging him to stop and sucking in air she had neglected to breathe. His heated breath puffed against her skin as he slowly trailed his lips in a line across her cheek.

"A week feels an impossibly long time to wait to make you my wife." His voice was deep with the passion of their kiss.

Her heart broke its rhythm, and her face flamed anew. Of course they would consummate their marriage after the wedding, now that it was for love, rather than political convenience. But suddenly the nearness of that intimate act made the walls of the storage room seem to close in on her. She pressed her back against the door to gain an inch from Ash, who still hovered close.

"Aniri?" His ragged breathing had quieted, and he peered at her. "You do still want to go through with the marriage, don't you?"

"Of course." But with war on the murky horizon, the needs of both their countries should take precedence. "I just thought we might put it off for a while."

Ash's face fell and he took a step back. "Put it off."

She reached a hand out to him, but stopped before touching his chest. "It's just… what are we going to do about the second skyship? If the *Dagger* has been built, and there's going to be war, we need to prepare—"

"If there's going to be war," he said with a frown, "I want to have my Queen by my side. And the alliance with Dharia cemented by our marriage."

She nodded. "Yes, of course. That makes sense." Then why did she feel so hesitant?

Ash sensed it immediately. He leaned away from her, searched her face quickly, then turned to intensely examine a box of ribbons on the shelf next to him. "I wondered if, once the adventure was over, once the drama of the escape and the treaty-making had ended, once we returned to Jungali… if you would reconsider. If you would regret a decision made in haste, in the heat of the moment." He sent a sideways look to her.

Aniri's mouth worked, but no words came out. The decision to marry Ash *had* been hastily made. And her judgment had a less than stellar reputation. It was her urgent desire to believe that Devesh had loved her, that they belonged together, which had nearly brought disaster to Jungali, Dharia, and all the people she loved.

Ash looked away again, now studying his boots. "I can understand how a Dharian princess might not be truly happy living in a backward mountain province—"

That propelled her forward. "It's not that." The troubled look in his eyes wrapped pain around her heart. "I'm just *worried*, Ash. With this second skyship, the possibility of war… My sister is with child, and trapped in a country we may soon be at war with. It's clenched my heart since the moment I realized Devesh's lies might be truths after all."

Ash's eyes lit with hope up until the mention of Devesh's name. "Aniri." He gripped the wooden shelf next to him, his fingers digging in the cascades of fabric there. "You seem to want to forgive him for things that I would throw him in the dungeon for."

She frowned, confused. "I'll be the last to forgive Devesh for holding me captive while General Garesh drugged and kidnapped me. But that doesn't mean *everything* he said was a lie."

Ash took a breath and turned back to her, his face serious. "We can't trust in anything he claimed."

His words scraped at her nerves. "I know I was foolish to believe the things he said—"

Ash's serious look softened. He gently touched her cheek with his finger. "It wasn't foolish to believe in someone you loved. He just wasn't worthy of it. Or of you."

She swallowed, the warmth of his hand soothing her. "All I know is that Dev was a master at weaving lies with truth. Perhaps the Samirians truly were using the skyship to distract us from the invasion they're planning. Only the invasion from the east will be by air and skyships, instead of by sea with their trade fleet, as he claimed."

"That's possible," Ash said with a sigh. "But we have to be careful word doesn't slip that we suspect another skyship. I've arrested those involved with General Garesh, but there are many more Samirians still living and working among us. Even *Karan* is Samirian."

Aniri drew back. "Surely you don't suspect him. He saved my life."

A small smile finally found a place on Ash's face. "I owe him my life as well. Karan is above suspicion. I wanted to check with you first, but I think it wise to bring him into our confidence with this."

Aniri nodded, relieved. Karan would understand the gravity of the situation. "Did he mention anything about another skyship when he was working with you and your brother?" Ash's brother, Tosh, had helped Karan design the *Prosperity* before the young prince was murdered. Aniri still hadn't found the right time to tell Ash that Garesh might have been behind his brother's death as well.

Ash shook his head. "No, I would have heard about it, if he had. But Karan could have valuable knowledge about the Samirians' capabilities when it comes to building another skyship on their own."

"Not least how they would get hold of sufficient navia gas."

Ash smiled. "Precisely. How can the Samir have skyships of their own, if all the lighter-than-air gas is in Jungali? It was the discovery of the gas in Sik province that inspired the partnership with Samir in the first place—our resources married to their technology."

A trickle of hope worked its way into Aniri's heart. "Perhaps the skyship plans were just the dreams of the ambassador and General Garesh. Oh, Ash… if that were true, it would end there. We have the plans, Garesh is dead, and the ambassador has fled." She dropped her gaze to the white decorative lamps that crowded the bottom shelf. "But that's probably just more of my wishful thinking." Her foolishness from before still burned shame in her cheeks. She didn't want her heart to lead her again into believing things that were plainly not true to those with clear eyes to see.

"It's good to hope for the best," Ash said softly. "But we must prepare for the worst. And one thing is certain: we're not ready for war. Our own skyship is still depleted of navia. And the burning glass has been damaged by a certain princess who is handy with a sword."

Aniri grimaced. "Can Karan repair it?"

"We'll need to send the skyship back to Sik province, but yes. And while I dislike the idea of using such a powerful weapon, if the Samirians mean war, we'll likely have need of it."

"Dharia needs to prepare as well. I brought my aetheroceiver. I can message my mother." Aniri had brought the clockwork device back with her from Dharia, while the Queen still had its twin. Their wireless messages over the aether were the most secure way to quickly warn her mother of what they knew.

"You cannot send this over a communique, Aniri!" Ash sighed and ran both hands through his dark hair. "I'm sorry. You're right, the aetheroceiver is relatively secure, but you cannot be sure who will be on the receiving end. And it is imperative we keep this quiet. If the Samirians suspect we know, they will be forced into action. And we're not ready for that."

Aniri held out her hands. "But the Queen can help us. She has spies, many in Samir—"

"And spies in her court as well."

He meant Devesh, but of course there could be others. Aniri balled up her fists. "I will travel back to Dharia to tell her myself."

Ash's shoulders dropped. "And if you run home when you should be making preparations for our wedding, the people will wonder if there is trouble in the royal household."

Aniri made a graceless noise of frustration, brushed past Ash, and strode the length of the small room. She peered up at the arch at the end, picturing her and Ash, Dharia and Jungali personified, standing underneath it, exchanging their vows. It was a prudent match, but that wasn't why they were marrying—was it? She had made the decision on a whim and for love. But maybe those were the same thing. Maybe love was as foolish as any of the decisions she had made to date. A shudder ran through her. She had only known the prince a few weeks, and he was right: there had been nothing but adventure and intrigue and daring feats during that time. Was she merely swept up in it? And now that war loomed, how could she possibly know for sure?

"*Is* there trouble in the royal household, Aniri?" Ash had remained at his end of the room. His arms were folded across the black-embroidered finery of his jacket, and his bronzed face seemed darker with the scowl carved in it.

She bit her lip, hesitating, then took slow, careful steps toward him, stopping by a box overflowing with gauzy fabric. "Perhaps we should postpone the wedding." She sped up at the fall of his shoulders. "Only until we can resolve this matter with the second skyship and whether we will soon be at war." But, in truth, that would give her time to settle her heart as well. To *know* this was the right choice, without the uncertainties of war tangling it.

"And what then?" he asked coolly. "Shall we marry to make an alliance for the sake of winning a war?"

"No," she said harshly. "I mean, yes! But not for that reason." She flung out her hands in frustration, knocking the box of fabric so that it cascaded the filmy fabric on top of her. She fought it back, growling as she disentangled from it.

A smile warmed the chilled look on Ash's face. "Your mother will be here for the wedding in a week," he said gently. "That's enough time for me to dispatch spies to Samir and begin to ready us for war, if need be. In the meantime, let the preparations for the wedding distract you."

Heat rose in her face as she pushed away the sheer fabric clinging to her. "I can't bear the thought of planning a party when my sister and mother might be in danger."

Ash stepped closer and carefully pushed the last bit of unruly material back into the box. He peered down into her eyes. "Do you wish to cancel the wedding?" he asked softly.

She took a deep breath. "No."

"Then let us move it up. Get it behind us so we can focus on the future."

Aniri swallowed. It was a sensible idea, yet... "It will take at least two days for my mother to arrive. Priya will probably die of heart failure if I tell her that's all the time she has to prepare." She didn't mention that her heart was attempting to hammer its way out of her chest. *Two days.* It would clear the way for them to deal with the looming possibility of war, but it seemed to hasten an already hasty decision, sending her hurtling toward something that was more like an abyss than a wedding.

Ash smiled. "The people want a celebration,

Aniri. Let's give it to them. It will reassure them that the worst is behind us."

Aniri tried not to let her rising alarm show. "Two days, then." Her heart continued to slam against her chest. Two days to reassure it that she was making the right decision. Two days of patience while Ash unraveled the mystery of the second skyship. But while Ash might think the wedding preparations would distract her, she knew better. She would have to find something that would truly settle her heart, and there was only one thing for that: finding a way to get her sister Seledri out of Samir before war was upon them all.

Chapter Two

Aniri climbed the spiral steps of the slim, white-granite tower, pressing herself against the wall to let the Jungali sailors pass with their burdens: copper tubing, machinery bristling with gear teeth, and crates of every size from teetering small boxes to ones that took two porters to ferry down the steps. The captain of the skyship was in the dungeon along with the others who conspired with General Garesh, so it must be Master Tinker Karan who had ordered all the activity. It seemed he was offloading the entire contents of the skyship.

Which must mean he was trying to lighten the ship for takeoff.

Aniri increased her pace, afraid she wouldn't catch him before they departed for Sik province.

Ash had already agreed to bring Karan into their confidence about the second skyship, but the prince was busy arranging spies and planning a wedding. Aniri had broken the news of the tight deadline to Priya, and after a minute of shrieking, her hand-maiden had disappeared in search of the necessary goods to make the wedding happen. Which left Aniri with an opportunity she had no intention of wasting: a moment to catch Karan and grill him about the Samirian capability to build a skyship of their own.

When Aniri reached the top of the tower, the mayhem was even more pronounced. Dozens of young men and women—a couple she recognized as guards from her stay in the palace before—scurried across the open stone terrace to batten down lightweight items that threatened fly away in the gusty breeze. She understood their haste: anything that worked its way loose would be lost to the thousand-foot cliff that bordered the estate. Less comprehensible was the frenetic pace of everyone else. A few were dressed in tinker outfits—rugged work pants, leather-laced boots, and suspenders holding up belts laden with tools—but most wore the uniforms of palace guards or black, military-styled jackets with double-rowed buttons left half-undone, as if they were hurriedly thrown on before reporting for duty. All moved as though Devkalaka herself—goddess of change and war—was bearing down on them with a blade in each of her six hands.

The skyship loomed over the entire enterprise. Its billowing gas bag was slack for want of enough lighter-than-air navia gas to fill it, and the wind tormented it into shuddering waves of brilliant blue. The narrow, wooden platform on top rocked dangerously, but she couldn't see the brass butterfly, or the burning glass, as the prince called the beautiful weapon that almost destroyed her home. It must be laid flat to keep it from blinding everyone. The ship itself was tethered by thick ropes to the parapets of the tower, and they snapped as the wind constantly tested them. Along the sides were a half dozen fins, like masts with folding sails turned sideways, but they were battened down to save them from the gusts.

A hasty parade of people along the gangplank offloaded goods. Aniri picked her way past the busy workers, none of whom gave her a second glance in her adventuring clothes—she had quickly changed from her royal attire into the same rough pants and leather-bound boots as the skyship crew. Karan was nowhere to be seen on the deck, gangplank, or terrace. Knowing him, he would be deep inside the ship, most likely the engine room—she only hoped she could get him alone for a short while.

Aniri waited for a gap in the stream of workers along the gangplank, then worked her way across, ignoring the precipitous drop to the forested canyons below. The distant mountains were still frosted with snow at the tips, even deep in summer as they were, but all of that was lost once she plunged into the relative darkness of the ship's below-deck corridors. She had learned the layout mostly under duress, but it was still familiar. The narrow, rivet-bound hallways and bulkhead doors reminded her of a Samirian submarine. She ducked under low-hanging brass tubes, pattered down a metal-grated staircase, and dodged a couple of tinkers hurrying through the hall, schematics held in front of them, before she found the engine room. This was where they had first seized the ship from Garesh's men, committing acts of mutiny to counter his acts of treason.

The two-story engine room was less frenetic than the rooftop, with only Karan and a couple of tinkers at one of the six-foot-tall control panels, and two crewmen busy feeding shovels of coal into the twin brass engines at the back. The room wasn't as smoke-filled as the last time she was aboard, but the heat of the engines made Aniri wish her leather jacket wasn't quite so snug. She loosened the top straps and stepped closer to Karan and his tinkers. Karan was massive compared to their slim builds, but his thick, bronzed fingers were nimble as they danced across the metal panel of needle gauges and toggle switches. It was clear who was the Master and who were the apprentices.

"When we start up the blades, don't be gawkin' at your crewmates, aye?" His voice was low and gruff. "Startup's when we're most a danger of over-heatin', so watch your gauges and be alert. We haven't the parts here for fixin' her, not till we get back to the airharbor, so don't be wrecking my ship before then."

"Aye, sir," the two tinkers, one male and one female, said in unison. They were young, a year or two older than Aniri, and she had only just passed her eighteenth birthday. Karan was a few years older, but the corners of his deep brown eyes had wrinkles which made him seem wise past his days.

She didn't think he had noticed her, but then he grunted out, "Whatcha standing there for? Get to unloadin' like the rest of the—" He cut himself off when he looked up. "Ah, fresh! Tired of the palace life already? Lookin' to join the crew?"

She smiled broadly. "Do you have a need for shiners? I might have some experience in that area." Polishing the beautiful but dangerous panels of the butterfly wasn't what she came for, but it might give her a chance to draw Karan away from the prying eyes of engine room.

He smirked and shook his head, but he directed his words to the tinkers, who stood looking between them with wide eyes. "Get to work, you lot." He waved them off. "We'll not be getting' into the air on the power of your gawking alone." They nearly tripped over themselves backing away and scurrying to the far end of the control panels. But they stayed there, still watching Karan and Aniri. And still within earshot.

He turned his attention back to her. "I'd prefer if you kept your distance from the burning glass, fresh. I'm still figuring how to fix the mess you made the last time." His smile was teasing, but she knew how he felt about the ship. Even the parts that could "rain down fire from the sky" as he put it.

"A different job then," she said brightly. "Maybe up on the bridge? I'd love to learn more about the skyship, and I won't be in the way." She glanced at the tinkers. They were trying to appear as though they weren't straining to hear their conversation over the clattering of shovels and boilers building steam.

Karan's smile softened. "I'd love to have ye as an apprentice, Aniri, but I'm full up with fresh lookers who don't know a toggle from a check valve." Karan checked a gauge on the control panel next to them as he talked, then pushed down a large-handled lever labeled "rudder." It clunked when it reached the bottom. Karan checked the gauge again. "With Garesh's men in the brig, I'm a bit short on crew. Had to scrounge from the kitchen for this lot." Nodding to himself, Karan held up a leather gauntlet on his beefy forearm. It was festooned with dials and tiny sleeves for minute tinker tools. He drew out a pencil, made a tiny notation on an even tinier pad of paper, then stowed the pencil again. "Don't know how Ash expects us to get off the ground in this state with no respectable crew, but he's all fired to get back to the airharbor and make repairs. Though, can't say I blame him for that part."

"How soon are you leaving?" She might have to outright ask for a moment alone. With all the activity, they could be departing at any moment.

"Truth is, we're ready now." He gave a small, mysterious smile. "But I've a bit of business to finish before we get aloft." Aniri's eyebrows rose, but before she could ask, he continued on, "But there is one position we need to fill by the time we get the *Prosperity* in top form again." Karan smiled wide. "We're in need of a captain, fresh. Perhaps ye could take a shot at it?"

He was mocking her.

"I'm not even qualified to captain a shashee," she said. The shahee were large, slow-moving animals, traditional Jungali war beasts, and the physical incarnation of the mountain goddess Devpahar. Any Jungali child could probably direct the shaggy creatures given a tapping cane and a way to hold on.

Karan gave a deep, rumbling laugh. "Don't sell yourself short, fresh. You seem to do best in a pinch." His eyes were glittering with humor, and Aniri winced. She didn't mind his teasing, but it wasn't much of a credit to her to get out of a pinch of her own making. Especially when it put other people at risk.

"Yes, I excel at ruining perfectly good sabers and burning glasses at the same time." She didn't regret tossing her father's saber onto the burning glass to stop its ruinous progress toward the capital, but she was concerned that Karan might not be able to fix it again. As Ash said, they might have need of it. "What will it take to make the butterfly operational?"

Karan sobered. "Well, that sword of yours was high-tempered Samirian steel. It made a fine mess when it turned to slag. We'll likely have to cut the burning glass crystal again. A tricky business that, but better than mining another, assuming we could even find one. Huge spot of luck stumbling on the first one, so best not to count on that."

"What about the butterfly wings?" As Aniri recalled, when her father's saber melted, some of it splashed on the brass plates that directed the sun's energy to the crystal.

"Those are easier done. All told, should be done within a week. But the prince says I've only got two days. Don't know quite how that's going to happen, but those are my orders. Supposed to be back in top shape in time for your wedding, fresh." He smirked again. "Don't want to be freezing my parts in Sik province while you're having all the fun in Bhakti."

Two days. Her stomach hollowed out with the reminder. She didn't want to delay Karan's repairs, but she had no time to waste. She glanced at the tinkers, who had slowly crept closer to them. "Do you have time for a word alone, Karan?"

"I suppose." But then a light pattering and rustle at the door behind her caught his notice. His face lit up, and this time his smile was all joy.

Aniri turned to find her handmaiden, Priya, carefully lifting her skirts over the bulkhead door. Her dress was layers of cream-colored silks that took the full width of the door, topped with a corset that dripped in lace, but left her shoulders bare. Aniri cringed as Priya tiptoed across the coal-dust covered floor in tiny satin slippers. This was finer wear than she normally donned for tea. What in the name of Devkasera was she thinking, wearing it on a skyship?

"Priya! I would have returned for your preparations. You didn't need to fetch me, especially in *that*." She gestured to Priya's skirts which were still hiked up off the floor.

Aniri's words, indeed her presence, seemed to catch Priya by surprise. "My lady! I didn't expect you here." She darted a look to Karan.

"I can see that." Aniri knew the romance between Priya and Karan had blossomed since they worked together to engineer Aniri's rescue, but she hadn't had time to query Priya about it in the whirl-wind of events.

Priya recovered, dropped her hold on her skirts, and clasped her hands together. "But this is even more perfect, don't you think, Karan?"

"Well, I offered to make her captain," Karan said, "but she was having none of that. Royalty should do, though, don't you think?"

"Should do for what?" Aniri frowned.

Priya skittered to close the space between them and took Aniri's hands in hers. "Karan and I are to be betrothed," she said, breathless. "Will you be witness for us?"

"I… what?" Aniri dashed a look to Karan, her heart missing a beat.

He looked very pleased with himself. "That bit of business I told you about."

"But… you…" She swung back to her hand-maiden and dropped her voice to a harsh whisper. "Priya, you can't be serious. You can't marry Karan! You only just met." That familiar squeeze on her chest grew tighter.

Priya arched her eyebrows and pulled herself up to her full height. "If it's good enough for my lady, it's good enough for me." She made a small curtsey and grinned a secret smile for Karan. He chuckled, and the bottom dropped out of Aniri's stomach. She had only told Priya that the wedding date was moved, not her misgivings of it. Aniri wasn't sure whether her nuptials were a hastily-made mistake, but she was certain that this was nothing short of disastrous.

She turned to Karan intending to forbid it, but stalled out at the adoring look he was giving Priya. Instead, she said, "Karan, I... I thought you were leaving."

"I'll be back, fresh," he said, still looking at Priya. "In time for your wedding, and with any luck at all, mine as well."

Priya squeaked with happiness and dropped one of Aniri's hands to take hold of Karan's. "Say you'll do it, my lady. It would mean ever so much to both of us."

Karan's face lost its humor, and both he and Priya looked expectantly at her.

Aniri swallowed, lost for words, but unable to say no in the face of their happiness. "I... what do you want me to do, exactly?"

Priya dropped Aniri's hand and took both of Karan's. His hands were enormous compared to her delicate ones. He was a giant next to her, dressed in oil besmirched tinker's clothes that tarnished her perfectly neat cream-colored skirts just with their nearness.

Priya gazed up into Karan's eyes, but her words were for Aniri. "We want you to witness our betrothal, my lady." She glanced at Aniri. "It's a Samirian tradition. The exchange of betrothal gifts and a witness to it."

Aniri nodded even though she did not approve of this at all. "But why must you betrothe so quickly?" she couldn't help asking. She struggled to keep her desperation to stop this out of her voice. But her words seemed to go unheard as Karan and Priya gazed at one another.

Karan dug into one of the many tiny leather-satchel pockets on his tinker belt. He withdrew a key on a thin leather cord. It was slender, with a square tip and clockwork mechanisms at the head that sprouted tiny wings.

He held it up before Priya with a dead-serious look. "Priya, I give you the key to my heart. Take right care of it until I return and we can be properly wed in the eyes of the gods and our families."

The solemnity of his words tormented Aniri, but Priya glowed as Karan placed the necklace over her head. He drew back, leaving a gentle kiss on her cheek along the way. Priya then fished into the cream-colored fabric swept over her shoulder and came out with a long, brown cord of cut leather. A small gear was attached to the end.

Karan's eyes danced as she commanded in a stern voice, "Hold out your arm."

When he did so, she wound the length around and around his wrist, fashioning a rough bracelet and saying as she went, "Karan, with this cord I bind my soul to yours, until you return and we can be properly wed in the eyes of the gods and our families." She fixed the loose end to the gear piece, so that it held in place. His smile had softened as she spoke, and once she was done, he took her delicate face in his large hands and kissed her.

It was done before Aniri could think of words to stop it. And it was so intimate and sweet, she felt guilty for wanting to do so. The heat in her cheeks tempted her to duck her head away, but as apparent witness to this betrothal, she forced herself to watch as her new friend and rescuer Karan gave his love to her oldest friend and hand-maiden. She blinked back her tears and kept her objections to herself. But what did they know about each other? How could they possibly pledge their hearts and souls when they had only known each other over the high drama and daring adventures of the last few days? What horrible mistake was she being witness to? And was she truly about to do the same herself?

As Priya and Karan broke their kiss, Aniri looked away, embarrassed by all of it: the kiss, the vows, and most of all, her thoughts. Her own betrothal was far less solemn, having taken place with no witnesses and sealed only with a kiss. But now that it was done, it felt more binding than the leather cords around Karan's wrist. She shook her head. Now was not the time to be having second thoughts—not with war looming and so much at stake.

Priya grinned at Karan, released him, and skipped to Aniri's side. "Oh, my lady! It was even more wonderful with you here." Then Priya threw her arms around Aniri, and Karan very much chuckled at her surprised response. She did her best to put off her shock and hug Priya back.

"It was... my honor to be here for your betrothal, Priya." She cast an imperious look to Karan. "I dare say the prince's Master Tinker will not be tempted to break his vow now that he knows the future Queen of Jungali would have his head for it."

Karan's chuckle broke into a full guffaw. He

struggled to rein it in. "Fresh, I'd be far more afeared of Miss Priya's reaction than yours."

She couldn't help but smile at that. "As it should be, I suppose."

"And now, my lady." Priya tugged at Aniri's adventuring jacket. "We must get you out of these clothes. There is much to be done and scandalously little time to prepare for a proper royal wedding."

"Now that my bit of business is done," Karan said with a smile, "it's time for this ship to be lifting off as well."

Aniri sighed. She couldn't plausibly delay him without stirring all kinds of suspicion. Her questions would have to wait until Karan's return. "Are you quite certain, Master Tinker, that you'll return in two days' time? I'm still quite interested in learning how your ship works."

His great brow wrinkled up. "As soon as she's in right shape again, you can have all the lessons you like, fresh."

Aniri nodded and pulled in a breath. "I'll hold you to that, Mr. Karan."

His frown grew deeper, but Aniri ignored his puzzled looks and let Priya lead her from the engine room and back to the palace where her future awaited.

Chapter Three

IT HAD ONLY BEEN A DAY, but the endless parade of people and wedding items was driving Aniri to distraction. It was as if her mother's court had been replicated in the Jungali mountains, only now Aniri was the center of attention, rather than the rebellious Third Daughter who would occasionally show up late for tea. The whirlwind of activity just built a sense of increasing dread with each hour that marched forward, as though she were on a train hurtling down the tracks with increasing speed. There was no time to think about whether boarding was wise, and no seeming way to get off, regardless.

She hadn't seen Ash except to select the local dancers for the wedding celebration and to receive the nobles come to present their wedding gifts. She supposed it was keeping with tradition to limit contact between the bride and groom in advance of the wedding, but it seemed silly in light of how much time they had already spent together—or how little, her heart reminded her. And it left no opportunity for her to gauge whether it was foolishness to marry so quickly, or whether following her heart in this case was the best course for all. Ash was right that the preparations were distracting, but not in a way that settled her heart.

As the Jungali people trickled in from the other three provinces—Sik, Rajan, and Mahet—the prince's home province of Bajir was mostly concerned with the finer details of the wedding preparations. Aniri's room was heaped with samples of foods for her to evaluate, gifts the Bajirans hoped the royal couple would bestow on their guests, and vase after vase of wild mountain flowers. The blossoms transformed her room into a perfumed mountain meadow and distracted her from the onerous job of being fitted for her wedding dress at the frenetic hands of Priya.

Aniri stood on a small platform with the enormous skirt of her dress draping nicely for her handmaiden's attentions. Aniri's short, snow-white corset was heavily jeweled along the edges, leaving her midriff and shoulders bare. The skirt billowed from where it sat low on her hips, the undercoat of blue satin covered with layers and layers of sheer white fabric. Deep-blue, teardrop-shaped crystals weighted the hem, each one a royal raindrop dripping to the floor. The whole dress gave the impression that Aniri was afloat in a bejeweled cloud. The sweep of sheer white fabric over her shoulder completed the illusion that she was somehow not quite real, just a puff floating over the brilliant blue Jungali sky.

Priya fussed over the dress, pinning and repinning and adjusting things Aniri couldn't even see in all the layers.

When her handmaiden stepped back to examine her handiwork, Aniri ventured, "Are we done?"

Priya simply scowled and dove back in to the frothy dress.

Aniri took a giant calming breath, which only made Priya squeak with indignation. "Do not move, my lady!"

"We've been at this an hour, Priya. I might lose my mind if we don't finish soon."

Priya climbed back out from under the layers to

give Aniri a tiny scowl. "My lady, this is only the first fitting."

Aniri's mouth fell open. "The first? How many will be required? I promise not to change shape before the wedding tomorrow."

"As many as necessary to make sure my lady is perfect in every way."

Aniri gritted her teeth. "I'm afraid there are not enough fittings possible to achieve that."

Priya just shook her head and lifted several diaphanous layers over her head so she could work on the snug inner skirt hanging from Aniri's hips. "Perhaps my lady needs an adjustment to her temper as well as her gown."

Aniri sighed. "Perhaps."

Of course she couldn't tell Priya of her true concerns: not about the haste of her marriage, especially given Priya's betrothal to Karan, nor about the Samirians, their possible skyship, and her sister across the sea who might be caught in a war between them. Aniri had messaged both her sister Seledri and their mother, the Queen, but neither had expressed anything but pleasantries about the upcoming wedding. Seledri was beside herself that she couldn't attend, but other than that, nothing. Yet aetheroceiver messages were of necessity brief and colorless—who knew what their notes were leaving unsaid, just as hers were.

At least the Queen would arrive this evening in time for the rehearsal. Aniri would have to meet privately with her mother as quickly as possible. Perhaps the Queen could use some pretext to convince Seledri to come home again, at least until the danger of war had passed. Ash's spies had already reached Samir—soon, they should have knowledge of whether the Samirians were capable of creating a second skyship on their own. Then she would know the depths of their troubles.

Or perhaps all her worrying would be for nothing.

Priya fought her way out of the dress's layers. "My lady, I will need you to slip out of your gown for the moment while I make these adjustments."

"Praise be to the gods," Aniri said under her breath.

Priya lifted the shoulder sweep carefully away. Aniri unhooked the back of the skirt and wriggled it down until she could step out of the voluminous fabric moat that surrounded her. She saw no way to exit other than leaping over the yards of material, so she did.

Priya let out a small shriek when it seemed Aniri

might not quite make the edge. Her handmaiden held the giant sweep of sheer fabric in one hand and pressed the other to her chest as if her heart had stopped. Then she scowled and stalked toward Aniri. "My lady definitely needs a break."

Aniri grinned and turned her back so Priya could undo her corset. "Can you spare me for an hour? The prince has refurbished a fencing hall for me, and I've yet to set foot in it."

Priya made a small sound of impatience as she worked the thousand tiny hooks at the back of Aniri's corset. "No more than an hour. I still need to prepare you for tonight's rehearsal."

"I promise," Aniri said, her heart light. When Priya set her free of the last hook, Aniri raced to dig out her fencing attire, still buried in the many cases they had originally brought from Dharia—back when she had no intention of staying, but had to pack as if she did. It was fortuitous now, and she hastily pulled on her canvas breeches and thin-soled, leather boots. Her fencing jacket went over a lightweight undershirt, but she just grabbed her chest protector, foil, and fencing glove and ran out the door before Priya could change her mind.

The palace had become less of a mystery to her as she flitted from one appointment to the next.

The highest levels were reserved for royal apartments and guest rooms, the midlevel for public
gatherings like the rehearsal, with the lower levels
reserved for household staff and kitchens. These
levels extended below the streets outside, carving
deep into the mountain rock, and somewhere in the
depths lay the dungeon and Garesh's men. It was
slightly unsettling to have them so near, but she
supposed it was better than summary execution. Or
returning them to Sik province where they could
enact further insurrection.

The fencing hall was on the top floor, down the
hallway that gently curved to follow the mountain's
sheer edge. Ash had fenced as a boy, along with his
brother, Tosh, but the hall had been left to disuse as
the boy princes grew to men with responsibilities.
Her thin fencing boots made no sound as she stole
down the hall, although she attracted the curious
glances of a pair of guards along the way.

With Ash's mother and brother both passed on,
the royal apartments were mostly empty. The guest
rooms would remain likewise vacant until her mother's entourage arrived this evening. Aniri passed the
still-damaged guest room that was her first in the
estate—the scent of the fire lingered, and the soot
marks from the attempt on her life still marred the

edges of the door. At the end of the hall was the prince's private quarters—rooms she had yet to visit. In less than a day, those rooms would be hers as well, and she and Ash would consummate their marriage here in the palace, as was customary. That thought sent a surge of uncertainty through her, and she quickly looked away, searching for the entrance to the fencing hall.

She found it just two doors down from the prince's room and stole up to it, as though she were getting away with some indiscretion. Gathering her chest protector, foil, and glove all in one hand, she quietly turned the knob. With a glance down the hall and no one to see, she pushed the door open, snuck inside, and turned to quietly close it.

"Aniri!"

The voice startled her so badly, she dropped her things. As her sword clattered on the polished wooden floor, she turned in the direction of the voice, and only when she saw him standing there, did she recognize the prince.

"Ash," she said, breathless and trying to calm her heart. "You startled me."

He stood at one end of the training room, which was easily three times the size of her guest room, and a quick look confirmed they were alone.

Behind him was a table arrayed with swords and a glass cabinet that spanned the narrow length of the room. It held weapons, armor, and what looked unsettlingly like instruments of torture.

Ash smiled broadly and set down a saber he had been holding. "Are you spying on me again?" He was dressed for fencing: a high collared jacket, fitted breeches, and lightweight fencing boots. But he was missing a chest protector, and there was no one else in the hall. An automaton, made of brass and steel and clockwork, stood at the opposite end—perhaps that was his intended partner.

"I was just making my escape from Priya and her ministrations for a moment." As Aniri bent to pick up her things, her fencing jacket fell open to reveal her rather thin shirt underneath. A blush ran up her neck, and she wished she had fully dressed before venturing out. She awkwardly juggled her things, trying to find a graceful way to fix her shirt with her hands full.

Ash strode over from the table, a bemused smirk no doubt for her gracelessness. "Is your hand-maiden holding you captive?"

"She torments me with corsets and wedding gowns." Aniri decided to rest her foil against the door and drop her glove back to the floor while slipping the chest guard over one shoulder. "What are you doing here? I thought you no longer fenced?"

"I'm thinking of taking up the sport again." His smile dropped away as he arrived in front of her. He reached to the bottom of her fencing jacket and wrapped it tight at her waist, then slowly fixed the brass buttons, one at a time, as he worked his way up her side. It flashed unbidden memories of Devesh back home, although he never dared to dress her like this in the fencing hall. Then again, she had never shown up for lessons half-dressed.

By the time Ash reached the buttons at her neck, her face was on fire. She shouldn't be embarrassed—once they were married, he would do much more than button her jacket—but somehow that didn't keep the fluster from her face. He must have seen her blush, because when he finished fastening her buttons, he lightly brushed his cool fingers across her heated cheek. She ducked her head, absurdly feeling embarrassed for feeling embarrassed.

If he noticed, that didn't stop him from lifting the second strap of her chest guard over her other shoulder and reaching his arms around her to hook it in the back. This time, his cheek swept hers as he worked. It seemed to take far longer than necessary.

When he finally pulled back, he whispered in her ear, "I've wanted to fence you ever since you pulled a blade on me."

She swallowed. "I don't remember threatening you with a sword."

His amber eyes were afire. "I remember it quite well." His tone brought the memory hurtling back of the night in Mahet when they shared a room, but not a bed. She had to look away, because it flamed her face anew, but he quickly brought her back with a gentle touch to her cheek. "Aniri, what's wrong?"

"Just a bit... nervous, I suppose." Her sister Seledri would be laughing herself silly if she saw Aniri blushing this way, alone with her husband, on the eve of her marriage. As if she had never clutched a man in a fevered embrace. True, she was still chaste, as was expected, but that didn't explain her heated face. It was her uncertainty that had her quivering at the thought of sharing a bed and all that intimacy would mean. If her sister were here, perhaps she would reassure Aniri that all women had the same doubts as she. But, then again, maybe not. Her sister had never had the benefit, or perhaps curse, of a choice in the matter.

"Me too," the prince said quietly.

She drew back and tossed him a skeptical look. "You hide your nerves very well, Prince Malik."

He grinned. "I've survived a mutiny and a saber duel on top of a skyship with you. I imagine a wedding is only slightly more treacherous."

She took a deep breath. "Honestly, a saber duel sounds much less nerve-wracking. At least then I knew who we were fighting. Do you have any word from your spies in Samir?"

His smile faded. "Nothing as yet. We took care to encrypt the aetheroceiver transmissions, plus my spies have devised a code such that, if intercepted, the messages would be unintelligible. Even so, they've made no mention of a Samirian skyship. There are general rumblings of fear in the Samirian countryside about the *Prosperity* and the new treaty between Jungali and Dharia, but nothing that would indicate they are preparing an imminent invasion. Their fleet, the sea-bound one, appears to be following their already planned trade missions. But the Samirians are very clever. They could be arming their ships in a way my casual dock worker spies would not be able to detect it."

"The Samirians are also well known for their distrust of strangers. Perhaps your spies cannot hear what the people would not say to someone unknown."

"Indeed." He pulled back from her. "They are also excellent liars."

He was referring to Devesh, which only made Aniri purse her lips. "If our alliance is causing unease, we may be provoking them into preparing for war, even if they had not intended one before."

"That is also true." Ash sighed. "Once Karan returns, I will gain his counsel on the Samirian capabilities. I didn't want to send him off to Sik province without time to discuss it properly and with no means to do anything about it. If I didn't think it would be considered an act of war, I would simply have him fly the ship over the sea to Samir to take my own measure of their intentions and ability to wage war against us."

"Perhaps, once the wedding is finished…" Aniri half hoped she might be on that flight.

"Perhaps. But you are right, first things first."

His gaze dropped to her lips and a quiver shot through her again, surging back the nervous feeling from before.

Ash's gaze traveled back to her eyes, and he gave her a shy smile. "I have something for you. A gift."

"A gift?" Her throat tightened as she thought of Priya and Karan and their touching betrothal. "Are we supposed to exchange gifts? Because I don't have—"

"Aniri," he cut her off. "It's all right. There is a very old tradition where the bride and groom exchange gifts, but this isn't that. I mean, it doesn't have to be that. This is just something I wanted to give you. I was going to present it after the rehearsal, but now that you're here…"

He took her hand and led her to the table. There was a wide assortment of blades: a scimitar that looked very old, with a plain and ancient iron grip; a saber with a heavily jeweled and odd-looking handle; and half-dozen regular foils, some with dazzling filigree grips and others with functional steel ones. He picked up the jeweled saber and held it out to her on open palms.

She took it and stepped back, gripping the ornate handle, afraid it might be awkward or uncomfortable, but the stones were so perfectly aligned and smoothed that it felt like the finest polished brass in her hand. The balance was perfect, although the blade was slightly heavier than she was used to. That would only give it more power once she became accustomed to it.

She twirled it, tipped it forward, and thrust at an imaginary foe to the prince's left. When she stepped back from the lunge, she said, "It's a beautiful weapon, Ash. Thank you."

"Do you truly like it?" He watched her carefully as she swung the blade again.

"Of course. It's perfectly balanced and easy to grip."

He stepped closer, and she pointed the saber to the floor, safely away from him.

"I had it made special for you."

She held up the jeweled handle. "It has a rather unusual grip for a saber."

He gently wrapped his hand around hers, where she held the grip, then looked in her eyes. "That's because it's actually a dagger handle."

She frowned. "A dagger?"

He edged closer, brushing her hair back and slipping his fingers through it. "It was Tosh's."

Aniri drew in a breath and frowned at the handle still clasped in their two hands. "The one you found him with?" Ash's brother had been set upon by Sik marauders. Ash had kept Tosh's blade, believing he had used it to defend himself. Aniri suspected General Garesh had been the one to push Tosh out of the window he supposedly fell from, but now hardly seemed the time to mention it. "I can't take your brother's knife."

She shook her head, but he stilled it with a soft caress of her cheek. "When I realized you had thrown your father's saber into the burning glass, I knew you had destroyed something much more than the two weapons. Your father's blade was a promise for the future—a promise that was broken even before you tossed it into that fire. Tosh's blade was a promise, too, one I made after my brother's death: that I wouldn't use it to seek vengeance in his name, but would create peace instead. You, my love," he said, stroking her cheek again, "helped me keep that promise. I had it made into a saber as a new promise to you: that the future we forge together will be everything you want. Everything you deserve. I want to give you that future, Aniri, if you'll let me."

Words fled her, and tears blurred her eyes. With her free hand, she pulled his face down to hers and kissed him. Every reason she ever had for loving him came rushing back to her, and she poured every single one into her kiss. She held nothing back, and he pulled her close in return. For a long time, they were lost in kisses and touches. When they finally broke their fevered holding and nuzzling, the smile on Ash's face settled her heart in a way she had been grasping for but couldn't find.

She could make many worse mistakes in her life than marrying this noble prince. And for a brief, shining moment, she had no doubt that, together, they could find a way to keep peace in all three Queendoms.

Chapter Four

When Aniri returned to her room, Priya's scowls were even darker. Apparently the wedding dress—which had been hastily made over the last day—wasn't meeting her exacting specifications.

"We'll have another fitting tonight," Priya said as she helped Aniri into her rehearsal gown. It was a much simpler but more colorful affair, and felt truly Jungali with its breathtaking contrast of colors: a bright purple corset hooked over sweeping folds of orange embroidered fabric. Priya's rehearsal attire was similarly vivid with a deep rose corset and a winter-blue dress.

Priya hastily laid an orange jewel in Aniri's hair, then whisked off to find their slippers. Aniri righted the teardrop that hung on her forehead and called across the room, "I'm sure they will wait for us, Priya."

That must have been the wrong thing to say, because Priya returned with the slippers and an even deeper scowl. She quickly pulled hairpins from somewhere deep in her corset and threatened Aniri with them. "You will not be late for your own wedding. Not if I have anything to do with it."

Aniri sighed as Priya tugged her hairpiece loose and repinned it. "It's only the rehearsal, Priya."

"And our only chance to practice the Jungali customs before tomorrow."

"Are they really so elaborate?"

"No, but they must be perfect."

Aniri didn't wish to quarrel, still floating on the warmth of the prince's kisses, so she kept quiet until Priya had wrestled her hair into submission and declared her fit for royal company.

"Has the Queen arrived?" Aniri asked as they left her room and strolled toward the stairs to the rehearsal room below.

"I've heard that the Queen of *Dharia* has already arrived at the rehearsal," she said with a haughty lift of her chin. "The Queen of *Jungali* has yet to make her appearance."

Aniri laughed. "I'm not Queen yet, Priya."

Although a trace of her former nervousness chased away the laugh. Being Queen would require so much more than holding Ash in her arms until they could no longer breathe properly. It would require responsibility and dignity. And forging the future her handsome prince had promised they would have together.

That thought sobered her rather completely.

As they lightly pattered down the white-granite stairs, Aniri asked, "Have you heard word from Karan? Do you expect him to return in time for the wedding?" She wished him there, for her sake and Priya's, but even more she and Ash both wanted to question him about Samirian skyships.

"Oh," Priya exclaimed as they reached the foot of the stairs. "In all the rush, I forgot to tell you, my lady. Karan has already returned, and his skyship is *a right beauty now.*" Her imitation of Karan's deep, rumbling voice made Aniri's laugh bubble up again.

Giggling and rushing, they made a less-than-graceful entrance into the hall where the rehearsal and wedding would both take place. Aniri practically ran into her sister, First Daughter Nahali, who stood by the rear door with her Dharian nobleman husband, Ekan.

"Still artful in making an entrance, I see,"

Nahali said with a small smile, looking her over from head to toe. Aniri was painfully aware of how colorful and Jungali-like her dress was compared to Nahali's more subdued gold-and-green embroidered corset and skirts. Her loose-fitting sweeps of fabric didn't quite hide the bump that signaled a new Queen in the making. Or if it was a boy, a new prince, not to be made King unless Nahali failed to deliver another First Daughter to eventually take her place.

Priya pressed her lips together and took a step back, but Aniri straightened and stood tall to face her brilliant and commanding sister. Nahali would never have made such a graceless entrance: she was far too *regal*. Something Aniri never thought she possessed, until Ash had pointed it out. Only he had called it *arrogance*. And he was right.

"You can be assured the wedding will be properly royal," Aniri said, not entirely reining in the sarcasm. "Just wait until you see the dancing." She managed to keep the smirk inside.

"I'm sure Aniri has been rushing about with important duties." Ekan flashed his ridiculously gorgeous smile, the one that made all the women at court fan themselves, even though Ekan only had eyes for Nahali. The perfect First Daughter wouldn't accept anything less. "Have you killed any bad guys lately, Aniri? Rumor at court is that you single-handedly skewered the general with your father's sword before disabling the sky weapon with it."

Nahali gave him a sideways look. "You know perfectly well the general merely *fell* to his death." She turned a cool look to Aniri. "We're just lucky our Third Daughter didn't tumble off the skyship as well."

Heat surged up in Aniri's face, but she managed to keep her face neutral. "I was lucky to have Janak to ensure my safety."

"Indeed. It's fortunate Mother sent him with you, although he barely seemed to survive your escapades."

Aniri struggled to conjure a civil response to that.

Priya leapt to her rescue. "Oh, look, my lady. The Queen and Mr. Janak have already arrived." She pointed to the front of the room, and for the first time since entering it, Aniri drew her attention away from her imperious older sister and took in the changes that had been wrought throughout the room for the rehearsal. A myriad of chairs had been brought in, readying the room for many more guests than they had at the engagement party, and a small elevated platform at the front was clearly the center attraction. Her mother and Janak were having a hushed conversation in an alcove to the side, their heads bent close enough together to call the discussion intimate. Aniri tried to tamp down her hopes that romance had bloomed in the short time she had been away. Janak noticed Priya's outburst and gave them a small nod to indicate he and the Queen would join them shortly.

Near the platform, the prince gathered with Nisha and two young girls who must be her daughters. The adults talked quietly with a woman dressed in the plain robes of a priestess, while the girls decorated their hair with flowers stolen from the scattered baskets on the platform. Guards held posts at the two entrances, front and back, and more were outside—Ash had increased security throughout the palace due to the high concentration of royalty in one place. But otherwise the room was empty. It struck Aniri with a jab of sadness to realize that Nisha and her girls were the only living representatives of Ash's family.

Behind them stood a life-sized statue of Devrakama, the god of passionate love. His bulging muscles, broad shoulders, and narrowed hips were the picture of male beauty, while his piercing gaze was a force of masculine passion she could feel from across the room. The love god's bare granite chest was draped in several garlands of real flowers, the waxy white-petaled kind she and Ash fed to each other at the engagement party. The statue's six hands grasped still more flowers, except for the one holding a slender spear wrapped in flower vines and tipped, according to the myths, with a poison that would keep two lovers perpetually rapt in passionate love.

"Well, that's… *charming*," said Nahali. "Devrakama should bring a certain Jungali flavor to the ceremonies. I do hope we won't have to offer up anything other than flowers."

Aniri scowled. She had no idea what the ceremony involved, hence the rehearsal, but whatever the Jungali customs, she prayed that Devrakama would banish her older sister's arrogance. Or at least restrain Aniri's passions before she said something she regretted.

A nudge from Priya jostled Aniri out of her glare just as the Queen and Janak arrived at their side. Her mother swept Aniri into an uncharacteristically warm hug, and Aniri hesitated only a tiny moment before returning the affection. Janak stood slightly back from their reunion, the gruff look on his face inscrutable as always. He was the Queen's *raksaka*, the stealthy protectors of royalty and occasional assassins, and he guarded her mother's life with his own. Aniri knew he secretly loved the Queen, but his impassive face gave no hint of it. They were both dressed as if for high tea in her mother's court—the Queen in muted golds and lavenders, Janak in his characteristic black, but with a royal jacket. They appeared not at all weary from their travels deep into the Jungali mountains, but Aniri regretted the rush to wed that brought them here. It had only been a few days since Aniri was at Janak's bedside, wondering if he would survive, yet here he stood, his bearing as filled with controlled power as it ever was. If he was still suffering from his grave injuries, it didn't show.

When the Queen released her, Aniri said, "I'm so glad you're here, Mother."

She held Aniri by both shoulders. "Well, of course I'm here," she scolded, but lightly. "How can we join two families without the family members being present?" Of course, their wedding was more than that, but Aniri loved that her mother saw them first as family, second as nations. She impetuously pulled her mother into another hug, and the

Queen's shoulders shook with a small laugh, but she was smiling when Aniri pulled back and ducked her head slightly in embarrassment.

"How are you faring, Janak?"' Aniri asked softly.

"Well enough to perform my duties, your most royal highness." It wasn't what she meant, but a small tip of his head and a tiny raise of an eyebrow meant he knew that. At least she hoped he did. She would have to sequester him soon to express her true concerns, but first, there were more pressing matters.

She took the Queen's hands in hers. "Mother, there are some things I need to discuss with you." Aniri cast a furtive look to the alcoves that lined the room, wondering if she could justify pulling her mother aside for a quick discussion of the Samirians, their possible skyship, and how she could convince Seledri to come home.

The Queen squeezed her hands and smiled. "And many things I wish to talk to you about as well. But I believe there are some ceremonial duties which need to come first." She glanced to the front, and sure enough, Nisha and the prince had finished their discussion with the priestess and were watching them expectantly.

Aniri held back her sigh of frustration. "Very well. Let's not keep them waiting." The sooner the rehearsal was finished, the sooner she could speak with her mother alone. Or possibly with Janak. He was her closest advisor, still, even if he hadn't yet expressed his true feelings.

Aniri led the way to the front. The controlled sparkle in Ash's eyes made her both smile and blush, but fortunately, Nisha intercepted her first in an enthusiastic hug. Her dress was as colorful as Aniri's and Priya's—pure Jungali blue with purple drapings and not even a corset to contain them—while her hair flowed unbound around her, matching her exuberance. She stepped back to introduce the others.

"These are my daughters, Nikhita and Tissa." As Nisha said their names, they popped up from the platform where they had been playing with the flowers and pressed their hands together to bow.

"Arama, Queen Malik," the older one, Nikhita, said. She was perhaps ten, with lively eyes and her mother's beauty.

Aniri couldn't help smiling and pressing her hands to bow in return. "Arama, Princess Nikhita."

The younger one, who was maybe eight, tugged

on Nikhita's elbow and loudly whispered, "But she's not Queen yet, is she?"

"Tissa!" Nisha said. "Aniri will be our Queen soon enough."

Tissa looked to Aniri with wide eyes, pressed her hands together, and bowed.

Aniri held back her chuckle, but she could hear Ash's quite well. She bowed to Tissa with a show of solemnity. "I would be delighted to be your Queen, Miss Tissa. But first, I must marry your uncle." Then she winked at Tissa, who grinned and then hid behind her big sister's sky-blue dress.

Nisha shook her head and then turned to the priestess. "And this is Sage Padma."

Padma bowed. "Arama, Princess Aniri. I look forward to joining you and Ashoka together before our gods and your families in accordance with our most sacred traditions."

Aniri smiled, bowed in return, then shot a look to Ash. A flush went through her—she was fairly sure it was excitement, not nerves—but she hoped he would help her through the ceremony. For his part, Ash was still grinning at the girls and making faces for them.

Nisha must have seen her hesitation. "Don't worry, Aniri. I'll walk you through everything." She smiled wide and motioned all the family repre-senting Aniri's side toward the front door. "We'll start with the entrance. The bride's family mustn't enter the wedding hall until the groom's family has consecrated it for her."

Nisha's daughters, Ash, and Sage Padma stayed behind as the rest were herded into the hall by Nisha. Aniri smiled at the slightly awkward look on Janak's face, as if he wasn't sure if he belonged in her entourage, but was unable to leave the Queen's side in any case.

As Nisha shuffled them around and lined them up, Aniri edged over to Janak's side. "My mother should have an escort for the ceremony," she said quietly, low enough that only he would hear over Nisha's chipper exposition about the formalities. "To be honest, I was afraid she might bring one of those charming but vapid courtesans she favors."

He frowned. "Courtesans are useless for most things, when they're not being downright dangerous."

He was referring to Devesh, who Janak had suspicions about from the beginning. And, of course, he had been right all along. Whereas Aniri had been as foolish as Janak had believed. Still, she inwardly triumphed at his bristling. Her mother's habit of keeping courtesans would come quickly to an end, if she knew of Janak's love for her: Aniri was certain of it. Getting Janak to admit as much would be the challenge.

"It's a good thing you're here, then," Aniri said. "Having the Queen's most loyal raksaka by her side is a fitting way to attend my wedding." She gave him a small smile, hoping it wasn't too much.

"My lady should pay attention or she'll embarrass the crown," he said gruffly, staring straight ahead.

Aniri grinned. Janak shuffled forward as Nisha beckoned him with a rapid flutter of fingers. She had finished lining them up: the Queen and Janak first, followed by Nahali and Ekan, then Priya, and finally Aniri. Her sister, the First Daughter, held her place stiffly, as if offended by Nisha's ordering them about.

"Now remember your placement," Nisha said, "as I won't be here to shape you up for the ceremony tomorrow. My place will be inside with Sage Padma, performing the consecration to make the wedding hall sacred for the wedding rites. When it is your time, the doors will open, and your procession will begin. Today, just follow me, and I will show you."

She flung open the doors, held her skirts, then walked backward through the door. The entire entourage dutifully followed her in a stately procession that circled the perimeter of the room, keeping to the alcoves along the edges until they had gone the length of the room, traversed the back, and come forward again. Nisha stopped when she reached the platform. Ash stood next to the priestess at the far right with one of the Devrakama's garlands in his hand. He caught Aniri's eye, even with the crowd of people between them, and grinned. She smiled in return. Nisha's girls were busy scooping fallen flower petals and hurrying over to toss them on Aniri's head, only they weren't quite tall enough and the flowers merely fell on her dress. Aniri bit her lip to keep from laughing.

Nisha was still directing. "Now the bride's family must part, making room down the middle for her to pass." It took a moment of shuffling, but they managed to make an aisle for her between them. "As Aniri passes, you should reach out to touch her shoulder. A gentle blessing that she goes with your fondest wishes for a rich and fruitful future with her new husband."

Aniri's heart skipped a beat with that word: *husband.* But she managed a tentative step forward.

Priya, whose eyes were shining, reached out to touch her shoulder, whispering, "My lady," before choking up and saying nothing more.

It made Aniri's throat close up, and all the nerves that had been banished by Ash's kisses come flooding back. Her heart pounded harder with each slow step. Fallen flower petals crushed under her slippers as she passed Nahali and Ekan, both of whom touched her without a word. When she reached her mother and Janak, she was in serious danger of crying, not least because tears were already leaking from her mother's eyes.

Aniri swallowed her way through it and floated past their touches to arrive in front of Ash. The smile had dropped from his face, and his eyes had gone wide. Was he suddenly as unsure as she was? Or was it just the agitation quivering through her that made her think so?

A small hand tugged at Aniri's elbow. Tissa stood there, her innocent face beaming as she handed up a garland of flowers to Aniri. The priestess came to stand on one side of Ash and Aniri, facing their future audience, which for now was just a sea of empty chairs.

"Wonderful," Nisha said, appearing on the opposite side. "Now is the exchanging of the garlands, where you show that you accept each other as husband and wife and pledge to show mutual respect for the full extent of your lives. Afterward Sage Padma will lead you in recitations, your vows, and the final ribbon ceremony. But, first, the garlands. Aniri, the bride always starts."

Aniri looked at the garland and Ash's height and nervously thought of Janak's words about embarrassing the crown. She tentatively reached toward him, but Ash must have quickly figured it out, because a tiny smile snuck on his face, and he bent low to make it easier for her. She still had to reach up on her toes, but she managed. His smile grew as he straightened and leaned forward to place his garland of honey-scented flowers over her head.

Just as they turned to the priestess to see what came next, the front doors to the rehearsal hall flung open. A tall, young man in a palace guard uniform rushed in and hurried to Ash's side. Nisha's scowl said this wasn't part of the ceremony.

The man cupped a hand to Ash's ear. His breathless whispers were not quite loud enough for Aniri to hear. Ash's eyes went wide, and his jaw clenched. Then he nodded to the man, who stepped back, a wild-eyed look on his face, like he wasn't quite sure what to do now that he had delivered his message.

Ash took her hand and gripped it tight, but then turned to face everyone. "Someone has made an assassination attempt on the Second Daughter of Dharia."

All the air went out of Aniri's chest in one giant crush of horror.

Chapter Five

THE GASP that went around the room with Ash's words barely registered in Aniri's ears over the steady ringing in them.

Someone tried to kill Seledri.

Ash's hand squeezed hers tighter, but she pulled away and covered her mouth. "Is she alive?" Aniri asked him past the muffle of her hands.

"I think so."

"You *think* so?" Her hands flew away from her face and formed fists. "What does that mean? Tell me what happened, Ash."

She could feel her mother and Janak at her back, as well as the others, everyone pulling in close to hear what he had to say.

Ash gestured helplessly. "All I know is that someone tried to assassinate her. If she had been killed, I'm sure there would have been word of that."

He tried to take her in his arms, but her body was too tense for it. She nudged him away, stepping back from her mother and Janak as well, suddenly feeling like she was going to suffocate with the pressure on her chest. "How can we not know for sure if she's alive?" She pointed a finger at the messenger, who stood nearby, looking even more pale than when he came in. "You! How did you hear of this? What exactly do you know?"

He looked to the prince for confirmation, then hastily said, "All I know, my lady, is what came over the wire. News from Samir that the First Son's wife was subject to some kind of attack. Some say poisoning, others say a viper was let loose in her room. Still others say an armed assassin. I don't think they know for sure, my lady. Just..." He looked to the prince again.

"Just *what*?" Aniri held herself back from striding over to shake the words out of the man.

"It's just that... no one has seen Princess Seledri since the attack, my lady."

Ash turned to her. "She's probably just shaken

by the attempt. Just resting until she's able to make a public appearance again."

Somehow this enraged Aniri even more. "My sister would show her face if she could. She's brave and strong and…" Tears sprung out and choked off her words.

Ash hugged her in spite of her arms crossed tightly across her chest. "Of course she is."

Aniri blinked away her tears, finally noticing the distraught look on her mother's face. Janak hovered at the Queen's side, torment scarring his face, like he didn't know if he could console her or not. Aniri reached out a hand, which her mother took.

"She has the baby," her mother whispered, and then she didn't seem to be able to go on. Janak looked like he might explode. He slowly put a hand on her mother's shoulder. "Your majesty, I'm sure they've taken her to safe keeping somewhere. Until they can be assured it's safe to appear in public."

The Queen nodded, but Aniri wasn't at all convinced. She didn't want to worry her mother further, but there were forces at play here that the Queen didn't realize.

Aniri gave a pointed look to Ash. "We need to *discuss* this."

He grimaced, hesitated, then said to the Queen,

"Your highness, I believe we should meet in private to discuss the implications of this act for our respective countries."

Her mother was still reeling, but she raised her eyebrows at the urgency in Ash's voice, along with everyone else in the room. Aniri only hoped she wouldn't object.

"Aniri?" her mother asked, and there was a lot in that question. *What do you know about this? What are you keeping from me?*

"Mother, please." Aniri glanced at the others hovering near them. The priestess and Nisha stood at a respectful distance, Nisha's girls frozen behind them, watching with gaped mouths. Nahali and Ekan huddled close, Ekan's hand resting on Nahali's belly and future child. Priya was stricken, holding back, but hanging on every word. Aniri returned to her mother. "We need to talk in private."

Her mother nodded, and Nisha sprang into action, ushering everyone from the room.

Nahali hesitated, looking back and forth between their mother and Aniri. "Mother, if you would like me to stay——"

"No, Nahali." The shock was wearing off their mother's face, and the normal cool demeanor that the Queen wielded in matters of state was slowly returning. "I will let you know if there's something we need your counsel on."

Nahali bristled under that dismissal, but Aniri couldn't bring herself to care, one way or the other. She was laboring to breathe. Frightening scenarios where Seledri was already dead or mortally wounded crowded her vision. Aniri grasped Ash's hand to steady herself while everyone departed. When the final guard followed after, closing the door behind them, Aniri realized Janak still stood by her mother's side. But Aniri would hardly be the one to order him away, even if she wished to. Which she didn't.

"Mother," Aniri said breathlessly, "we believe the Samirians may have another skyship."

The Queen drew back. "How do you have knowledge of this? And what does this have to do with the attempt on Seledri's life?"

Some of the tension released from Aniri's shoulders at the commanding sound of her mother's voice. The Queen would take control of this situation and make it right. And she would see the next obvious step: that her sister needed to be recalled from Samir and brought home.

Aniri rushed out her explanation. "Garesh

brought the Samirian ambassador's aetheroceiver onboard the *Prosperity*. After we took over the ship, I opened it up." She stalled out for a moment, trying to decide how to explain that Devesh had given her the code. Then simply pressed on. "Inside was a schematic for a second skyship, the *HMS Dagger*."

"A *second* skyship?" The Queen threw a concerned look to Ash.

He put up his hands. "I had never seen the plans before."

"Ash didn't know about the burning glass, either, Mother. Obviously the Samirians were at least *planning* on building a second ship."

"Or they already have one," Janak cut in. "But how is this connected to the attempt on the Second Daughter's life?"

Aniri bit her lip and glanced at Ash. He tilted his head to indicate she should tell her mother everything. "Mother, Devesh told me the Samirians were using the skyship as a diversion. That they were planning to invade Dharia."

Her mother's face colored, and Aniri felt the heat of her anger before she opened her mouth. "And why did you think that *wasn't* something I should know?"

"I... I didn't know where the lies ended and the

truth began." And she was embarrassed to have been taken in so fully by Devesh's kisses and promises. "I thought he had simply been trying to forestall my wedding to Ash, and I... I just didn't think it mattered." Aniri cringed as the words came out. They were the words of a child. A foolish child.

Her mother let out a breath, her anger cooling into exasperation. Somehow that wounded Aniri more, that her expectations were so low. "Aniri, you should have told me."

"I would have." *Eventually*, she thought. "Especially once we found out about the second skyship on our trip back to Jungali—"

"We both wanted you to know," Ash cut in. "But it seemed prudent to keep our suspicions off the wireless."

Janak slipped a look to Aniri that made her cringe even more. "That, at least, was a wise decision."

The Queen took a deep breath. "We need to discuss further how to prepare for the possibility of war with Samir. But they've been our allies for a century. We're trade partners. We intermarry. We may have a sea between us, but the lifeblood of our countries is deeply intertwined. I find it hard to believe they would suddenly put everything we've built together at risk—"

Ash cut her off again. "My spies have already informed me of the unrest in the Samirian countryside that the mere presence of the *Prosperity* has brought on. Even if the royal house was not preparing for war before, your majesty, it has certainly entered their thoughts now."

"That is no doubt true," the Queen replied. "But I still do not understand, Aniri, why you think this attempt on Seledri's life is connected."

It seemed obvious to Aniri, but then she had yet more information that she had not shared with the people she loved. She wrung her hands, but forced the words out. "Because General Garesh and the people he conspired with have already killed a royal." She turned to Ash's puzzled face, bracing herself... this was probably the worst possible time for this to come out, but there was no denying the connection anymore. "Ash, I've been meaning to tell you... I think General Garesh was involved in your brother's death."

Ash leaned away as if Aniri had slapped him. "How could you possibly know that?"

Aniri grimaced, feeling the weight of that secret doubly so now. "When Garesh had me, well, he bragged about killing royals. He as much as admitted to having Tosh murdered to clear the way for using the skyship as a weapon."

Ash's mouth dropped open in disgust, then he rubbed his hand across his face, as if he could wipe away the horror of his brother's death, as well as his disbelief that Aniri had kept knowledge of his brother's murderer from him.

Aniri winced, then reached out a hand to him. "Ash, I'm sorry—"

He stepped back, avoiding her touch and running both hands through his hair. After a moment, he nodded to himself and said softly, "He's dead." He turned back to her. "Although now I wish I had run my saber through Garesh before he fell." He paused. "You're sure it was Garesh? No one else?"

"I'm not sure of anything." The pain in Aniri's chest grew worse. "But I think Garesh and whoever he was conspiring with inside Samir, including the ambassador, were definitely capable of assassinating a member of the royal house. And the ambassador… she could have returned to Samir, in spite of what my sister said." Aniri stopped, running out of words as she imagined Seledri falling from a window in some dark estate deep in the Samirian capital.

Ash fisted up his hands, then released them and put one on Aniri's shoulder. "Aniri, I'm sure Seledri is fine."

"You don't know that!" She pulled away and turned to her mother. "Seledri could be on her deathbed right now. Why else would she not make an appearance to reassure the people? Something awful has happened, Mother, I can *feel* it. I won't believe she's well until I see her with my own eyes. You must find a reason to bring her back to Dharia."

"I'm as worried as you are, Aniri, but I can't simply order her home. Not without undermining the one major political connection we have with Samir. Especially if the threat of war is as great as you think."

"Political connection?" Aniri asked, incredulous. "Mother! Someone is trying to kill her. They may have already succeeded."

"Aniri." Her mother's commanding voice returned, but Aniri no longer wished for it. "We can, and absolutely should, ask for assurances that she is still alive. But she's carrying the future heir of Samir. I cannot imagine they would endanger the child, if nothing else. Which is what war would do. That alone should give them serious pause."

Aniri turned away from her, hands balled up in frustration. She stared at the looming love god, Devrakama, laden with flowers and a sultry stare. There was no possibility she could endure a wedding while her sister may be lying dead in a hostile country. Or in danger still. Who was to say the assassins wouldn't try again? And her mother hadn't seen the fervor on Garesh's face. The sneering hatred for royals. Or the ambassador's cool acquiescence to her kidnapping and possible death. She didn't understand the kind of people they were.

Aniri turned back to them. Janak, her mother, and Ash were giving each other knowing looks, as if they expected her to do something foolish. Childish. Well, she wouldn't disappoint them.

"I'm going to Samir."

There was a moment when all eyes were on her, but no one spoke. Then her mother and Ash both protested at once.

"Aniri, you'll only be putting yourself—" her mother said, while Ash said, "The wedding is tomorrow—"

They stopped, looked at each other, and in that half-beat, Janak spoke up. "I'll go with you."

The gush of relief through her wasn't enough to fend off the hurt look in Ash's eyes.

"She's my *sister*, Ash."

He said nothing in response, but his gaze roamed her face. She didn't like how that made his mouth turn down even more.

Her mother put a hand on her shoulder. "Aniri, you have a wedding and an *alliance* to make. Wait a day, be married, then we can send a delegation from both our countries—"

"I'm *not* going to throw a party while my sister may be lying dead in Samir." A sudden heat ran through her. Even though she knew her mother hadn't left her father dead in Samir all those years ago—that he had actually run away from his family instead and she merely covered it up—her mother didn't know she was privy to that family secret. And years of carrying the anger of that abandonment still lived in her heart. If her sister was still suffering from the attack, or gods forbid actually dead, she would hunt down whoever was responsible and drive a saber through them. If that was childish, so be it. She couldn't live with herself otherwise.

The wedding could wait.

"Of course you won't." Janak's low voice was rough with emotion, but Aniri had never loved it more. "However a simple alliance could be cemented now. The families and priest are gathered. That is all that's required."

Now? Aniri's heart stuttered then raced as if it wanted to leap out of her chest and hide. Moments ago, she had been practicing at a wedding, but it wasn't real. There had still been time to back out— except now Seledri's life was in danger.

Aniri had run out of time. She swallowed down her nerves, steeled herself, and turned to Ash. "We should marry now. Before I go."

But the grim look on his face didn't change. "The Jungali people will be suspicious of an elopement." There was more he wasn't saying, and it made Aniri draw back.

"Aniri." Her mother's voice had gentled. "You're marrying a head of state. It's not something you can do behind closed doors." She gave Janak a look that said he was already in trouble and just dug deeper. "The people need to know the alliance is legitimate. If you are married in secret, it will work against the very confidence you are trying to build between the two peoples."

Aniri looked back and forth between Ash and her mother. With all their concerns for the politics, they were not so different. No wonder her mother was ready to adopt Ash and so readily agreed to their marriage. Her delight that it had been for love seemed shallow now, rooted less in her happiness for Aniri than in her approval of her choice.

"Then the wedding will have to wait." She said it with a tone that she hoped signaled the discussion had ended.

"Aniri." Whatever inner turmoil had been roiling through Ash had finally reached his face. "Can I speak with you a moment?" He took her hand, hardly waiting for her agreement, and towed her toward the back of the rehearsal hall. It was sufficiently large that even empty, with his boot steps resounding off the marble floors, they might reasonably have a private conversation in the rear alcoves.

When they reached as far as they could go and still be in the room, Ash pulled her close and lightly cupped her cheeks. The torment was still plain as he dropped his voice to a whisper. "I would go with you, but—"

"I don't expect you to—"

"Aniri." He said her name like it hurt him and dropped his hands from her face. "I *would* go with you if I could possibly go." His voice was still pained. "I know you well enough to know that nothing I say will stop you, but I can't help thinking that you're leaving because…" He paused, then straightened. "Because you've changed your mind. About the wedding."

"Ash, I haven't." But her words made her squirm. They were far too close to her own doubts. "We'll have our wedding when I return, I promise."

He frowned, and she wasn't quite sure if he believed her. But he only frowned and said, "They've already tried to kill you once. And now your sister."

"I'll be fine," she said, relieved he was only worried about that. "Janak is going with me. You can send a legion of guards along if you like. I'm only going to check on my sister, then I'll return." She didn't mention that she had every intention of bringing Seledri back with her, but she would meet that challenge when she got there.

"I'll send a legion of guards and a skyship as well. With a fully functional burning glass, and a promise of swift and deadly retribution should anything happen to my Queen." He looked pained again. "Aniri, please don't do this."

"You could come with me."

"I *can't*," he said, his voice hiking up. "Certainly not the way I'm going to send you. You're not yet

Queen, and Seledri is your sister. Your arrival by the swift transport of the skyship is merely a concerned sister coming to visit the Samirians' beloved future Queen. You have no authority to wage war… yet. But if I were to come, aboard the warship we just confiscated from a rogue group of Samirians… while tensions are high… it would be seen as something entirely different. It would be a provocation. Besides, your mother and I truly do need to make preparations, now that she knows about the possibility of war with Samir." He stopped, looking frustrated. "My duty is here, Aniri. But if you leave, you're taking my heart with you. Please stay. Marry me tomorrow in front of all our people. I promise we will get reassurances that Seledri is fine another way."

"I have to go, Ash." She said it quietly, hoping he would understand.

He stepped back from her, biting his lip to hold in words Aniri was sure she didn't want to hear. Emotions warred across his face, until finally he said, "Of course you must do what you think is right." He bowed slightly, hands pressed together, but said nothing more, simply brushed past her to rejoin her mother and Janak at the far side of the room.

Tears burned at the back of her eyes, and the pall of Ash's anger hung over her in his wake. Doubt fluttered up inside and battered her heart. But when she thought of her sister possibly lying dead in Samir, she couldn't picture herself doing anything other than seeking her out and bringing her home.

Chapter Six

ANIRI STOOD on the deck of the *Prosperity*, staring down at Ash on the terrace and hoping she wasn't making a terrible mistake. The look on his face certainly said he thought she was.

The walkplank had been pulled in, and the crew busied themselves with unlashing the tie downs to set the *Prosperity* free. The sailors were dressed in blue jackets the color of the Jungali sky with twin rows of crisp steel buttons down the front. The uniforms were new since their return from Sik province, and they made the Jungali crew appear a proper royal navy. The sailors' shouts, the thrum of propellers in the thin mountain air, and the wind buffeting dull thuds against the gas bag above made calling farewell to her husband-to-be a pointless endeavor, so she simply held his gaze as the last ropes were cast off and the ship rose swiftly in the air. The movement was so sudden that Aniri had to grip the wooden railing to keep from tumbling to the deck. Boots pounded their way past her and down below decks as the ship put a hundred feet, then two, between them and the highest tower of Ash's palace.

Her future home and future husband. And she was leaving them.

He had wanted her to stay. Begged her, practically. And yet still she was leaving. The hollow feeling in her stomach wasn't from the rise of the rapidly ascending ship. It was the haunting feeling that she couldn't trust her own heart. It seemed no matter where it led her, she ended up the fool for it. The ache in her stomach lasted well after she could no longer see Ash watching her go.

The ship continued its steady rise, but now the delicate folding sails had fanned out and were turning the ship, pointing the bow east toward Samir and giving her an expansive view of the Jungali mountains. The setting sun in the west tarnished the snow-capped peaks with reddish-orange, and their lengthening shadows drew the valleys deeper and more mysterious. The skyship was fast, but they had to cross mountains and a sea before reaching Samir.

Karan said the sailors could rotate through shifts, and night travel was possible with a star navigator adapted for air travel from the Samirian Navy, but the main problem was fuel. The ship could fly from Bhakti, the capital of Jungali, to Mahatvak, the capital of Samir, on one load of fuel. But they would have to refuel before making a return trip. The ship simply couldn't fly when laden with all the fuel it would take to make the entire journey. So the *Prosperity* would stop at the Dharian coastal city of Chira—it was a shorter flight than to the Dharian naval docks, but still had rich stores of coal for refueling.

All of which made her wonder about the Samirian's capabilities: if the *Dagger* had been built, could it reach Dharia, or Jungali for that matter, without refueling? And if not, where did that leave them in terms of war? The sea between Dharia and Samir was relatively small compared to the breadth of land between the coasts and the inland capitals. The Samirians might be able to cross the water and return without refueling, but they wouldn't be able to venture much farther inland. Aniri would have to ask Karan for further explanation—Ash had revealed the possibility of the second skyship to him and shared the schematics for the *Dagger*, but there had been no time to query Karan further about his thoughts.

The air cooled as they rose and picked up speed, whipping through Aniri's traveling clothes even with her latched leather jacket, heavy breeches, and knee-high boots. When she could no longer see the granite cliff where Ash's estate perched, she turned away from the biting wind and followed the rest of the crew below. The hallways were clear as most had already reached their stations, or their bunks to rest before their shift later in the night. The evening air was untroubled, not shaking the ship as much as the last time she was aboard, but Aniri still glided her hand along the brass rails leading forward to the bridge. Gaslamps had already been lit, and their flames quaked with small tremors from the engine vibrations.

When she reached the bridge, it was lit with an odd combination of waning red from the sun, dancing yellow from the gaslamps, and white effervescence from the twin full moons. Both Raka and Indu shone through the lattice of windows that wrapped the length of the bridge. In the center of the room, Karan in his tinker clothes, bent over an expansive table, studying an assemblage of sheet maps. Along the back, one sailor in a blue uniform stood by a large brass-belled horn and another manned a bank of needled gauges. At the front, by the windows, a third sailor stood with a strange brass device mounted on a pivoting base.

The instrument was roughly triangular in shape, but bristled with so many lenses and mirrors and knobs, it was difficult to discern its main function. The sailor using it peered through a miniature version of the aetherscope Aniri kept on her private rooftop observatory. Only he kept tilting the tiny scope left and right and fore and aft, in small motions, as if he were balancing it, all while making minute adjustments to the knobs.

"Are ye able to get yer fix, Mr. Tarak?" Karan asked in his typical rumbled voice.

"Aye, sir," the crewman at the tiny aetherscope said. "The air's as smooth as glass tonight. Sighting Raka at 50 degrees, 30 minutes, point six, sir." He lifted his face away from the scope to look back at Karan. "What's your time?"

Karan leaned over the table to peer at a time-keeper in the middle. It had a large dial and a small one, both encased in industrial metalwork like it had just been ripped from the wall of a seagoing ship. "Seven minutes, three seconds past the hour, Mr. Tarak." He picked up a pencil and made a note on a slim piece of paper.

Tarak waited as Karan shuffled the papers, apparently looking for one and not finding it. "Do you want me to plot the fix, sir?"

"No, Mr. Tarak, I'm quite handy at me tables still."

"I didn't mean—"

"Carry on, Mr. Tarak." Karan waved him off without looking. "Go on and shoot the second moon."

"Aye, uh…" Tarak stalled out when he finally caught sight of Aniri standing in the threshold of the bulkhead door. Even in the flickering light, Aniri could see he was young, only a year or two older than her. His brown eyes grew wide, and Aniri guessed he knew exactly who she was, although she had never been on the bridge or met him before.

Karan looked up from his papers. "What's yer trouble—" He cut himself off at Tarak's look and twisted back to see what had his navigator searching for words. "Ah, fresh," Karan said when he saw her. "Was wondering how long it would take for ye to work yer way up to the bridge."

"I don't want to interrupt your work." Although

curiosity was like a physical force drawing her inside the room.

"Not to worry, fresh. We can work up a line of position even in the presence of royalty." Karan's smirk made her both relax and flush a little. He turned back to Tarak. "Do me proud, Mr. Tarak, and take the angle of Indu while I work these numbers."

Tarak jerked a little in surprise, then hastily turned back to his instrument. "Aye, sir."

Karan returned to sorting through the many sheets. Some were indeed maps, but others were tables of long, precisely rendered numbers. A thick, leather-bound book labeled *Her Majesty's Nautical Almanac* sat at one corner of the table. Aniri watched as Karan found a sheet with a large circle marked in degrees that had also been crossed with spaced-out vertical and horizontal lines. Within the circle was a tiny x labeled "dead reckoning." Karan worked quickly, flipping open the Almanac, consulting a table of numbers, then drawing two intersecting lines across the circle, one marked "Actual Position, Raka" and the other labeled "Line of Position, Raka."

"Are you plotting the positions of the moons?" Aniri didn't understand celestial navigation, but she knew the navies—both Dharian and Samirian— used the positions of the stars as they hung in the aether to guide them. Perhaps they used the moons as well?

"No, fresh. I'm plotting *our* position. But, aye, the moons help us find it." He raised his voice to call out to Tarak. "Ready for the next fix, Mr. Tarak. At your leisure."

Tarak replied immediately, "Indu sighted at 40 degrees, 10 minutes, point two."

Karan glanced at the timepiece, whose translucent face didn't quite conceal the multitude of tiny clockwork gears behind it. "Time is ten minutes, fourteen seconds past the hour." He bent over his tables and the Almanac again.

"Our current heading gives us good sights for three stars between the clouds," Tarak said. "I've got a good view of Chitra on the port side. Shall I shoot that next, sir?"

"Aye," Karan said without looking.

Aniri kept her voice low, peering at Karan's plotting sheet as he worked. "I'd like to know more about the skyship, Karan. How she works. Her capabilities. Navigation as well, when you have time."

Karan didn't answer until he plotted another set

of crossed lines labeled for the moon Indu. "I told ye, you can have all the lessons you like, fresh." He glanced up at Mr. Tarak, who was busy adjusting the star navigator to peer out the left side of the bridge windows. "However, Captain Tarak is probably best for teaching navigation."

"*Captain* Tarak?" Aniri asked in a whisper. "But he's a *boy*, Karan."

"You always were a right quick one, fresh." Karan chuckled.

She made a face at him. "I mean he's no older than I am." She didn't realize they would be traveling with a crew who didn't have much more flight time than she did.

"Aye." Karan sighed, throwing a glance around the control room to the other crew, who Aniri guessed weren't much older than Tarak either. "When Ashoka sent me off to Sik province to get the ship back in shape, he insisted on routing the Samirians from the crew. I knew we'd had a spot of trouble with the ambassador, but I figured it was that fool Garesh who had a mind to start a war. And he was *Jungali*. Sik province at that. Still, I followed orders. Trust me when I say Tarak's the best of the lot, and by a nautical mile, too. He's been navigating and building tables and maps for us from the start two years ago. Sharp lad."

Aniri shuffled closer to Karan along the edge of the table and dropped her voice. "What if we were to encounter difficulties in the air?" By which she meant another skyship. "Is *Captain* Tarak capable of command in that situation? I mean, Karan, it doesn't make any sense. By all rights, *you* should be Captain of the *Prosperity*."

He smiled. "Thanks for the vote of confidence, fresh, but my place is in engines. Besides, I'm also a Samirian, in case ye forgot."

"But that doesn't matter——"

"I know you mean well by it, fresh. And 'course now I understand Ashoka's concern a spot better. I know I have the prince's confidence. Wouldn't be on the ship, if I didn't. And he's trusting me to train his new aerial navy officers. Grand honor, that is. But I'd rather train 'em up while we're the only thing the sky, if you take my meaning."

"I had a few questions about that as well." Her priority, of course, was ensuring her sister was safe from harm, and hopefully removing her from Samir altogether, but taking advantage of the trip to investigate the Samirian's skyship capabilities was an opportunity they couldn't pass up. She glanced at the crew and kept her voice low. "Given our limits on range, it would seem that much of Dharia and Jungali are out of reach—that any *unwanted* incursion would of necessity be one way."

"Aye," Karan said, keeping his voice low as well. "Which isn't the best for a war time mission. Range is a tricky thing, but we built the *Prosperity* for commerce, not war, and her range is from Bhakti to Kartavya, one way. I've looked over those schematics from Ashoka. Those plans are no different than the *Prosperity*, which means any ship built to those specs would have the same range."

"So a round trip would be limited to, say, port to port?"

"Aye." Karan glanced down at the map spread before him on which he was plotting their course. It showed the ports of Dharia and Samir relatively close across the short sea, compared to the vast country of Dharia and the distant northern mountains of Jungali. "Which is a fine thing for ruining your neighbor's navy, but not much for taking over a country. Unless that country is Samir."

Aniri frowned and peered at the map again. "Because Samir is so much smaller than Dharia."

"Far easier for Dharia to be the one makin' those unwanted incursions."

She looked up. "But we have no intention—"

"I know, fresh. But I'm not the only one who can read a map." He sighed. "When we were building the *Prosperity*, we had all kinds of specialized parts shipped over from Samir. Once we land, those backdoor supply channels are a good place to look for any unusual trade. But schematics aren't the same thing as a ship, fresh. Even the *Prosperity* has a few tweaks you won't find in any plan. And if I was still workin' for the Royal Guild of Tinkers in Samir, I'd be designing a different ship than the *Prosperity*. And building it as fast as I could put gears together."

Aniri nodded and cast a look around the bridge crew. They were ignoring the whispered conversation at the mapping table, as far as she could tell. A little louder, for the benefit of the crew, she said, "Still, I'd feel better if I knew more about how the *Prosperity* works."

"As soon as we're done sighting our location, I'll be happy to turn you over to the Captain for lessons." He smirked, then pulled back suddenly at something over her shoulder.

A glance back showed Janak had appeared from nowhere. He was apparently at pains to keep his stealthy raksaka reputation intact, in spite of whatever grief his injuries may still be causing him.

"If your most royal highness can spare a moment from your aeronautical studies," Janak said, "we have a few things to discuss."

She didn't know how much Janak had overheard, but their mission wasn't exactly a secret from him. "Of course. I've yet to find my cabin for the trip, but I assume Priya will be there." She wasn't sure when, or if, they would make Priya aware of the secret part of their mission.

"Then perhaps we can take a stroll elsewhere," Janak said.

Priya would find out later, then.

"Above decks will be less than comfortable, fresh," Karan said. "The galley should be clear for at least an hour. Cook won't be prepping for dinner until then."

She nodded her thanks and followed Janak from the bridge. They were quiet down the two flights to the galley. She finally noticed a slight hesitation in his steps on the stairs—not quite a limp, more a favoring of one side. It made her stomach clench. Why had she agreed to have Janak on this trip? Surely there was someone else who could provide security. But of course she knew the answer: her mother would trust no one else like she would Janak. And, despite her concerns, Aniri was selfishly glad to have him with her.

The galley was empty, just as Karan had said. There was only a trio of wooden tables that could seat maybe a dozen sailors at once. The crew was small, and probably ate in shifts, too.

Janak eased into the seat opposite her, slower than she would have expected, sparking new concern. "Are you sure you're well, Janak?"

"My injuries will heal." He narrowed his eyes. "Your foolishness, on the other hand, appears quite possibly terminal."

She returned his glare. "Ensuring my sister's safety is not foolishness." She felt the rightness of that statement in her heart, but at the same time feared he was right. The anger and hurt on Ash's face still haunted her.

"No, but upsetting the political balance between three countries who may be on the brink of war most certainly is."

Aniri pushed back from the table and crossed her arms. "I thought you came because you supported me in this."

"I came because the Queen would worry excessively about you if I didn't."

Aniri threw her hands out in exasperation. "I have an entire guard and a skyship to protect me. I'm simply going to ensure that Seledri is well, then return. A few days at most."

Janak didn't move, but his dark eyes bored into her. "The Queen worries—and I can't say without reason—that you might do something more foolish than that."

Aniri's eyebrows hiked up. Did Janak and her mother already guess her plans to bring Seledri home? Not that she had any idea how to accomplish it, or even if Seledri would be willing to come, but Aniri wanted to ensure her sister had a way out of the enemy territory that Samir might soon become. She met Janak's inscrutable stare with her own, not wanting to tip her hand. Perhaps she could throw him off.

Aniri leaned forward again, putting her elbows on the table. "Have you told her?"

Janak frowned. "Told her what?"

"Have you told my mother that you love her?"

Janak's mouth fell open, then he shut it in a thin line and studied the sworls of wood grain on the table.

"I haven't told her, either," Aniri hastily added.

"About that, or that I know the truth about my father."

His attention snapped back to her. "I told the Queen you are now aware that your father isn't dead."

She leaned back. "You did?"

"She's worried that your rush to Samir has as much to do with that as with your sister. And I'm concerned that you keep the secret your mother has suffered under for years."

Her mother thought she would try to find her father.
Should she?

The thought honestly hadn't occurred to her, yet now that it had, a slithering itch of agitation ran up her legs and forced her to stand and pace away from the table.

"Aniri." Janak's voice carried warning. "Tell me you aren't thinking of—" He cut himself off.

Aniri turned to study him: he was clearly ailing, fist clenched on the table, visibly struggling with emotions. He came not to watch over her, not to rescue her sister, *but to keep the Queen's secret safe.* She didn't want to be angry with him, but it surged up inside her anyway.

He ground his fist into the table and said through clenched teeth. "It was my mistake to let you know. Believe me, I regret that. In a moment of… *weakness*… I betrayed the Queen's confidence. I have sworn your handmaiden and Prince Malik to secrecy. I believe they both understand the gravity of the situation, but you…" He stared up at Aniri from the table. "You are known for making decisions that may not be the most prudent."

His words were a blade slicing through her heart. She turned away, pacing and trying to choose words she wouldn't regret. Finally, she stopped in front of him, hands on hips. "That's why you haven't told her. Isn't it?"

Janak clenched his jaw and looked away from her demanding stare. "The Queen thinks you will run after your father. She actually has great confidence in your ability to find him, even though no one else could. And the hope in her eyes when she spoke of it…"

Aniri could see the pain that caused him, and it made her heart clench. "My father left her. Left *us*. He might as well be dead. He's nothing to us now." She hadn't thought of it that way before, but it was true. As much as she wanted to know *why* her father had chosen to leave them, in the end, the why of it didn't matter. He left them all the same.

Janak shook his head. "I'm afraid he remains something to the Queen."

Aniri took a seat again. She wanted to reach a hand across the table to Janak, but she didn't think he would allow it. So she balled hers up on the table, mirroring his. "He's just a memory that she clings to because she has nothing to replace it."

Janak looked to her, and the glimmer of hope was almost worse than the pain. "I think it's more than that, Aniri."

Aniri. He never called her that, and it tore at her.

"How can it be more? *You* are the one she trusts. *You* are the one she sends to make sure I'm not an even bigger fool than normal. You are by her side every day, whereas he's just a bad memory, an embarrassment she's had to carry for years."

He shook his head sadly. "You don't hear the way she talks of you, Aniri. How proud she is. How much you remind her of him—of the good parts. The parts she wishes to remember. She still—" He stopped and pressed his lips together, like he had already spoken too much.

"She still what?" This time Aniri reached across the table to grab Janak's clenched fist. "Tell me, Janak."

"She still clings to the idea that he never truly left. Never abandoned her. That somehow, something went wrong. He wandered off in the night. He was lost or kidnapped perhaps."

Aniri's heart clenched, and she drew her hand back. "Is that possible?"

Janak gritted his teeth. "It is a fairy tale she tells herself because the truth is too bitter." Then his face softened. "But it's not one I can bring myself to take from her."

Aniri was still reeling. "You said… you said he left a note. She can't deny that."

Janak rose up, pushing away from the table in disgust. "Yes, he left a note, but notes can be faked. He had protection—I was there as his raksaka—but my tea was drugged. It might not have been your father himself drugging my tea, even though he was the only one I wouldn't have suspected. It could have been assassins or kidnappers. By the time I awoke, your father could have been spirited far away, against his will. The Samirian Queen Mother assured us no one in her court had knowledge of his whereabouts, but they could have been lying. If it was a conspiracy, our Queen could never have uncovered it without launching a full scale war. And if he was taken, why then… he could have *escaped*.

He may yet still be alive, living in the shadows in Samir, just waiting for the chance to return."

He was laying out the logic in the Queen's voice now, but his voice was bitter. Aniri could picture it, this argument they had, Janak and her mother, over whether her husband had truly abandoned her. Or whether he had been taken by the Samirians who then covered it up, for some unknowable reason. The woman Janak loved was still fighting, eight years later, to hold onto a version of the past that would forever exclude Janak from her life.

Aniri could only imagine the pain on both sides of that fight. "You don't believe any of that," she said softly.

"No." His shoulders dropped. "If he loved her like she wants to believe, there is nothing save death that could have kept him from returning. Nothing that could have kept *me* from returning."

"But you are *raksaka*," Aniri said with a small smile. "He was only a man."

He gave a short laugh that more resembled a huff.

She edged forward. "My father may or may not be dead, but either way, the man who *was* my father is gone. I'm only going to Samir for Seledri. You have my word on that."

He stared into her eyes for a long moment, studying her. Then he gave a short nod. "I hear you have plans to become a tinker along the way."

"Only in my spare time." She kept her face serious, but a smirk flashed across Janak's face. He believed she was telling the truth about her father, and she was. But all this talk of him only strengthened her resolve to get Seledri out of Samir. Her father had abandoned them long ago; she wasn't going to do the same to her kind-hearted sister.

WHEN THE SKYSHIP stopped in Chira to take on coal, Aniri thought she would see the famed black lava flows or glittering sand beaches, but the night was pitch dark, the twin moons had set, and she was exhausted from hours of instruction on the operation of the *Prosperity*. Sighting tables, needle gauges, and ship schematics swam in her thoughts as she dropped into a bunk in the room she shared with Priya. She didn't even change out of her traveling clothes, just kicked off her boots and nearly fell asleep before her head hit the pillow.

What felt like minutes later, but must have been at least a few hours, Priya shook her awake and urged her to change into attire suitable for meeting royalty. They were deep inside Samir, past several low-lying mountain ranges and the boroughs that were nestled between them. The air was rougher now, making it difficult to keep her balance while she struggled into a corset, skirt, and slippers. Priya gave up pinning her hair after several attempts. Instead, Aniri just donned a hair jewel matching her subdued orange-and-red dress.

They climbed the stairs to the deck in time to see the skyship sail over the wall of the Samirian capital of Mahatvak. The city was buttressed by granite mountains on one side, and a massive stone wall surrounding the rest. The ship flew low—perhaps only a few hundred feet above the buildings—and sound carried crystal-clear through the air, bringing the rattling of steamworks, the laughing voices of children, and the calling of street vendors hawking their wares. It was like Bhakti, Ash's capital city, with the buildings jammed together and constant motion in the streets, only Mahatvak was five times the size and didn't have the color of Jungali. A haze of brown muted the city, and the acrid stench of burning coal wafted up to them. Through the smoke, Aniri could see even the buildings lacked color. The metalworks and masonry Samir was famous for— carved stones, bricks, and riveted steel columns—

were uniformly gray or brown or a dirty sort of ivory.

Priya leaned over the railing and waved to a group of children who were looking up at the skyship and pointing. "Hello!" she shouted, as if the strangers below were her fondest friends. "Hello, people of Samir!" Of course, as far as she knew, the Samirians were their allies and had been for a hundred years.

As they sailed above the city, many of the citizens waved back, but many more shielded their eyes against the morning sun and simply stared. The ship's shadow passed over them, and it made Aniri shiver. She could imagine a skyship sailing over their city, one that had a weapon on board capable of destroying it, wasn't the most pleasant thing to see on this bright, sunny morning.

Aniri pulled back from the railing. "I'm moving forward for a better view."

Priya remained behind, waving to the crowds and gawking at the sights. Aniri worked her way around the Jungali sailors as they darted along the deck, unwinding coiled ropes to prepare for docking. Karan had messaged ahead and been cleared for an approach to the Samirian royal household. That alone—that the Samirians were willing to let them fly the skyship straight into their capital city and dock at their estate—gave Aniri a wash of relief. Surely, if they were planning war with Dharia, or Jungali for that matter, they wouldn't be welcoming a skyship with open arms deep into their country.

Aniri found Janak at the bow. Most of the deck was occupied by the glass-encased bridge, which had a sailor on top waving nautical flags, one in each hand. He dangled over the edge, a line attached at his waist for safety, signaling someone with flags of their own on the parapets of the estate.

"I think Seledri must be all right," Aniri said to Janak. "They wouldn't be welcoming us so warmly, allowing us to dock right at the palace, if there was any trouble afoot."

"Or they are glad we're bringing our one weapon within arm's reach," Janak said wryly.

"They could have forced us to land in a field outside the city. Surely that would have provided them with more advantage for attack, if they were of a mind to. And kept their palace far from any danger."

Janak looked surprised she had given it any thought at all.

Aniri scowled at him. "I'm attempting to better my education in political matters."

"Well, that will certainly be a relief to all our Queendoms."

Aniri shook her head. Janak's temper hadn't lightened much after their discussion, and he seemed to grow more tense as they approached the palace. It was a glittering, dark gray behemoth, carved of granite and fortified with steel from the Samirians' resource-rich mountains. The castle had a myriad of slender towers that ended in needle-sharp spires, like daggers sheathed in the craggy granite mountain behind them. There were also rounded domes, arched windows, and stone terraces, but even those were topped with metal spikes, as if the estate were a giant quilled beast that stood defensively against any attack.

"Where are we to dock?" Aniri asked, suddenly concerned.

"It *is* a rather unfriendly place for a gas bag to perch." Janak pointed off to the left, what Captain Tarak called the port side, and there an extension of the castle ran along the mountain: it was a series of rooms, a single story tall, carved straight from the rock. They were far from the spires, which made the extended balcony at least a plausible place for docking, but Aniri couldn't imagine their purpose otherwise.

"Whatever are they for?"

Janak eyed the apartments. "High security prisons? Secret meeting rooms? The royal suites?" He glanced at her. "I can see the strategic advantage of having a fortress which has only one, highly guarded entrance."

"It just looks… odd."

"The Samirians are known for their metalworks and their cleverness, less so for their aesthetics. Their designs always serve a purpose."

Aniri nodded. The skyship drifted closer, and she glimpsed a half dozen guards and a lone figure who might be royalty on the balcony. The ship slowed and turned sideways, cutting off Aniri's view. Shouts from the opposite side of the ship sounded like the Jungali crew were casting lines.

Janak carried the Queen's aetheroceiver tucked under his arm. Its twin would remain with Captain Tarak and ostensibly provide wireless communication with the skyship while they were on the ground —but it was also a lifeline to signal for help, should they need it.

It reminded her of the other aetheroceiver on board—the one with a twin in Ash's office. He had given it to Karan, but the first message had been for her, arriving not long after they departed.

ANIRI: BE CAREFUL. RETURN QUICKLY.

Aniri had transcribed the message herself, working the symbols into letters on the thin scroll of parchment. She could feel his anger between each word. He had practically begged her to stay, to marry him in front of all his people. Instead, she had fled, running off to rescue her sister from a country and a husband she didn't love.

Aniri wasn't forced into marriage, like her sister, but maybe her betrothal to Ash was an ill-fit union as well. She had thought she was in love with Devesh, but that turned out to be a love built on lies on his part and wishful thinking on hers. At least she and Devesh had the advantage of time together, whereas nearly every moment with Ash had been filled with intrigue and drama. When the threat of war receded, what would they have binding them together? Perhaps Ash was right: a princess from the plains and a prince from the mountains were too unlikely a match. His steaming hot kisses in the fencing hall might convince her heart they were meant for each other, but clearly her heart had proven to be as flighty as bird; she couldn't help but wonder if she could trust it at all.

Aniri shook her head, breaking free of her reverie.

Janak's curious stare made her flush, but he quickly held out his free hand, gesturing her to go ahead of him. "After you, your most royal highness. If all is well with your sister, perhaps we can be on our way within the hour. The less time we spend within blunderbuss range of the Samirian seat of power, the better."

Aniri nodded and turned to lead the way to debark. As soon as she ensured Seledri's safety, she would ask her sister if it was common to hesitate so much before a wedding. Wasn't that a sign the marriage was poorly chosen? Her lovely and love-burdened sister hadn't been given a choice, but Aniri was certain she would have wise counsel about this.

Meanwhile, Aniri needed to focus on the problem at hand: spiriting Seledri out of Samir. An hour was considerably less time than she might need. Perhaps she could offer to give her sister a ride in the skyship—surely the Samirians couldn't object to a sightseeing tour of their city from above—and then simply make for Dharia and hope they were out of range before her plan was detected.

She couldn't see Karan agreeing to that. Not when it risked having his ship shot down. Nor would Janak, given it would likely be an act of war. Aniri had spent the hours flying over the sea to Samir casting for a plausible reason to bring Seledri home, but she had come up empty.

By the time Aniri and Janak cut through the midsection of the ship and emerged at the walkplank, Priya had joined them. The wind was quiet next to the immense rock cliff that abutted the palace. The fins of the skyship were tucked for docking, and cables lashed the ship to the balcony, holding the walkplank steady enough. Rope handholds had been strung across it, making the crossing somewhat less treacherous than before.

Aniri went first, facing the welcoming party and recognizing Seledri's handsome Samirian-prince husband immediately. Pavan's face held an uncertain smile, and his dark brown eyes were wide with the wonder of the skyship before him. He was dressed all in black, from his shiny leather boots to a stern, high-collared jacket. The diagonal slash of coal-black buttons across his chest glinted in the morning sun. As Aniri approached, his smile warmed. He pressed his hands together and held them high with a slight bow, the most formal of greetings.

"Princess Aniri," he said, in a grave tone, "The country of Samir welcomes you."

Once safely on the solid ground of the balcony, Aniri returned the formal gesture, bowing slightly with her hands held together by her forehead. "It is my honor to be welcomed to your country, Prince Pavan."

He immediately dropped the formality and reached a hand out to take hers, guiding her away from the walkplank and toward the palace. Aniri felt Janak close at her back and trusted that Priya, Karan, and the sailors acting as royal guards trailed behind her. Karan had wanted to stay with the ship, rather than leave it in the hands of young Captain Tarak, but Karan's secret mission to assess Samirian capabilities would not be served from the air. He had donned a blue Jungali sailor uniform, and hoped not to be recognized in his disguise as a royal guard. They left enough crew on board to fly the ship, in case of emergency.

Karan had convinced Aniri that the range of the skyship was an important secret to keep, even if the details of the *Prosperity's* design were already known by some—it was precisely who knew what that was at issue. When the skyship was still a highly secret project, the Samirian ambassador in Jungali coordinated all communications and the flow of goods and people between the two countries. Even Karan didn't know who within Samir had knowledge of the secret airharbor in the northern Jungali mountains. As a precautionary ruse, Karan wished to keep the actual fuel usage of the Prosperity a secret, even as they arrived in Samir. He had requested coal provisions for the return journey, and already a line of mechanized carts had formed along the balcony. The carts were unlike anything Aniri had seen before: Samirian workers pumped long handles up and down, cranking some clockwork inside that propelled the cart forward. It struck her that this was technology that had never made its way to Dharian shores.

Pavan hooked Aniri's hand over his arm in a gentle and friendly way. "I am so glad you came, Aniri. Seledri will be beside herself with joy." The warmth of his hand and his voice, and especially the mention of Seledri's name, made her almost weak with relief.

She squeezed his arm. "I came as soon as I heard. I hope you understand, Pavan. She is so close to my heart, and with the baby... I simply needed to see her with my own eyes."

His smile faltered, just for a split moment, but it was enough to make Aniri's heart lurch. She had forgotten: the last she had heard, Seledri had not told her husband about the baby-to-be.

"I... I hope I haven't misspoken." Aniri bit her lip and studied his face.

It crinkled into a sad kind of humor. "I'm not surprised you knew of the baby before I did." He frowned. "Although I will admit that I had hoped, once she had a baby on the way, it would... change things."

The torment on his face clearly said it had not. Then Aniri realized: *he knew.*

It was obvious Pavan's love for her kind-hearted sister was a true one, in spite of their arranged marriage. He was First Son to a Queen with no Daughters—normally he would wed a Samirian noble, just as First Daughter Nahali had found a suitable husband amongst the Dharian court. As Second Daughter, Seledri should have wed the Second Son of Samir, or if there hadn't been one, another high-ranking Samirian noble. By tradition, the marriages of Second Sons and Daughters cemented the relations between the two countries without upsetting the normal order of ascension. But Pavan had asked for Seledri's hand, and Second Son Natesh was rumored to have already fallen in love with a Samirian noblewoman. The Queen Mother allowed it, for the sake of both her sons, but everyone knew the match would never have occurred had Pavan not fallen in love with the beautiful, soulful-eyed Second Daughter of Dharia.

Aniri had never been sure if Pavan knew Seledri's heart—that she had fulfilled her duty, but hadn't yet grown to love him. But now Aniri realized: of course he knew. How could someone *not* know when their love wasn't returned?

Pavan seemed to force a smile. "I still hold onto hope that, perhaps, when the baby arrives..." He swallowed, then continued on. "I didn't know she was with child until she returned from Dharia. She speaks of you constantly, Aniri, and the difficulty of being away from home. I see the toll on her face. She misses you and Dharia very much, and with the baby now, well, that just cements her place here even more. I can understand why telling me was difficult for her. Of course, I *do* wish she would have told me sooner. Maybe then, this wouldn't have happened." The handsome angles of his bronzed cheeks drew sharper.

"Is it really so dangerous for her to be with child?" She didn't understand why that would be, but she would use any excuse to bring Seledri home.

They had reached the end of the long balcony and approached the palace proper. The gray granite walls were intricately carved, a veritable lace of stone that allowed light into the palace but kept out the elements. The large, arched doorway was rimmed in riveted steel with an elaborate clockwork mechanism at the center. Pavan inserted a key from a long chain around his neck. The gears shifted and clicked, then sprung the heavy stone door wide under its own mechanical power. Inside was an even larger second door, illuminated by the diffused light filtering through the embroidered stone. Sentries guarded the door—their oversized pistols had dark Samirian-wood handles, but the barrels were a mass of clockwork and pistons, the function of which could only be to make the guns more lethal.

The door behind the guards began to whir and click as they approached. It swung open, and across the threshold strolled a younger, and even more handsome, version of Pavan. Aniri had only briefly met Natesh, the Second Son of Samir, at Seledri's wedding, and that was two years ago, when he was still a boy. Now he was a man, with the same angled cheekbones and dark brown eyes as his older brother, only his still sparkled with the unspoken mirth of youth. His asymmetric jacket was unbuttoned, baring a casual silk shirt underneath, and his broad smile had an unabashed charm, as if he hadn't a care in the world. Which Aniri understood all too well: with no Daughters in Samir to take the throne, a Second Son wasn't quite as extraneous as a Third Daughter, but almost.

"Well, if it isn't the dashing Third Daughter of Dharia come to visit our very home," Natesh exclaimed, taking her hand in his and bowing deeply to touch his forehead to it. It was a bit presumptuous but also very gallant. His words and the intimate touch managed to work a grin out of her. His smile dampened only slightly when he straightened. "Stories of your intrigues and adventures raced across the sea to entertain us. I'm only sad it took a near tragedy to draw you to our beautiful country."

"I've been meaning to visit for some time." Which was true, although with the intent of seeing her beautiful sister, not the countryside. "I will have to make arrangements to return for a lengthier visit soon." She only hoped that would actually be possible.

Natesh slowly let go of her hand, and his smile settled into something just short of a smirk. "It's my fervent hope that you do."

"I'm sure Aniri would prefer to meet with her sister without further delay." Pavan tugged her away from his charming younger brother.

Natesh beamed again. "Yes, of course. I'm sorry to keep you, Aniri. Please give Seledri my regards." He stepped aside to let them pass, and Pavan urged her forward through the massive doorway. They wound through a series of polished granite hallways with gleaming brass-trimmed windows and somewhat stuffy portraits of Samirian nobles. Pavan and Aniri led her entourage of Janak, Priya, Karan, and the half dozen royal guards, not to mention Pavan's royal escorts as well. It was quite a crowd, but they made good time through the palace.

Aniri waited until they had left Natesh well behind to bend her head close to Pavan and ask, "What did your brother mean about giving Seledri his regards? Does he not have occasion to see her rather often?" It struck her as a strange thing to say, even more so because Seledri had so recently been attacked. Surely he had seen her since then, if only to give his regards in person.

Pavan caught her eye, glanced back at the others, and kept his voice low. "Seledri has been quite selective about visitors since the attack. She's simply not feeling well enough to entertain."

Aniri's heart climbed into her throat. "Pavan, please tell me she is all right."

He took her hand again, wrapping it around his arm and drawing her closer so that their whispers wouldn't carry. "She's fine, Aniri, I promise. But with the baby and the poisoning—"

"She was *poisoned?*" Aniri sucked in a breath.

Pavan squeezed her hand. "She's all right now, as I told you. I thought you had already heard."

Aniri let out her breath. "Messages have a way of jumbling with rumor when they cross two continents and a sea. I wasn't sure at all what had happened. Which was why I was in such great haste to get here."

He patted her hand. "And I am truly glad you did so. I'm sure you will brighten her spirits." He smiled, but that didn't calm the stuttering of her heart.

Aniri's imagination flew back to the last time she saw her sister: Seledri had seemed close to a death-like appearance then, even though she was merely pale from the rigors of travel and carrying a child. But it highlighted her sister's more delicate nature. Aniri fought a surging panic in her chest and steeled herself to be a comfort, not react with horror, should Seledri be in a similarly stricken state. But questions still tumbled through Aniri's mind. She should ask them now, rather than make Seledri endure them.

"How did this happen?" she asked Pavan. "The poisoning."

"Somehow her handmaiden did not properly check her food before Seledri consumed it."

Aniri's stomach clenched. "Was she very ill?"

"For a short period, yes."

"But she has recovered?"

"Recovering."

Aniri's stomach tightened further with each question. "And the baby?"

Pavan hesitated, but Aniri could tell it was from emotion contained, not a reluctance to answer. "The healer assures us the baby is fine."

Aniri glanced back at her solemn entourage, then dropped her voice. "Do you know who is behind it?"

"No." There was great frustration in his voice, a

coiled anger that reminded her of Janak, only Pavan's nature was more gentle, so it seemed to hold less deadly potential. "It begs belief that anyone would want this, Aniri. You know your sister. She's kind-hearted and sweet-tempered to a fault. She earned the people's love from the moment she set foot in Samir."

Aniri could feel the fear radiating from him: for Seledri, for the baby, for the near-tragedy that almost stole everything dear to him. "There must be someone you suspect."

Pavan took a breath. "The handmaiden has disappeared, so yes, she is a suspect. Trust me, I've deployed every resource in the Queendom to find her. And the Royal Guard has been tasked with hunting down anyone who may have had access. I've also put round-the-clock guards on Seledri's room while she rests." He paused to glance at her. "I don't know for certain who did this, but I have every intention of making them pay for it."

Aniri nodded, her last doubts fleeing on those words. They were the ones she would use, and they resonated in her heart. It certainly seemed that her worst fears were unfounded, and that Pavan had things well in hand.

They slowed as they approached a white granite

door that had been carved with more geometric designs, only these did not penetrate the rock. Pavan brought the whole group to halt.

"If you don't mind, Aniri, I would prefer just you to come inside. Like I said, I'm trying to minimize her visitors, so she can get the rest she needs."

Aniri felt Janak materialize by her side. "Your highness, I insist on accompanying you."

She held up her hand. "It's all right, Janak. I'll just be a moment." She smiled a little, chiding him. "You can break down the door if I don't come out soon."

Janak only frowned, not at all amused. "I'm certain that Princess Seledri will understand, given her recent encounter with assassins and near death." His hard look told her he had no intention of taking her *no* for an answer.

Aniri glared at him, then turned an apologetic look to Pavan. "He'll make less trouble if we allow him to come. I promise my overzealous raksaka won't disturb her."

Pavan seemed uncertain, looking back and forth between Aniri and Janak, but then acquiesced with a tip of his head. Using a ring-key on his hand, a different one than he used for the outer entrance, he unlocked the door to Seledri's room. Pavan held the door open just wide enough for Aniri and Janak to slip through, then followed them inside.

Seledri's room was spacious, with a window to the outside streaming in the morning sun. Dozens of heaping bouquets of flowers filled the room with their mixed perfumes. Dark Samirian furniture formed a sitting area to one side, next to an empty fireplace. A large four-postered bed dominated the middle, draped with heavy netting and gauze all the way around, such that Aniri couldn't see through to discern her sister within.

Janak drifted to the window to check something, perhaps if assassins could make the climb, while Pavan closed the door, then hurried over to intercept Aniri before she reached the bed. Perhaps Seledri was sleeping, and he wished to wake her first. Instead, Pavan took Aniri by the shoulders. The apology in his eyes made her heart seize up.

She glanced to the bed again. There was no motion inside, none that she could see anyway. "What is it, Pavan?"

"Seledri's not here."

Chapter Eight

"WHAT DO you mean she's not here?" Aniri pulled out of Pavan's grasp and tried to open the heavily draped netting around her sister's bed. When she couldn't find an opening, she hoisted it up over her head.

There was a body in the bed, gray with death, and packed with bags of ice around it. The scent of whisky hung over it like a cloud. The body's face was misshapen and splotched, but there was no mistaking it: this wasn't her sister.

Breath rushed out of Aniri, and she tumbled backward into the netting, grabbing at it to hold herself up. *This is not Seledri. This is not Seledri.* The thought pounded through her head, but she forced herself to lean forward again, to study the body's face once more, just to be certain.

It wasn't her.

A scuffle, a thump, and a strangled sound came from outside the netting, then a hand reached to grab her arm through the layers of gauze. Aniri fought against it, jerking and kicking at the unseen person holding her from the other side, but it was useless: their grip was iron strong.

"Aniri." The admonition was Janak's. "It's only me. Are you all right?"

"Yes!" She still railed against his hold, the panic of being constrained fighting through any reason that told her he was trying to help. "Let go of me, Janak!"

He did, slowly, then he grabbed a fistful of the netting and raised it over his head, enough that he could lurch inside the hanging shroud. In his other hand was Pavan's throat, his eyes bugged and mouth gaping but unable to breathe.

"Janak, release him!" Aniri tugged at the solid rock that was Janak's hand choking her sister's husband.

Janak didn't move except to cast a look at the body on the bed. "Is that the Second Daughter of

Dharia?" His cool tone of voice convinced Aniri that Pavan's life hung on her answer.

"No," she said hastily. "I'm certain. Queen's breath, release him!"

Janak dropped his hand, and Pavan grabbed at his throat, sucking in air, coughing and wheezing. Aniri went to him, digging him out of the drapings as he struggled to breathe again. His hands covered the already-red marks shaped like Janak's fingers on his throat. Once free of the netting, he knelt to the floor next to another body. It was a man in a Samirian guard uniform, passed out next to the bed. He hadn't been in the room before, causing Aniri to quickly glance around the room for more. The door they came through was still closed, but a second door—seemingly a hidden one, the way it appeared to fit precisely into the wall of Seledri's bedchamber—stood ajar leading to steps beyond.

Pavan tried to rouse the guard, but he didn't move. "Did you kill him?" He wheezed as he pushed up from the body and the floor. A coughing fit took him, and he was forced to bend over, hands on knees, gasping.

Aniri stared at the guard, then looked to Janak for an answer.

He emerged from the curtain of gauze and,

with one swift motion, hoisted it over the top of the bed to clear it out of their way. Then he loomed above the still-bent-over Pavan and his inert guard.

"Your guard is lucky I decided he was too weak of a threat to kill." Janak picked up a small brass pistol that Aniri had missed lying on the floor. He tucked it into the back of his raksaka uniform and stood in front of Pavan. He didn't touch the prince, but the threat of it forced Pavan to peer up.

"I believe some explanations are in order." Danger laced Janak's voice.

Pavan straightened, a hand still holding his throat. Aniri winced as she saw it was already starting to bruise, but he seemed to be recovering his breath.

He gestured to the dead body in the bed. "The woman is Seledri's handmaiden." His voice was still raspy, and he had to pause to wheeze in more air. "They were very close. She was poisoned with a meal meant for Seledri."

"Where is the Second Daughter?" Janak's voice remained clipped with tension.

"I've hidden her away." Pavan turned apologetic eyes to Aniri. "I'm sorry for the deception, but I promise you, she is fine. I had to secret her away. There is no way the assassin could have accessed her food without the help of someone within the palace. And I suspect they were not simply after Seledri, but the baby. The attempt was made shortly after we announced the new heir-to-be."

Aniri's heart was still pounding. "I want to see her."

"I know. I'll take you to her. But you must leave your entourage here." He indicated the multitude still lingering outside Seledri's room, not Janak. Clearly Pavan understood Janak wouldn't be leaving Aniri's side under any circumstance now. "Tell them you wish to spend some time with your sister. They may retire to the common rooms and refresh themselves. I'll see to it they're attended to. But it may take some time for us to reach Seledri's hideaway, and we must use stealth in getting there." He paused to swallow, something that seemed quite painful for him now. "We must take care to maintain the ruse that she remains here, resting in her room."

Aniri glanced at Pavan's guard at her feet. "Is that why you're keeping the handmaiden's body here? And guarded?" She left unspoken the question of why the guard attacked Janak, assuming he must have been attempting to save the First Son from Janak's iron fist. Something Aniri could have told him would be ill-fated.

"He suspects another attempt will be made on the Second Daughter's life." Janak's voice had lost much of its tension. It seemed he believed Pavan's story as well.

"Yes. And I want any further attempts to be made *here*... where I have the ability to capture the assassin and find out where the conspiracy lies and who is involved."

Aniri raised an eyebrow. "Don't you have raksaka in your employ?" Thwarting assassination attempts is what raksaka lived for. She couldn't imagine any standing by idly while letting a mere palace guard lay in wait for one.

Pavan grimaced. "I cannot be sure of their loyalty."

Janak looked like he wanted to strangle the First Son anew.

Aniri jumped in. "I can't believe Samirian raksaka are so different than Dharian ones. They live to serve the crown."

"But which part of the crown?" Pavan's voice was still recovering but the growl in it wasn't from his near-choking.

Aniri drew back. "You suspect the royal family?" It was incomprehensible to her. She would risk her own life for any of her sisters, even First Daughter Nahali. *Especially* First Daughter Nahali, since an assault on her wasn't just an attack on her family but her country and its future as well.

Pavan glanced at the door. "We can discuss it further once we're on our way to see Seledri. That *is* what you traveled across the sea for, isn't it, Aniri? I want to assure you of her safety, and perhaps gain your assistance. The backing of Dharia and Jungali would be instrumental in an internal fight for the crown."

Aniri's eyes were wide, but she nodded her assent. Meanwhile, Janak had already moved to pull down the curtain of gauze and straighten the netting to hide Seledri's dead handmaiden. Pavan bent to attempt to awaken his guard, who was moving his head, but not yet fully roused. Between Pavan and Janak, they carried him to the couch and laid him out.

Janak returned to her side, and they approached the door together.

He gave her a stern look. "We will assure Seledri is alive. Then we will be leaving." She was certain he wanted nothing to do with the internal politics of Samir. Aniri nodded, but her sister's life was on the line. She had no intention of leaving Seledri in a viper's nest of political intrigue in a foreign country. Janak should know better, if he believed she would agree to that.

Nevertheless, she opened the door just enough for her and Janak to slip through, with Pavan following close behind. Priya and Karan were huddled together near the Jungali sailors acting as royal guards. They seemed wary, hands on their pistols, as the Samirian guards surrounding them did the same. As if they thought her entourage might start a riot at any moment.

Priya stepped forward, but Aniri stayed her with a hand. "Princess Seledri is doing well," she said with as much confidence as she could muster, "but I wish to spend some time attending to her privately. I will only require my personal guard. Please bear with me." Aniri caught Karan's gaze, which was jumping between Aniri and Janak's impassive face. She gave Karan a small nod, which he returned.

Priya shuffled forward in spite of Aniri's words. "Are you sure my lady doesn't need assistance?" Her pitched voice and wide eyes said she didn't understand at all what was happening, but it was worrying her. And Aniri couldn't blame her handmaiden for feeling that way—worry was still wringing echoes through her body as well. Aniri reached out to reassure Priya, who grabbed fast onto her hand and drew close.

Aniri whispered in her ear, "Tell Karan to proceed." Then she pulled back and added, louder, with a forced smile. "I'm counting on you to keep our crew out of the ale, Priya."

Priya nodded vigorously. "As you wish, my lady."

Pavan was artfully keeping a hand over his neck to hide the bruising from Janak's hold, but he managed to whisper a few commands to an aide, who then scurried off. Aniri waved to the assemblage, gave Priya one last reassuring smile, then returned to Seledri's room, determined to find a way out of Samir for all of them.

Chapter Nine

WHILE PAVAN REVIVED and reinstated his guard, Aniri quickly searched Seledri's wardrobes for attire that would allow her to pass for one of the Samirians in the streets below—since that was their apparent destination.

The hidden doorway in Seledri's room led to a spiraling stone staircase, a secret passageway through the mountain castle that was dank and dripped water on Aniri's boots as she followed Janak and Pavan. The air grew more foul as they spiraled deeper into the bowels of the mountain. Finally, the stone steps emptied into a tunnel carved from the bare rock. Trickles of water wept down the walls and gathered in the center. The three of them followed the tiny stream, their torches casting orange licks of light around them. The low ceiling and tight walls forced them to walk single file.

Pavan had given them dark, heavy cloaks with hoods to hide their faces, but even those didn't ward off the pervasive chill. Janak still had the aethero-ceiver clenched in one hand, but she wondered how truly secure a communique would be in the heart of the Samirian capital, where surely there would be other aetheroceivers which might intercept their transmission. With any luck, they wouldn't need to find out. And they would be back before their entourage had tired of the Samirian hospitalities.

"This tunnel is ancient," Pavan called from the front. His voice echoed off the hard surfaces. "It was designed to provide an escape for the royal family in the event of a siege, back in the days before Samir was a unified country, and the prov-ince lords still fought one another."

"Is the door in the Second Daughter's room the only one leading to this tunnel?" Janak asked.

"Yes," Pavan said. "No one has used it for a century, and I only know of it because Seledri's bedchamber used to be mine as a child."

"And we're the only ones who know Seledri's handmaiden hasn't run away, but is lying dead in Seledri's room?" Aniri asked.

"Only a few people know the true state of things. As soon as I realized what had happened, I was at a loss as to whom I could trust. The handmaiden was already dead. There was no use calling for a healer. Instead, I brought in two of my most trusted guards and immediately spirited Seledri away. I kept the tunnel a secret mostly out of habit, but it was the perfect way to remove her from the dangers of the royal estate, where any of a hundred people could present a danger to her and the baby. And as you'll see, even if the tunnel were discovered and compromised, Seledri is hidden in an innkeeper's room distant from the tunnel itself. She's safe because no one knows where she is."

Pavan cast a look down the tunnel to Aniri. "I'm taking a risk even bringing you to her, Aniri. But I need your help to keep her from harm."

Aniri almost suggested that there was nowhere in Samir safe enough for Seledri, but she decided the moment wasn't right. Yet. "You know I want nothing but the safekeeping of my sister."

He smiled and turned forward. "Which is why I was so happy to hear you were on your way. The people have been restless with this news of your new skyship, not to mention the burning glass and the destruction it wrought in the attack on your country. I've tried to reassure them of our bonds, through marriage and treaty and a hundred years of peace, but it hasn't done much to settle them. And then with the attempt on Seledri's life…" He paused and threw her a grateful smile. "You coming here so quickly, in peace and concern for our future Queen, and in the skyship no less—I can't tell you the effect it has already had in reassuring my people."

That wasn't her intent, of course, and who knew what Karan would find in his attempts to ferret out the Samirians' plans to build another skyship, but now didn't seem the right time to bring that up either. "Dharia and Jungali wish for nothing but peace with Samir." At least that much was true. It struck her that she could plausibly speak for both countries while, in truth, having no authority in either.

The tunnel came to an abrupt end, turning upward to form a vertical shaft with a ladder disappearing into darkness above.

"There's a hatch at the top," Pavan said. "I'll go first to ensure we're unnoticed." He pushed back his hood, and with his torch in one hand, awkwardly climbed the ladder. The light showed a circular door not far above. He reached the top and cracked it open to peek, then signaled them to follow.

The door was hidden behind a copse of red-berried bushes. The bright morning sun nearly blinded Aniri as she fought her way out of the shrubs, but Janak's hand at her elbow steadied her. They emerged into a small clearing behind a long line of gray-walled Samirian-styled buildings. Pavan raised his hood and gestured them to follow through a narrow alley that led straight to the bustling streets of the capital.

Their muted brown cloaks and hoods didn't stand out too harshly—it seemed everywhere the colors had been drained from the marketplace. The business facades were gray granite trimmed with steel, much like the palace, and even the street vendors had carts crafted from the dull metal. A tinker shop across the cobbled road was alive with wind-up toys, as well as larger steamworks that reminded Aniri of the Samirian ambassador's dancing automaton. A three-wheeled cart ambled, only without a beast to pull it. Like the coal carts in the palace, this vehicle was propelled by the pumping action of the driver, who stood on a small platform and sent the lever up and down, trundling her trunk full of goods down the street. Another cart passed by, this one with passengers instead of cargo.

Aniri shuffled closer to Pavan. "What manner of transport is this?"

"The pamgari?" Pavan asked, surprised. "Oh yes. Seledri says you don't have them in Dharia."

"I suppose it would put our beast masters out of business."

Pavan grinned. "In Samir, we're a smaller country than you. We have relatively less land, which means less grazing for beasts and less arable land for crops." He gestured over his shoulder to the distant palace and the looming mountain behind. "Whereas we have an almost unlimited source of metals and coal. If we can mechanize something, we do."

Aniri nodded as another pamgari trundled, by carrying a bushel of star-shaped fruit. "I can see that."

"Our destination isn't far," Pavan said, gesturing ahead, "but I'd prefer we spent as little time on the streets as possible."

He pulled his hood lower on his forehead, no doubt hoping to not be recognized. Her gawking at Samirian technology wasn't likely to help either. Aniri tugged her hood down as well and picked up her pace. Janak followed silently beside her as they wove through the considerable foot traffic along the lane. She dodged mothers with mechanized strollers and workers bearing crates for their shopkeepers. Aniri avoided making eye contact, but had to skirt a small child on the loose, which made her glimpse ahead and see something that froze her heart: a dark-haired man with the high, bronzed cheekbones and dark eyes of every other Samirian, only this one she knew far too well.

Devesh. He met her gaze but didn't linger, no look of recognition on his face.

Aniri dropped her gaze, her heart pounding. Could it be him? Was it possible? Devesh had fled Jungali with the Samirian ambassador. Her sister assured her that he had not returned to the capital, but in this teeming city, how would she have known? More importantly, had he recognized Aniri?

She peeked from under her hood again, but the figure was long gone. She glanced at Janak by her side, but his purposeful stride showed no sign of anything amiss. Maybe her eyes were playing tricks on her. There must be thousands of young men in Samir who were Devesh's age. He had spoken of how large his family was. Surely, it was just a resemblance. Besides, if it was Devesh, he would have shown some sign of recognition. She was sure of that. And, regardless, he was gone now. She kept her gaze on the ground in front of her, calming her heart and focusing on the street turns as they went —two left and one right—in order to not be completely off kilter in this foreign city.

Soon, they reached an inn whose weathered wooden door Pavan quickly pushed aside. The customers inside were a considerably rougher sort than the citizens outside. Most were men, with a few well-armed women holding court, and all were dressed like adventurers returning from hard travel: riveted and scuffed leather vests, loose and torn shirts, breeches of weathered canvas. Aniri guessed all manner of illegal services could be procured here.

Pavan strode to the bar at back and made a whispered request of the barkeep, whose rolled-up sleeves did a poor job of hiding the bulging muscles and series of scars on his forearms. If those weren't intimidating enough, the dagger, saber, and snout-nosed pistol strapped around his leather-waisted shirt would do the job.

Aniri kept her head bowed, hoping the hood would be sufficient, and turned to face Janak at her back. He was so close, she nearly bumped into him while he performed a slow scan of the other patrons. Janak was a coiled spring ready to explode at the least sign of trouble, but most of the customers had already dismissed them and gone back to their whispered conversations or slow consumption of various ales and liquors at hand.

The barkeep reemerged with a woman dressed in a stylish deep brown corset and trim skirts. Aniri guessed she was the owner by the automatic scowl on her face for the three strangers who appeared at her inn making whatever special requests Pavan had whispered. But when she saw the First Son peering from under his hood, her face relaxed, and she motioned for them to follow her around the end of the bar and toward a dusky stairwell. As they climbed the stairs and passed several closed doors, Aniri slowly realized just what kind of establishment they were in.

In her mother's court, courtesans like Devesh were considered skilled entertainers and accomplished social creatures. They were accorded a place of honor for their companionship, even though it was understood that their services often crossed over into the soft arts of love. It was all respectable and accepted as the natural course of things, with ladies of the court as well as royalty enjoying the courtesans' games and skills. That Aniri had fallen in love with one was her own foolish doing, but it wasn't as if it had never happened before. Courtesans often "retired" from the profession after wooing a lady of the court; indeed, that was the sole ambition of many. That Devesh would be one of those, having won the heart of the Third Daughter, was just one of her many assumptions that had turned out tragically wrong—the added insult being that, according to him, *all* courtesans were spies.

Perhaps that was true at court, but here, in this darkened inn buried deep in the capital of Samir, the courtesans likely provided only their most basic service. And Aniri suspected they weren't only male, but female as well, judging by the customers below. She shuddered to think of the desperation that lay behind those closed doors—not ambition or courtly wooing, but simply a means for survival by trading the only service left to them.

Her eyebrows arched, and she leaned closed to Janak. "I thought courtesans were banned everywhere but at court," she whispered. "Is that not true in Samir?"

"I suspect a great number of illegal activities

occur here." Janak didn't take care to keep his voice low, like she had.

The innkeeper scowled at him, but then glanced at Pavan and turned down another hallway, leading them past a dozen more closed doors before reaching one at the very end. She handed Pavan an ornate key for the Samirian-style clockwork lock in the door. Aniri glanced back: the other doors were not so similarly protected. A turmoil of emotions tripped through her, as she remembered their purpose. A scowl settled on her face for the kind of establishment in which Pavan had chosen to hide Seledri away. The innkeeper left them without a word or look back. Pavan knocked twice, then once more, then put the key in the door. The clockwork whirred to gain them entrance.

Inside, a guard in a rumpled Samirian palace uniform held the door as they filed in. Aniri quickly scanned the room for her sister. The guard was the only person in the shabby suite. It smelled of old leather and stale air, like the windows hadn't been opened in far too long. Hazy light filtered through gaudy curtains over the single window. A lone gas lamp hung near a small couch. Next to those were a table and chairs for eating, but no sign of her sister.

Then she spied another door on the left. "Is she in there?" Aniri asked Pavan in a rush.

He nodded and strode over to knock briefly, then open it. Janak hung back by the guard securing the door, while Aniri was a hair's breadth behind Pavan. Over his shoulder, she saw her sister lying on a large bed that nearly filled the tiny room. The only light was a dimmed gaslamp that left dull shadows in the corners and made it difficult to see.

But Seledri's warm brown skin seemed as gray as death.

Chapter Ten

ANIRI HELD HER BREATH, frozen at the doorway of Seledri's room. Her sister shouldn't have already taken to her bed, and that unnatural pallor… Aniri prayed to Devkasera, mother goddess of Dharia, and any other goddess who would listen, for Seledri to open her eyes. While Aniri was fixed in place, fear clenching her heart, Pavan hurried to his wife's side, and gently shook her awake.

Her sister sleepily blinked up at her husband. "Pavan." Her voice was thick.

Aniri's breath released all at once, relief flooding her body.

Pavan beamed and helped her sister as she eased up to sitting. "I've brought you a visitor."

Seledri frowned and pulled back from Pavan's

touch, then looked to the door. Her shock at seeing Aniri stilled her momentarily, then her hand flew to cover her mouth, like she might cry. That unlocked Aniri, and she crossed the room in two large strides, climbing across the bed to reach her sister more quickly.

"Aniri!" Seledri reached for her.

Aniri hugged her sister, hard. She bunched up the red silk of Seledri's loose-fitting bedclothes, and it occurred to her that she might be holding Seledri wrong, squeezing too tightly for the baby. But the need to hold her sister was too much to let go.

"You're here." Her sister's delicate frame shook, her face buried in Aniri's hair. "I can't believe… you're here."

Aniri held her tighter. "I'm here." She kept hold of her sister a moment more, then she had to see Seledri's face. Her eyes were shot with red and rimmed with tears. Her smile was far too tremulous. "Tell me you're well, Seledri. Please."

"I'm fine." Seledri gave short laugh that sounded uneven, like she might be crying instead, then pulled Aniri into another hug. "Everything's going to be fine now that you're here."

Aniri's eyes pricked, but the strength with which

Seledri held her was reassuring. Aniri glanced to Pavan, whose smile had grown even wider.

"Could you…?" Aniri wasn't sure how to politely ask him to leave.

But he dipped his head and seemed to understand. "Take your time." He backed away from the bed, and the door clicked as he closed it behind him.

Aniri loosened her hold on her sister and eased back on the lumpy bed, but Seledri didn't let her get far. Her hands went to Aniri's face, and she could feel them shake.

"Gods, Aniri, am I dreaming this? I think maybe I've summoned you on the power of my wishing alone."

"Of course I'm here. I came as soon as I heard." Seeing her confident, wise, funny sister in such a state—distressed, trembling in her bed clothes, seemingly on the edge of a dark precipice —carved a hole in Aniri's chest. She took Seledri's hands from her face and held them. "Are you truly, well? You don't look it."

"No, no, I'm fine." Seledri put a protective hand over the small bump on her belly, which had grown since Aniri had seen her last, but was still just beginning to show. "Thanks to poor Alisha. She paid a terrible price—" A hitch in her sister's voice cut her off.

Aniri's heart squeezed. She couldn't imagine how distraught she would be if Priya took poison meant for her. "I'm so sorry about your handmaiden. Pavan said she was dear to you."

Seledri's gaze sharpened. "What did Pavan tell you?"

Aniri frowned. "Only that your handmaiden was poisoned and he didn't know whom to trust, so he secreted you away."

Seledri leaned back against the headboard. Her eyes—the deep brown ones that were always filled with warmth and made Aniri feel loved with just a glance—were dull and weary, a film of fatigue drawn across them.

Unease climbed into Aniri's throat. "What's wrong?" She glanced around the room—it was clearly meant for illicit activities, not securing the life of a royal. Her gaze dropped to the bump. "Is it the baby?"

"No." Seledri put both hands on her belly. "Well, maybe it is. I can't be sure." She took a deep breath. "I think Pavan may be behind the attempt on my life."

"What?" Aniri drew back, rocking the bouncy

mattress with her movement. She glanced at the closed door, but Pavan and his guard had more to fear from Janak than the other way around. "I don't understand. Pavan loves you. You're carrying his child, the future heir of Samir—"

"That's just it," Seledri said, then stopped, her eyes welling with tears. She blinked them back. "When I first told Pavan, he seemed overwhelmed with joy. His love for the baby, the sweetness of it… it captured my heart. I thought that, maybe, finally, I had found a way to love him." She looked away, past Aniri, beyond the walls of the tiny room. "Then something changed. He suddenly stopped talking about the workings of the Queendom. He withdrew and became distant. When we heard news of the skyship and the attack on Dharia, I could hardly drag answers from him about the fate of the ambassador and your courtesan."

Her sister's words seemed so at odds with the concern that had been plain on Pavan's face. "Why do you think he was acting so strange?"

"I think… perhaps…" Seledri seemed to struggle to get the words out. "I think Pavan may have taken a lover."

"*What?*" That made no sense at all. Her sister was the most beautiful among the three Daughters, but more than that, she was kind-hearted and sweet. And funny. And now she carried Pavan's child, giving him the one thing he needed to rule Samir, once his mother the Queen stepped aside. It didn't make sense to risk all of that with a lover. But there was undeniable heartbreak in her sister's eyes. "What makes you think all this?

"He hasn't just been distant," Seledri said, dropping her gaze. "We no longer share a bedroom."

In the haste of everything, it had escaped Aniri's notice that Pavan referred to the room as Seledri's room, not *their* room. Aniri gestured to her sister's rounded belly. "Well, that obviously hasn't always been true. Is it because of the baby, perhaps?" Aniri didn't understand why that would change anything, but Samirians were more *strict* in some of their customs. And she certainly didn't know all of them.

"That was what he said at first, that he wanted to allow me the comfort of my own bed. But then he was often missing from the palace. The keepers of the estate didn't seem to know where he had gone. I stopped inquiring because of the looks they gave me. As if they knew something I didn't." She took a shaky breath. "Oh, Aniri, I should have tried harder to love him. He didn't have to ask for my hand. He broke with tradition to make me his wife, and loved me so sweetly, and yet… I still didn't love him in return. I just *couldn't.* It was the one thing left that was truly mine to give, truly *my* choice."

Aniri reached out to squeeze her sister's hand. "You can't force your heart to feel something it doesn't."

Seledri shook her head, gaze falling to their hands. "When has it ever mattered what my heart truly felt?"

Her words cut into Aniri. "It has always mattered!"

Seledri looked up, sadness a deep well in her eyes. "Oh, little sister. You've always believed the heart should rule. It's one of the many things I love about you."

That cut even deeper. Aniri's heart certainly hadn't been a wellspring of good choices lately. Possibly ever.

Seledri took a breath and let it out. "But following my heart was never a choice for me." She shook her head. "Maybe if I had loved Pavan the way he wanted… but instead I made him wait and wait, and now…" She gave a bitter smile. "Now I'm afraid I've simply become too inconvenient to keep around."

Aniri could barely stand the tremble in her

sister's voice. "That doesn't make sense. You're carrying his child—"

"I am carrying a child who is half Dharian!" A flush of red darkened Seledri's face. She swung her legs off the bed and rose quickly, leaving Aniri off balance. Her sister paced and spoke rapidly. "In Samir, there is less love for Dharians than you might imagine. It is one of many things that divides the brothers. And there has always been a competition between them—I've seen it grow from a boyish taunting to a more serious thing. A more deadly thing."

"Competition for what? The crown? But Pavan is First Son." If the Samirians had different ascension traditions, surely she would have heard of it before now. But Pavan did mention not trusting his own raksaka—

"Yes, he is First Son," Seledri continued, pacing and gesturing as she spoke. "The only son of the Queen and her first husband, who is now deceased. The husband who was rumored to have been found with a lover before his untimely death."

"A *lover?*" Aniri was truly shocked. Courtesans entertained unmarried members of the court, but royal marriage was held sacrosanct. It wasn't simply a marriage, but the understructure of the country.

Her mind's eye flashed unwillingly to the image of Devesh stumbling out of the ambassador's bedroom, half dressed. Were Samirians simply incapable of fidelity?

"Yes, a *lover*. And then he died mysteriously in an accident while mountain climbing. The Queen soon took a second husband. One who has been supposedly more loyal, and who gave her a Second Son." The anger on Seledri's face rose again. "Apparently assassination is preferable to divorce in Samir."

Aniri's mind recoiled from the thought. Royals married for life—one reason why her heart quaked in the face of taking that step with Ash. She had to be *sure*, because there would be no changing one's mind after the wedding. But if a royal found themselves trapped in a loveless marriage, and found someone else to love… and were desperate enough… was death the only escape?

She shuddered. Then she realized her own father had left his Queen as well, faking his own death in order to run away from the court and its obligations. And they had been *in love*, at least at the beginning. Her shoulders fell with the weight of that thought. Was royal marriage nothing but a trap, no matter how it was arranged?

"Let's say, just for the moment, that Pavan wanted out of the marriage," Aniri said, hardly believing her own words. "But orchestrating an attack on you? And his child-to-be? He's such a… a gentle soul. I can't imagine it."

"I know! It begs belief." Seledri fluttered her hands, and the tears came back. "But it's no secret that the Second Son charms his mother, the Queen. And she's already broken with tradition once, in allowing her First Son to take a Dharian wife. She could give the crown to whomever she favors. But if Pavan found a Samirian to love, someone in keeping with tradition, someone who…" She choked up for a moment. "…actually returns his love…" She paused. "I've only ever been useful as a trading chip, Aniri. A pawn in the political drama of Dharia and Samir. I should never have pretended I could be anything else."

Aniri scrambled out of the bed to rush to her sister's side. "That's ridiculous. You have always been more than that."

Seledri grabbed her into a hug. "To you, my beautiful younger sister. Perhaps. Not to anyone else."

Tears were threatening to burst forth, but Aniri

managed to hold them in. "If Pavan can't see it, he's a fool."

"Pavan is not a fool," Seledri said bitterly, releasing her. "Tell me, what does the world think of my disappearance? Where is he saying I've vanished to?"

A sick feeling churned in Aniri's stomach. "He's telling people you've taken to your bed, still sick with the poisoning." She left unsaid that she had basically confirmed Pavan's story to her entourage and sent them away.

"How easy it would be for me, then, to take a turn for the worse. Once he's found a suitably convincing way for me to die. Did Pavan tell you who brought the food that contained the poison?"

"No." Aniri's chest tightened.

"He asked the kitchen to make a special dessert. I hadn't told him I had been suffering from sickness with the baby. So you see?" Her sister's hard look narrowed further. "He couldn't have known I would ask my handmaiden to eat it for me."

Aniri sucked in a breath. "Oh, Seledri."

"You can imagine my distress when it killed her."

The hardness in Seledri's face broke Aniri's heart.

Was it really possible? Could Pavan have poisoned his own wife and child-to-be simply to clear the way for a new one? What kind of people were these Samirians that they could even conceive of doing such a thing to someone they supposedly loved?

Then it hit Aniri like a slap to the face. They were people like Devesh.

"Seledri… I don't know what to say."

She reached out to grip Aniri's hands. "I need your help, Aniri."

"Of course. Anything."

Fervor burned in Seledri's eyes. "You need to get me out of Samir."

Chapter Eleven

"You want me to do *what*?" Janak asked in a tone of voice that clearly said Aniri had gone mad.

"Knock out the prince and his guard and help me secret Seledri away on the skyship," Aniri said as evenly as she could. She had explained everything, but Janak simply looked back and forth between her and Seledri, as if trying to decide which Daughter had gone mad first in hatching this far-fetched and ill-considered plan.

"You brought the aetheroceiver, yes?" Aniri pressed on. "You can simply message Captain Tarak and have him meet us outside the city."

Janak was speechless for a moment, his mouth working, but no sound coming out. Finally, he shut his mouth, closed his eyes, and rubbed them, as if gathering patience. When he opened them again, his gaze settled on Aniri, and she could feel the weight of his judgment. He had found her guilty of this plan, probably figured she had intended it from the start. Which, really, wasn't too far from the truth.

"You want me to assault the First Son of Samir, kidnap Samir's future Queen and unborn heir, and spirit them away via skyship to Jungali," he said coolly. "In other words, you wish to have me start a war, and by your leave, your most royal highness, in the process abandon half the skyship crew, your Master Tinker, and your handmaiden to a country which will soon want our heads."

Aniri cringed. She hadn't thought about what would happen to Priya, Karan, and the others.

"All because your sister suspects her husband may be having an affair."

When he said it that way, it sounded even more foolish than Aniri already knew it to be. She bit her lip and looked to her sister. What hope had been in her eyes was now crushed into a dull glaze. Seledri pressed her lips tight and averted her eyes. She wouldn't force Aniri to look her in the face while she told her *no*. That they weren't going to help her.

That Aniri was going to leave her to her fate in Samir, whatever that was.

A pawn in the political drama of Dharia and Samir. Her sister deserved better than that.

Aniri turned back to Janak, steeling her voice. "I want you to protect the life of the Second Daughter of Dharia. It's your job."

Janak straightened, and Aniri knew she was perilously close to a line she shouldn't cross. His eyes were pitch black in the dim light, and his gaze roamed her face, taking the measure of her. She knew he would find her lacking. It was ill-considered and reckless and something only a child so naïve or willfully ignorant of the realities of life as a royal would demand. But she also knew she couldn't leave her sister under these conditions. It was an impossible situation, and she prayed Janak would help her find a way out of it.

Aniri held her face neutral even though every part of her was wilting under his stare.

The tension in Janak's shoulders eased ever so slightly. "I doubt the prince would attempt anything in our presence. If he has any ill plans toward the Second Daughter, he would wait until we have been reassured and departed again. Then a second assassination attempt, or success, could plausibly be blamed elsewhere."

Aniri held her breath, not certain exactly what that meant for them.

Janak tipped his head to Seledri, and Aniri thought she saw a softening of the tight crinkles at the edges of his eyes. "Naturally, we will not give him the chance to make such an attempt."

Seledri let out an audible gasp that was loud enough to cover Aniri's similar gush of breath in relief. Her sister threw her arms around Janak, who seemed slightly alarmed at the sudden contact. It took everything Aniri had to keep her grin in check, knowing that could easily make Janak rue his decision even more. Seledri pulled back quickly, sparing him from deciding what to do with his arms as they hovered mid-air behind her.

Janak cleared his throat. "Given that we have a small measure of time before we would have to return to the skyship or raise suspicions, perhaps we should message Captain Tarak and see if he could make arrangements to pick up our crew who still remain on Samirian soil."

Aniri nodded fervently. "Yes. That would be... prudent."

Janak scowled. Of course, nothing about this

plan was prudent. "I will wait until we have incapacitated the prince and his guard and made our way to the edge of the city before contacting Captain Tarak with our true plans." He looked over Seledri's loose fitting bedclothes, rich in their red embroidered silks. "Do you have more suitable clothing for travel, my lady?"

"I do," she said. "When Pavan brought me, he insisted I wear a heavy cloak. And he has since provided other changes of clothing, as the days wore on."

Janak's scowl grew deeper. "Truly the mark of a man bent on killing his wife."

Seledri's shoulders drooped. "I know you must think me mad, Janak—"

He cut her off by holding up a hand. "*Someone* is trying to kill you, my lady. I'm not certain it's the First Son. But then again, I'm not certain that it is not. The politics of your situation concern me far less than ensuring your safety. I'll do my job." Janak turned a hard look to Aniri. "Your job will be to handle the politics that may fall out from it."

Aniri gave him a sharp nod. Whatever befell from this decision would be squarely on her. She would accept it, broker a solution—or wage a war, if it came to that.

"I'll tell Prince Pavan you wish to visit a bit longer with your sister," Janak said. "That will give Captain Tarak time to retrieve the crew. A message to the captain about our impending departure shouldn't raise suspicions." With a short nod, Janak strode from the room and closed the door behind him.

Seledri hurried to a small armoire tucked in the side of the room. The furniture looked mismatched, like it had been brought in from elsewhere. Her sister quickly dug through it, pulling out traveling breeches, a loose-sleeved jacket, and a leather vest that was just shy of a corset. Finally, she pulled out a voluminous black hooded cloak. Aniri watched as she dressed, worry eating at her thoughts, now that the threat of abandoning her sister had receded.

"Seledri," she said quietly.

Her sister looked up from lacing her vest loosely around the bump that was Aniri's future niece or nephew.

"What if Pavan isn't the one behind your assassination attempt?" Aniri asked. "Are you certain you want to do this?"

Clouds of doubt crossed her sister's face. "I don't want to think it's him, Aniri. He's the father of my child. And if you'd asked me before the baby,

I would have said *no, Pavan isn't that kind of man.* He was one of the few who treated me like I was something *more.* Worth something beyond my duty as Second Daughter." The tormented look was back. "That's what I thought. Until the political winds shifted. Until having a Dharian wife was something less *politically sound.* And having a half-Dharian heir became something that would come between him and the crown he always thought would be his. Then… *then* he became just like everyone else."

Aniri caught a glimpse of the bitter pain in her sister's eyes before she pressed them closed, as if shutting out the awful reality of the idea. She took a deep breath. When she opened her eyes again, a steely determination had taken the place of the pain.

"I may be wrong, but I can't take the chance." Seledri rested a hand on her belly. "I've more than just myself to think about now."

Aniri cringed at her sister's words, but she didn't dispute them. Even Pavan mentioned he might be in a fight for the crown. It still didn't make sense, given his apparent pain about Seledri being in danger. But he was already telling lies to his people about her death. The rest could easily be a ruse as well. And if this was all a grand misunderstanding of words and actions, then words and actions might plausibly fix it. Apologies made. Fences mended. But if Pavan was truly a danger to her sister, well, there was no bringing Seledri's handmaiden back from the dead. Leaving her sister unprotected was the kind of mistake Aniri would not be able to fix, once it was made.

An hour passed as they waited to hear back from Captain Tarak about the recall of the *Prosperity's* crew. Janak remained in the main room with Prince Pavan and his guard while Aniri spoke quietly with Seledri. Some of the color came back to her sister's cheeks as they talked, and she even smiled once or twice as they spoke of her time in Samir. It wasn't entirely awful, but the stretches of loneliness and heartache were etched in the small downturns of her lips and the gallows humor that had replaced Seledri's always warm disposition. Pavan was right about one thing: two years in Samir had taken a toll on her beautiful sister.

Aniri was sitting cross-legged on the bed with Seledri when a muffled grunt came through the closed door to the main room. Before Aniri could work herself loose from the bed, Janak opened the door and held it wide, beckoning them out. Beyond him, Pavan and his guard lay crumpled on the floor.

"I take it Captain Tarak has boarded the crew?" Aniri asked Janak as she passed, her gaze fixed on the inert forms of the First Son and his guard. The guard's face held no expression, but the prince's was frozen in silent pain.

"Unfortunately, Karan has not yet returned to the ship," Janak said.

Aniri whipped her head around. "Where is he?"

"I imagine he is carrying out your royal highness's instructions."

Of course. She had sent him off to discern the Samirians' capabilities for war. Ones they may soon be discovering first hand. "Is there any possibility we can retrieve him before we depart?"

"I will message the captain about our new plans as soon as we have reached the edge of the city. For now, he's awaiting us at the palace."

A trickle of hope made her nod. "So Karan may yet find his way on board before we leave."

"It's possible," Janak said. "But it's more likely we will be forced to leave him behind. Then he'll have to find his own way to Jungali. Or perhaps he will stay here. He is Samirian after all."

"He is one of *us*," Aniri said.

"Understood." Janak's attention was drawn to Seledri, who was standing over Pavan's body, hand covering her mouth, tears glassing her eyes.

Aniri hurried to her side and grabbed her hand, tugging her away from the sight of her husband lying unconscious on the floor. "He's fine, Seledri." She cast a quick look to Janak to verify that, and he nodded. Aniri urged her toward the door. The sooner they left, the better.

"There's one more thing, your most royal highness," Janak said as he lifted the aetheroceiver off the dining table. He held out a thin strip of paper to her. "It's from Prince Malik."

Aniri took it and read the neatly printed letters of Janak's transcription.

ANIRI: HEAR SELEDRI IS WELL. MESSAGE YOUR EXPECTED RETURN.

Captain Tarak must have relayed the news back to Ash, or at least the story she told the crew. Aniri had never replied to his first message and neither could she respond to this one. Aetheroceiver communiques were necessarily terse: she couldn't tell if he was still angry, or merely impatient. But any response she could send would be meaningless —she couldn't tell him their true plans, not until they were well and truly away. And by then it would be obvious. Or possibly the news would race across the sea ahead of them, as it became known that they had taken the First Son's wife and child. Aniri supposed she could conjure a reassuring communique that was fit for spying eyes, but there was no time. She crumpled the slip of parchment, stuffed it in the pocket of her cloak, then put up its hood.

"How will we find our way through the city?" she asked Janak.

He raised an eyebrow for her obvious dodge on the subject of Ash's note. "During our flight in, I noticed the grid of the city's streets are neatly laid out, with the palace at the far eastern edge along the mountains and the main city gates to the west. We can orient to the palace, then follow the streets."

Aniri gripped Seledri's hand in a reassuring way. "Let us be on our way, then."

Janak held out his hand, gesturing for them to go first. Once they were out the door, he used a key he had obviously lifted from Pavan to lock the door behind them. Aniri dropped Seledri's hand as Janak gave her sister the aetheroceiver to carry, but stayed close to her side. They weaved through the hallways, past the closed doors of the courtesans and their desperate work, and down the dimly lit stairwell to the main floor.

The inn's customers had swelled in number and volume: the scuffling of boots and gruff voices fought to be heard over the sharp clinking of ale bottles and shot glasses. Aniri tried to stand tall while still hiding her face and working her way around clusters of patrons. Hopefully, no one would notice, or bother with, their quick retreat. She was only a dozen paces from the weathered front door when a cloaked figure, who had been leaning against the wall, pushed away and strode to intercept them.

Aniri tried to slip past him, but he stopped her with a single word. "Aniri." A chill ran through her body, and she stopped, nearly colliding with Janak behind her. The man's face was shadowed by a hood, but he quickly threw it back. "I just want to talk."

It was *Devesh*.

She gaped. At the same moment, a blur of motion to her side resolved into Janak. Before Aniri could blink, her raksaka had his hand on Devesh's throat, and her former lover was on his knees, his dark leather cloak dusting the floor around him.

The bar sounds stilled around them.

Seledri whispered, "Janak," with a warning tone. A nearby group with several leather-cloaked men and one heavily-armed woman looked on with interest, but didn't move to interfere. Aniri's heart pounded. She was certain Janak could handle any of them in a fist fight, but an image of one pulling a pistol on them—just like Garesh sending a bullet straight through Janak's chest on the skyship—flashed through her mind and made her heart stutter. Janak was armed, but the patrons had numbers on their side.

"Not here," Aniri whispered, tight and low.

Janak's face was splotched with anger, and she imagined he was already restraining himself, simply by the fact that Devesh was still breathing. A tension-laden second later, Janak released him and leaned back, still keeping his body between Devesh and the Daughters.

Her ex-lover coughed and choked but slowly worked his way to standing. The group of onlookers snickered and lost interest, returning to their ale bottles and furtive discussions.

Devesh rubbed his throat. "I just want to talk, Aniri, I swear." He glanced around. "Perhaps this is not the best place."

"Yes," Janak said, voice like ice. "Perhaps we should remove ourselves to an alleyway where I can kill your courtesan in peace, my lady."

Devesh's bronzed face paled, and his eyes grew wide. He looked rapidly between Aniri and Janak, as if he expected her to save him.

Even though Devesh had failed to lift a finger to save her from General Garesh.

Indeed, he had held her in his arms while Garesh drugged her. All the rage came flashing back at once, a heated volcano that scorched her face with shame at her own foolishness and anger at Devesh for pretending at love all while betraying her. Before she realized what she was doing, Aniri stepped forward and slapped him soundly with her open palm. It stung her hand and barely moved his face, but a flush of satisfaction coursed through her. She considered following it up with an actual punch to the face, but Devesh dropped his gaze and had the decency to look ashamed.

The chuckles and pointed fingers of their onlookers brought Aniri out of her haze of anger. "There is nothing you have to say that I want to hear." She kept her voice low, not wanting to put on any more of a show for fear they would all be recognized. And Devesh had already used her name once—she didn't want to give him a chance to do it again.

"Step aside, Dev." She left hanging the idea that if he didn't, Janak would force him to.

"Who *is* this man?" Seledri whispered to Aniri.

"My courtesan." Aniri used her most disdainful royal voice, and another flush of warm gratification filled her when he cringed. Seledri's eyes narrowed with understanding.

Devesh didn't move. "You have every reason to hate me. But I can help you."

"We don't need your help." Aniri stepped to the side, intending to brush past him, but Janak caught her arm and gently pulled her back.

"We can't leave him here, my lady," he said quietly. "We don't have that luxury."

She frowned, but then took his meaning. Of course, they couldn't simply let Devesh go. He knew who they were, and he had been working with the ambassador: not only might he foil their escape from the city, but he knew the very people who developed the plans for the second skyship. He was a danger to all of them.

Then she realized: Janak was serious about killing him.

Aniri's eyes went wide, and she flashed a look at Devesh. He must have taken Janak's meaning at the same time she did, because a panicked look seized his face. Before he could move, Janak locked a hand around his arm and pulled Devesh close.

"Don't make a scene," Janak said quietly, "and I won't be forced to kill you here."

Devesh's jaw clenched, and he gave a short nod, but it was hardly required. Janak frog marched him through the door of the inn.

Aniri and Seledri hurried to follow.

Chapter Twelve

THE STREET WAS bright with the midday sun, and hurried movements and swirling cloaks of the four of them would have drawn more notice had they stayed amongst the pedestrians and city traffic. But Janak hauled Devesh into an alley two shops down from the inn and shoved him up against the wall. Seledri and Aniri quickly turned the corner to follow.

Aniri's heart pounded like she had just climbed a mountain in the short walk to the dirty alley. It was empty of onlookers or witnesses. She loathed Devesh and hated the danger he brought to her country and those she loved. He had betrayed her in the most vile way. And yet she had once loved him. She couldn't bring herself to want him dead.

Devesh pressed his back against the rough cobblestone wall of the alley, as if he was trying to shrink into it and escape, even though Janak no longer touched him.

Her raksaka had stepped back, regarding Devesh coolly. "By your leave, your majesty, I'll dispose of this trash so we can be on our way."

Devesh's hands flew up, palms forward, begging for his life. "You can't let him kill me, Aniri." His voice shook, but he rushed his words out before Janak decided which fatal blow to strike. "Your father sent me to find you."

"What?" Aniri lurched closer to him, sure she had misunderstood his words.

"Your father wants me to bring you to him." He was still breathless.

"What are you... How did you...?" Words tangled in her mouth as her thoughts sped to catch up. Could it possibly be true? Did Devesh know where her father was?

"He's a liar and a Samirian, my lady." Janak stepped closer to Devesh, who tried to melt into the wall again. Janak's hand flexed, then curled half-closed. "Let me kill him."

"Janak!" Aniri's admonishment stayed Janak's

hand, but he only turned his cold anger on her instead.

"We have any of a number of reasons that justify it, your most royal highness. Not least that I see no reasonable alternative that would allow us to proceed with our plans."

"I just… I want to hear him out."

"Aniri." Her sister had edged up behind her. "What is he talking about? Our father is dead."

Aniri looked to Janak, who had eased back from his imminent strike on Devesh. He thinned his lips and gave a small shake of his head. Seledri didn't know about their father. Janak had called it a *moment of weakness*, letting the secret slip to Aniri. And now he was telling her to keep it from her sister. But Aniri couldn't bring herself to do that, not when their father might be here in the Samirian capital. Not when he might have, somehow, someway, sent Devesh to find her.

Her father is seeking her out.

It raised such a vortex of emotion that she was unable to speak.

"Aniri?" Her sister clutched the aetheroceiver to her chest, waiting for an answer. Devesh looked between the three of them. He would probably have blurted it out already if he wasn't afraid Janak would kill him for it.

Of course, it was possible Devesh was lying about everything. He had lied about so much, there was no way to be certain. Her father *was* out there somewhere, unless he had met an untimely death since he had run away from his royal obligations. She couldn't imagine he had travelled back to Dharia, where he would be recognized, or Jungali, where he would be immediately known as someone from the plains. But that didn't mean he was still in the capital. Maybe he had fled to some remote village in the many boroughs tucked between the mountains.

Aniri had promised not to run off looking for her father. And as tempting as it was to believe her father had somehow known Devesh and had sent him after her, none of that mattered. Her only purpose now was to get her sister safely out of the country.

Yet Seledri had the right to know their father still lived.

Aniri took her sister's hand and peered into her anxious eyes. "Our father is alive. There were no Samirian robbers who set upon him. He ran away from us, Seledri. I'm sorry to have to tell you like this."

Her sister leaned back, her face the picture of horror Aniri remembered feeling so keenly when she first found out. The haze of that moment had crippled her. And had sent her into the arms of Devesh, seeking solace. But this time, Aniri would share that burden, make it easier for her sister.

"But none of that matters now——" Aniri said softly.

"He's been watching you, Seledri." Devesh's voice was quiet but it roared through Aniri's ears.

She whirled on him. "We do not need any more lies from you!"

He held her gaze. "I didn't have to come after you, Aniri. When I saw you on the street, I could have just let it go. Walked away. But I knew, if you were *here*, in the city, then you had to be after *her*." He glanced at Seledri. "Or the rumors were true, and the Queen-to-be was in fact dead, in spite of Prince Pavan's claims. In which case… I know you, Aniri. You would be after her killers. And that was a dangerous course. I had to warn you——"

"Do not!" Aniri surged forward, a finger raised like she might impale him with it. "Do *not* pretend you care for me."

Again, he downcast his eyes, looking guilty, but Aniri wasn't pulled in by it. She knew it was all lies within lies.

"Of course, you have no reason to believe a word from me. I understand that." He looked up again, expression soft. "But maybe you'll believe your father."

"I don't believe anything you say." Aniri spit her words at him, but they were lies. She knew it as soon as they left her lips. Worse, she could see Devesh knew it, too.

"Aniri, what's all this?" Her sister's voice was shaky behind her. "Is our father really alive? I don't understand. Why did our mother tell us he was dead?"

Aniri cringed, but she supposed there was no avoiding it. "What could the Queen do? Her King left her. It would have weakened the people's confidence to know."

Seledri nodded, slowly. Her mind had to be still processing all of it. "And we were still girls, then."

"I think she thought to spare us with the lie."

Seledri let out a long breath. "That is so very like Mother, isn't it?" She narrowed her eyes at Devesh. "Can we believe this courtesan? That our father is still right here in Mahatvak? That he's been here all this time, but waited until *now* to make himself known?"

Aniri could hear the pain in her words. Their father was yet another person who treated Seledri with far less care than she deserved. Aniri didn't know what to say.

"Your father is worried about you both," Devesh said softly, drawing them back. "About the attempt on Seledri's life. About you, Aniri, getting tangled in it. Let me take you to him."

"You will be taking us nowhere." Janak's voice was as hard as the cobbled stones behind Devesh's head. "Do not be fooled by this, Aniri. Your father didn't want to be found eight years ago. I doubt he wants to be found now."

Aniri studied Janak's impassive face. It betrayed nothing of the turmoil this must be causing him. "Eight years is a long time." She couldn't say the words she wanted to: *you needn't worry about the King returning to his Queen.* Even if she and Janak were alone, she didn't know if she could voice them. Or if they were really true.

"Not long enough." The muscles in Janak's jaw twitched with how hard he was working to keep his words unspoken.

Hope was alive on Seledri's face. "If he's really alive, Aniri…"

"You cannot believe anything this courtesan tells you," Janak said. "He has nothing but ill intent in coming to find us. He is your *enemy*, Aniri. Do not forget it."

Of course Janak was right. Devesh had been working with the ambassador. He had knowledge of skyships and intrigues she could only guess at, and there was no doubt he was deeply entwined with the enemies of Dharia and Jungali. And yet… his words about her father had the weight of truth in them. Or maybe it was just her wishful thinking that her father now worried for the Daughters he had abandoned long ago. Aniri didn't know. She *couldn't* know the truth within Devesh's lies.

But one thing she did know.

She gave Devesh a cool stare. "He may be our enemy, but enemies have knowledge we can use to our advantage. Knowledge I'm sure we can extract given enough time."

Devesh's mouth fell open, and his face went ashen.

Janak lifted an eyebrow, but then gave her a small nod. "We'll bring him with us, then."

Aniri tilted her head in agreement. "Once we're

safely aboard the skyship, we'll have time to find out all he knows." She turned back to Devesh, who was looking quickly between her and Janak and frowning. "If you tell the truth, Dev, it will go easier for you. If not, when we get back to Jungali, I can't promise the interrogations will be any more pleasant." A lead weight settled in her stomach at the thought of how Devesh would fare in Ash's prison.

"Wait!" Devesh held up his hands. "I'll tell you whatever you want to know. But what is this about the skyship? You're leaving? Now?" He glanced at Seledri. "And you're taking *her* with you?"

Seledri dashed a wide-eyed look to her, and Aniri grimaced. She had just given away their plans. But it mattered little, since Devesh would be coming with them.

"You can come willingly or we can leave you in this alley." Aniri didn't have to say that he wouldn't be breathing if they were forced into that option. She turned to Janak, "We should make haste. Inform Captain Tarak we're on our way."

"Aniri, wait!" Devesh's voice hitched up a notch. "I'll go willingly. I'll answer your questions, just… come visit your father first." He glanced again at Seledri. "Before you decide to leave Samir. It's important you speak with him."

Aniri narrowed her eyes. "I haven't spoken with him in eight years. I'm sure it's nothing urgent." A sour taste rose in the back of her throat. The truth was this may well be her last chance to ask her father why he abandoned her and her sisters and their mother. But Seledri's safety was more important.

Devesh dropped his hands and stood straight against the cobbled wall. "Actually it is *most* urgent. It's regarding the assassination attempt."

Seledri edged forward and demanded, "What do you know about it?"

"I know you need to speak to him, my lady."

Janak coiled up a fist like he was tempted to strike Devesh again. "This courtesan is preying upon your hopes, your majesty."

Seledri ignored Janak. "How do you even know my father," she asked Devesh, "much less have his confidence in matters like this?"

"And why would he trust *you*, of all people, to come for us?" Aniri added.

Devesh held Aniri's gaze for a moment, his soft brown eyes pleading sincerity. "Because I've known him for longer than I've known you, Aniri."

She couldn't help it: some part of her believed him. She didn't trust him *at all*, but one thing she knew about Devesh: his ears and eyes were sharp. He was deeply involved in all kinds of matters—it was very possible he knew even more than he was letting on. And if he had information about the attempt on Seledri's life… they should find out what Devesh knew before they spirited Seledri out of the country and possibly touched off a war.

Janak watched her with expectant eyes, while Seledri's were filled with a wild kind of hope. Aniri's stomach twisted itself in knots as tight as her climbing ropes back home.

She turned back to Devesh. "If you're lying to me, Dev… it will not go well for you."

He visibly swallowed, then said, "I'll take you right to him."

They returned to the streets, walking briskly two by two through the bustling commerce of the midday capital, Aniri and Devesh in front, followed closely by Janak and Seledri. Janak had wanted to keep Devesh within arm's reach, but Aniri had questions she wanted answered before they reached wherever Devesh was leading them. Because if her father wasn't there, and it was some kind of trap, she had no doubt Devesh would be dead before she would have a chance to query him further. Besides, her questions were the kind she couldn't ask under torture, or the threat of it. Ones she shouldn't even ask. She certainly didn't want anyone else to hear the answers, even if they were lies.

"Why?" Aniri asked him.

He glanced at her, his warm brown eyes squinting against the sun. He seemed to struggle for an answer. Aniri waited, glad he didn't insult her by pretending not to know what she meant.

"My mission was to woo the naïve, rebellious Third Daughter of Dharia. With two of the three Daughters bound to Samirians, it would weaken the Queen's ability to resist Samir's demands."

"When you waged war upon us."

"Yes."

Aniri stared at the cobbled walk in front of them. The pain lancing through her chest was an echo of the first time he broke her heart, but it was still strong enough to feel fresh again. She knew he never loved her, that his betrayal began from the beginning, but hearing it from his own lips, finally spoken aloud… their unhurried pace was meant to avoid attention, but it served her well in that moment as her vision blurred on a well of tears.

Anger rose to fight them off. It was entirely intrigue for him, from the start. And now her interest should be solely intrigue as well.

"What reward did they offer you?" She kept her voice cool and measured like his. "Or were you merely in service to the crown?" *And the ambassador.* She left that part unsaid, but it added a layer of disgust to the sourness at the back of her throat.

"A place at court. The gratitude of the crown." He stared straight ahead. "I was a boy from a remote village with no skills and no prospects. It was an offer none would refuse." He paused. "I thought I knew, I thought I *understood...*" He stopped again, struggling. "I was foolish to think I could do this without causing harm."

"Oh, I'm quite certain I was the fool in that situation." The words were bitter ash in her mouth.

Devesh took her elbow to shift them right to avoid a merchant's table filled with clockwork toys, then they veered back to stay clear of a *pamgari* lumbering down the street carrying crates of vegetables.

He leaned closer, dropping his voice to not be heard by Janak and Seledri close behind them. "You were *not* a fool, Aniri. You were perhaps... a little naïve."

Aniri pushed him away, wrenching her elbow from his grasp. Janak surged closer. She held a hand up to stay him, then faced forward again.

Devesh glanced back, then added in the same hushed tone, "It was a credit to you, Aniri. It only meant you hadn't been corrupted by the cynicism of your mother's court." He took a breath. "Somehow you stayed separate from the political machinations and ambitious jostlings, and you were just… *you*. A girl with a kind and open heart who had lost the father she loved and who wanted no more than to escape all of it. And I took advantage of that for my own gain and for my country's. That makes me a fairly despicable person, Aniri, but it doesn't make you anything less than you already were."

He stopped speaking and stared earnestly at her. The tears had worked their way back into her eyes, so she avoided his gaze, keeping her head turned to examine the heaped baskets of flowers as they passed a merchant. His words were affecting her more than she wished, and it ran a tremble of fear through her. Devesh had always been able to say exactly what she needed to hear at any given moment. It was what made him so dangerous to her heart.

"Well." Aniri cleared her throat and summoned the haughtiness of First Daughter Nahali to her voice. "You needn't worry about my naiveté any longer."

"Aniri." He touched her elbow again, just briefly. "I am sorry. For all of it."

"It would have been more convenient had your regret come a little sooner."

"I *tried*," he said, pressing both hands to his forehead, then dragging them through his hair. "I didn't expect… I didn't plan to…" He took a breath, then pressed on. "When Garesh held that gun to your head, and I could see he had no intention, all along, of letting you live, I realized I hadn't just tricked you into falling in love. I had tricked myself into believing I hadn't."

She narrowed her eyes, glaring at him. "I suppose that came a little late as well."

He nodded vigorously, like he had been attempting to convince himself of precisely that. "I know. I know, I'm just saying that…" Then he shook his head, like he wasn't quite sure *what* he was trying to say. "I just wanted you to know that was why I helped you escape. Because I realized, too late, that I'd done the one thing I wasn't supposed to do: fall in love."

"You… *what?*" Anger rendered her speechless for a moment. She didn't believe his professions of love for one instant, but *helping her escape?* She turned and vented her full fury at him by impaling his shoulder with jabs of her finger. "*Escape?* You were the one who held me while Garesh smothered me in vapors. Whatever regrets you have, Dev, you cannot rewrite what happened!"

He took the onslaught like he welcomed her small assault. Like he deserved it. Which of course he did, but which only angered her further. She wished she could get away with punching him without attracting notice from the street. Instead, she attempted to rein in her fury, taking a breath, turning forward, and picking up their pace. They'd already walked several blocks, and the crowds had begun to thin as they left the main thoroughfares of the city.

It was foolish to hope for any real answers from him. "If your lies are going to be this transparent," she said coolly, "I'll wait to question you under less pleasant circumstances."

"I knew you wouldn't believe me," he said quietly. "But I thought, if you knew what happened, maybe someday you would understand."

"I understand quite well already."

"I mean about what happened on the skyship." He paused, and Aniri cursed herself inwardly but couldn't stop from glancing at him. When she did, he held her gaze with a serious look. "Who do you think informed the skyship's Samirian tinker that the Third Daughter of Dharia was being held in the captain's quarters?"

She tried not to react, but she couldn't help drawing back in surprise. Ash had told her someone from the embassy must have recognized her and informed Karan of her kidnapping. He took it as a sign that she had won the hearts of his people. But what if it wasn't his people at all, but... she refused to believe it. "That could have been anyone."

"Could it?" he asked. "Only a few people knew what had happened to you. I knew the Samirian tinker who had worked so closely with Prince Malik's brother would be loyal to the prince, if pressed. I knew the right word in his ear would find its way to the crown. I couldn't be sure of the prince himself, but he had opposed the use of the skyship as an instrument of war from the beginning, so he had every incentive to keep Garesh from starting one, not least by murdering the Third Daughter of Dharia, whom the prince had so artfully convinced to marry him." The bitterness in

Devesh's voice surged anger in Aniri, but he kept going. "I knew telling Karan would set in motion a plan to rescue you that might actually succeed. And it was all I could do. If I had confronted Garesh while he held you at gunpoint… Aniri, we would have both died in the ambassador's office that day."

She turned forward, her face flush with anger and… some other emotion she didn't want to examine too closely. She didn't want to believe him. She berated her heart not to believe a single word, because he had done nothing but lie to her. But belief wormed its way in regardless.

"I just wanted you to know," he said softly. Before she could think of something scathing to say in return, he added. "We're here, Aniri."

Devesh brought their small entourage to a stop in front of a shop with a weathered wooden door, but clean windows. Behind the clear glass was a tidy arrangement of coiled ropes, thin-soled leather shoes as well as nailed boots, and an assortment of pitons, slings, and some clockwork devices Aniri couldn't put a function to.

Her eyes went wide as she realized: it was a climbing shop.

Chapter Thirteen

IF HER FATHER had taken up residence in the capital, Aniri could too easily imagine him establishing a climbing shop to blend in with the local population. She glanced over her shoulder to Seledri and Janak behind her. Her sister's open mouth of disbelief told Aniri she understood, but it was Janak's stone cold stare at the door that sent her heart pounding.

Breathless with the possibility that Devesh had actually told her the truth, she quietly asked, "How is it that you know my father?"

Devesh edged away from Janak's hard, suddenly interested stare, and swallowed. "As preparation for my mission, I apprenticed for a time with your father. It was intended to glean information about you that might be helpful."

A sick feeling climbed the back of her throat. "Did he *know*? What you were?"

Devesh stared at his boots. "No. Not until I recently returned."

Aniri shook her head, tremors running through her as she stared at the shop. All the *why* questions came rushing to her at once. Why would her father leave his Queen? Why was the simple life of a shop-keeper so much more desirable than the crown? Was it worth abandoning his three daughters? Was it regret that sent him to seek her out now?

"He'll be surprised, but glad, to see you," Devesh said gently as he reached for the door. A small bell tinkled their arrival, but Aniri remained rooted on the cobblestones outside. The morning sun streaked through the front windows and threw shadows of coiled ropes and other equipment inside the dusky shop. Janak went first, with Seledri shuf-fling tentatively in behind. Aniri forced her legs to unlock, and she strode into the shop as if the idea of it didn't terrify her.

She breathed in the musky scent of braided fiber ropes and oiled leather. It brought a rush of memories tripping back: her father's voice on their climbs, his hand pointing to toe-holds, his smiling approval when she summited a small boulder that seemed a mountain to her child-sized self.

Always check your knots, Aniri.

She could hardly breathe.

Climbing gear hung on the walls, arranged into orderly groups of ropes and harnesses and leather goods on one side, metalworks on the other, and small islands with climbing shoes displayed in the middle.

"Just a moment," a man's voice called through an open door in back. A scuffle of boots scraped the polished wooden floor, then the owner of the voice hurried into the shop from the back room. He was dressed in work breeches and a short leather vest, striding toward them while cleaning something in his hands with a rag.

"These new crackjacks are a wonder, but the grease leaves quite a—" He was halfway across the shop before he looked up and met Aniri's wide-eyed stare. He stopped dead in a pool of light, the sun glinting on the turnbuckle device he held while keeping his face in shadow. But she could still see his quick, intelligent eyes, slender nose, and regal features. He was older now, and wore a tightly trimmed beard and mustache that made him seem foreign. More Samirian than Dharian. A sprinkling of gray had turned his midnight-black hair to frosted coal, but he was still unmistakably the serious-faced, handsome man from the ink portrait that sat in her mother's office. It was the face Aniri had mourned for years and hated for weeks.

Her father regarded her with awe. "Aniri," he said, sucking in a breath along with her name. "You are the picture of your mother." He said it like she was a ghost come back to haunt him, and Aniri felt it like a stab to her chest.

His gaze roamed over the party, a brief nod to Devesh, a narrowing of eyes for Janak, but when he caught sight of her sister, relief washed over his features. "Seledri! Thank the gods you are all right." He hurried past Aniri, leaving her gap-mouthed while he rushed to Seledri's side. He set down the rag and buckle and took her free hand, the one not clutching the aetheroceiver. "I was so afraid the rumors were true." He paused to take her in. "You're even more lovely up close." He seemed embarrassed by that, dropping her hand and stepping back. "I've only seen you from afar, and…" He sputtered out.

Seledri was blinking rapidly, as if she would cry at any moment.

Janak stepped closer to her. "And perhaps a little distance is in order now."

Her father's gaze swung to Janak and cooled ten degrees. "Janak."

"Tariq," he replied. "Can't say I'm glad to see you alive."

"Can't say I'm glad to see you in my shop," her father replied.

Aniri stepped toward them, still in shock at being ignored, but having no desire to see her father and Janak come to blows before accomplishing their purpose. Which she steeled herself to remember amid the swirl of emotions threatening to shut down her mind.

"Father." She meant it to be strong, but it came out a whisper.

He quickly turned to her. His hands rose like he would embrace her, then fell as he seemed to change his mind. "Aniri, I'm concerned for you, too."

Somehow his words set her teeth even more on edge.

"I would never have guessed…" He stalled out again. "I mean, I didn't expect to see you in Samir. When Devesh told me he had spied you in the city, I could scarcely believe him."

She had to force words past the closing of her throat. "Don't worry. I won't be staying long."

"That's not what I meant." He looked pained. "I just hadn't let myself hope. When I saw you last, you were just a small child—"

She couldn't stand it anymore: she couldn't keep inside the question that was burning her heart. "*Why?*" she demanded, taking a step closer to him. Her father leaned back, his eyes growing wide, but not quite retreating from her. "*Why* did you leave us?"

"Aniri, I didn't leave *you*, I… but, yes, of course, you would see it that way."

There is no other way to see it. But she kept those words trapped inside, waiting to hear him out. She would give him this chance, this *one* chance, to explain himself. She would find out what he knew about the attempt on Seledri's life. And then she would leave Samir and never look back.

A frown settled on his face, but somehow the serious look only made him more handsome. Refined and studious-looking. Aniri could easily picture her driven and capable mother falling in love with him. Janak's words came back to her: *Your mother wouldn't see him for what he really was.*

Aniri was determined not to make the same

mistake. She returned her father's stare, daring him to explain himself.

He drew in a breath, shifting to face both her and Seledri. Her sister's tormented look only bristled Aniri's anger more. Perhaps this was a mistake after all.

"I don't expect you to understand." Her father nodded, but it seemed to be for himself. "But I do owe you an explanation."

You owe much more than that. The words pushed against her throat, but she refused to let them out.

He took another breath, deeper this time. "As you may remember, I traveled a great deal, especially to Samir. Dharia was my birthplace, but the beautiful mountains of Samir have always called to me." He shrugged, a hand lifted to the walls of his shop and all the climbing equipment that crowded them. "The more time I spent here, the more I came to understand its people as well. And one in particular." He stopped, frowning again. He held Seledri's tormented gaze for a moment, but when he glanced at Aniri, he dropped his gaze to study the small mountain of climbing shoes next to them. Without looking at either of them, he said, "I fell in love with a Samirian woman. I didn't intend for it to happen, but it did. Your mother was busy with the crown and her court, and she would scarce have noticed."

Something painful dug into Aniri's palms. She looked down to find her fists tight as rocks, and her fingernails biting into her flesh.

"I was trapped." Her father was looking at her now.

Aniri locked her jaw and her body tight to keep from lashing out at him.

"There is no royal divorce. I certainly couldn't leave and marry a Samirian woman. It would be, quite literally, treason." A bitter smile turned his handsome face into something worse. Something painful for Aniri to look at, but he still held her gaze, and she couldn't look away. "And your mother is far too clever to not have found out eventually. Keeping it hidden from royal onlookers, not to mention raksaka, well, that was a dangerous thing unto itself." He glanced at Janak, and the coiled fury on his face sent a flush of warmth through Aniri. "There was a reason I traveled alone as much as possible. But in the end, it didn't matter."

He stopped. Aniri waited for more, but her father's lips were pressed tight, as if he was debating whether to tell the rest of his sordid story. She wasn't sure she wanted to know the details, and she was certain she wanted no knowledge of the woman who had stolen her father's heart. But how dare he say it didn't matter?

Seledri spoke it for her. "What do you *mean*, it didn't matter?" Aniri's flash of regret became a certainty—it was a mistake to bring her sister here, subjecting her to this trauma amidst running for her life, the baby, and her husband possibly arranging her murder.

This painful reunion needed to end, sooner rather than later.

But it was Janak who spoke to her father next. "You were found out anyway."

Her father grimaced, but nodded. "Yes. And by the Samirian royal family no less. I suppose I should have seen that coming, given she was a member of the court. But it still surprised me when the King himself approached me. And offered a way out."

Janak's eyes narrowed to slits. "One you couldn't refuse."

"I had no desire to embarrass the Queen," he said darkly to Janak, then turned to Seledri. "I had no desire to hurt any of you. But the choice was either to be exposed or to leave your mother. If I left of my own accord, the king personally assured I would not be found. He secured a village hideaway for a short time, then promised I could return to the city."

"Return to the city?" Aniri said, incredulous. The entire contents of her stomach felt like they might come up. "You mean return to your lover."

Her father's face twisted, as if Aniri was blaming him for something that wasn't of his own doing. "It was either flee," he said, bitterly, "or the king would have personally taken the news of the affair to your mother. That would have embarrassed the Queen, weakened her rule, and endangered relations between the countries. Not to mention, I would be living in a Samirian prison now. Or a Dharian one. If I was living at all."

His words and that look—as if he had no choice in the matter, as if it weren't something of his own doing—it chilled her heart, dousing the volcano of anger that had been building inside her. Somehow, her father did not think he was responsible for any of it.

Then a clear thought broke through: maybe she had made mistakes. Maybe, in Devesh, she had chosen the wrong person to love. But when it endangered her family, she never turned her back on them. She never betrayed or abandoned them. She knew, always, where the fault lay for the consequences of her acts, and she did everything in her power to amend them.

It seemed that following her heart wasn't always wrong.

Her father could have returned home to her mother. He could have apologized and begged forgiveness. Her mother would have taken him back, of that Aniri had no doubt. Even eight years later, after he abandoned her with no reason given, the Queen still held out hope. But instead, he chose the coward's way out and abandoned his family for his lover. Her mother may not have seen him for what he was, but Aniri certainly did: and he wasn't worthy of the Queen.

Aniri's fists uncurled. This man wasn't worthy of any of them.

"We should go," she said quietly to Seledri. "There's nothing for us here."

Seledri had small tears running down her face. She didn't object.

"Wait!" Devesh said, startling Aniri. She had forgotten he was there. And truly, she had no patience for his lies anymore, but his hands were out, holding her back from marching out of her father's shop. "I brought you here because you need to know the dangers to Seledri."

Aniri cursed herself inwardly. In all the turmoil, she had forgotten their purpose as well. She glared at her father. "What do you know of the assassination attempt?"

His defensive looks melted away, replaced by concern. "I know they are part of larger plans, ones that present grave dangers to not just Seledri, but all of Dharia." He turned a soft look to her sister. "I begged Pavan to tell you. Honestly, I was surprised to see you brought here by Devesh, rather than your husband. I thought sure he would have found the moment to tell you by now."

Seledri's eyes went wide. "Pavan *knew* you were here in the city? All this time?" She looked like every piece of her life was falling apart before her eyes. Aniri hurried to her side and took hold of her sister's hand.

"No, no." Her father held up his hands. "He only recently found out. Of course, the King has known all along. And I suspect the Second Son knows as well. But the King is not of a mind to share state secrets with the First Son."

Seledri nodded through her horror, as if this made sense to her. "The King is always working to bring *his* son, the Second Son, into favor with the

Queen. If he held a valuable secret like this, he would not share it with Pavan."

"And the runaway husband of the Queen of Dharia, hidden in a climbing shop, is definitely a valuable secret. Exposing me wasn't just a threat long ago, Seledri, it's an ongoing one." His voice turned bitter. "One I'm afraid he's waiting to use at the moment most opportune for Samir. Which may be soon. That's why I approached Pavan and revealed myself. He didn't know until then."

Seledri seemed to have lost all her breath. "So you don't think Pavan is involved in the attempt on my life?" she whispered.

"*Pavan?* No, of course not," their father said. "Once the baby was known, I revealed myself to him. Ever since, he's been coming here to visit. He keeps saying how he's searching for the right time to tell you."

Seledri covered her mouth with her hand, and Aniri could see her fighting to hold back tears. "It was *you* he was coming to see," she said in a whisper. "All those unexplained times away from the palace..."

Aniri squeezed Seledri's hand. Her husband, the father of her child, wasn't having an affair after all. And if he was searching for a way to reunite

Seledri with her father, it seemed unlikely he was trying to kill her as well. Amidst all the other horrors of the day, this must have seemed like a lifeboat.

Their father searched Aniri's face. "He knows how you feel, my child. I think he hopes to win your heart by bringing your long lost father back into your life. I told him I didn't think it would have the effect he hoped for."

But Aniri could see the effect plain on Seledri's face.

Aniri turned to their father. "If not Pavan, then who?"

"Most likely the Second Son," he said. "And now there are plans afoot that endanger both of you. Aniri, I would never have hoped for you to come to Samir, but now that you're here, it's better you stay. Dharia will soon be no place for a Dharian royal."

Aniri's heart cried out she would be returning to *Jungali*, and to a man far more noble than her father. She would be Jungali royalty, and proud of it. She was surprised how settled her heart was in that thought: there was a rightness to it that hadn't been there before.

But she wouldn't share the contents of her heart with a man who had abandoned his family and now inexplicably wanted her to do the same. Instead, she said, "What do you mean? No one is trying to assassinate me. And Seledri is far safer in Dharia, away from the Second Son's influence."

Her father pressed his lips together and glanced at Devesh. Aniri frowned. What secret were they contemplating keeping from her? But Devesh nodded, encouraging her father to speak it, and she quickly wondered why Devesh was orchestrating all of this: seeking her out at the inn, bringing them here, facilitating the reunion. And now, this last secret, whatever it was. Was it possible he actually cared for her? Or at least, had come to regret all his lies and deceit and intrigue, just as he said?

Her father drew in a breath. "The plot against your sister is just the beginning, Aniri. The Samirians' plan to wage war on Dharia. And soon they will have the skyship armada to accomplish it."

"An *armada*? As in more than one skyship. How many?" The horror of it mixed with a kind of disbelief in Aniri's mind. How was it even possible? It had taken many months and incredible secrecy, not to mention a supply of navia from the frozen mountains of Jungali, to construct *one* skyship. How could the Samirians already have a fleet of them?

And if they did… her head seemed to suddenly become light, floating above her shoulders. There would be no hope of fighting them. No possibility of even fending them off. They wouldn't have to have a burning glass to render her home into rubble. With an armada of skyships commanding the sky, the Samirians could do anything they wished.

"I don't know," her father said, bringing her out of a hazy image of burned villages and scattered armies. "I only know what Devesh has told me."

Aniri swung to look at him, but his face was open with the promise to tell her everything he knew. She frowned, still puzzling over *why*, but her father kept speaking.

"However, I know the Second Son is involved. He, and by proxy his father the King, surely hope to gain the crown once the war with Dharia has begun." He took Seledri's hand. "A Dharian wife of the First Son is not going to be Queen if we are at war, Seledri. I think they would have been content to let you live, had you not presented them with the threat of an heir half-Dharian, half-Samirian. It's possible to oust a First Son if that's all he were, but once he had provided an heir to the crown, especially if it was a Daughter, it would have been more difficult for Natesh to claim the crown." He glanced at the aetheroceiver in her hand, and turned to Aniri. "You must message your skyship. Tell them to return to Dharia now, before the fleet is mobilized and ready to attack. Make what preparations they can. But you and Seledri should remain here in Samir. If you return to Dharia, you will only be executed, along with all royalty in the land, once the invasion is complete. But if you stay here, I can secret you away. I've made friends, even beyond the royal household." He nodded to Devesh. "Friends who know many secret spots where a royal in exile might hope to live out their lives to their natural end."

Aniri shook off the horror of a Samirian armada and gave her father a look of disgust. "I will *not* hide while my country is destroyed." By country, she wasn't sure if she meant Jungali or Dharia. Either way, there was no doubt in her mind where her place was, even if it was to end in an execution.

Her father winced, but dared to take her by the

shoulders and look her in the eyes, as if he could convince her that way. "Please, Aniri. Think of what you're saying." He held a hand out to Seledri. "Your sister is with child. You are young. Between you, there are three lives with many years ahead of them. Someday, perhaps, you could return—a royal family in exile, three Queens who could return when the time is right to restore the Dharian monarchy. But if you go to Dharia now, it will end in nothing but bloodshed."

Aniri twisted out of his hold. "If my family is danger, you'll not find me running in the opposite direction." She nodded to Seledri. "Secreting my sister and her child, the future Queen, away is prudent... in *Dharia*. Where we will have far more friends than *enemies*." She wasn't sure where she counted her father in that tally, but the way his face fell made clear where he thought he lay.

"I understand why you wouldn't find much to admire in me." He said it with a sadness that threatened to pull at her heart, but she hardened it against that luxury. His mouth opened to say more, but then it gaped at something over her shoulder, out the windows of the shop. "Quickly!" He pushed Aniri to the side and rushed past her to the front door. They all pivoted to see what drew him. Outside, three figures were crossing the street.

Royal Samirian guards.

"Out the back," her father said, his hands fumbling with a key on a long cord around his neck. "Janak! Take them!"

In a blur, Janak and Seledri were gone, her raksaka rushing her sister toward the back door where her father had first emerged. Devesh tugged at Aniri's arm, but she stood frozen, watching as the guards arrived at the door at the precise time her father shoved in the key. A mechanical lock whirred, but the sound was quickly drowned out by the pounding on the door.

"Run, Aniri!" her father barked at her.

Devesh's tug became a forceful yank that unlocked her legs. She turned and ran with him toward the back. Devesh stopped long enough to shut the door to the main shop behind them, grabbing a key from a hook on the wall and hastening to lock it.

A crash sounded from the shop. It sounded of broken glass. Shouts and voices and a shuffling of feet. Devesh dragged her from the door.

"But, we can't—"

"Your father has bought us precious moments."

Devesh's voice was harsh as he shoved her past piles of boxes and equipment to another door standing open. Janak and Seledri were there. Aniri ran toward them. Just as she reached the alley a gunshot rung from inside.

Her heart seized, but this time she didn't stop.

Chapter Fourteen

My father has been shot.

Aniri didn't know this for sure, but her heart felt it: an icy fear that shoved out any other possibility, even though her head knew it might not be true. Aniri, Devesh, Janak, and Seledri ran hard the length of the alley behind her father's shop and down two others as well, before slowing to a normal pace. Once they broke out into the busy streets at the center of the city, they couldn't run as if they were fugitives. Aniri's legs itched with the need to go faster, the danger of the palace guards still haunting their backs. It seemed as though they scarcely moved through the thickly crowded streets, in spite of her boots pounding a steady rhythm on the cobbled walk.

Janak carried the aetheroceiver and kept his hand on Seledri's arm, but Aniri still worried. "Are you all right?" she asked her sister.

Seledri's breathing was a bit labored, but her voice was strong. "I'm fine."

"The baby?"

"We can both move faster, if called to again."

Aniri looked to Devesh up ahead, but he just shook his head and kept them at the same steady pace. Aniri stayed by Seledri's side. Janak swept his gaze ahead and behind, with an occasional glare for Devesh, who likewise scanned the streets, keeping a high alert while trying not to appear on the run.

Finally, Janak said quietly to Devesh, "My offer to kill you, should you lead the Daughters into danger, still stands, courtesan." His words were harsh, but his voice had a careful respect. Devesh was saving them from the palace guards. If the guards were part of some trap, Devesh was certainly not involved. Nor her father, who might have taken a bullet to buy them a few extra seconds to escape.

Unwelcome tears threatened her eyes, but she blinked them away. There was no time for that. "How did they know where to find us?" Aniri asked, both of Janak and Devesh. "And more importantly, where are you taking us, Dev?"

He ignored her first question, which was probably wise, given they were still on the streets. "I know a place where we can stay, at least for the moment. It won't take long for them to come after us, and the three of you hardly blend in."

Devesh had thrown back his hood and left his cloak to flap open, but he had the luxury of doing so. He was Samirian, and while the features of Dharians were not so dissimilar, surely the people would recognize their own Princess Seledri were she to stroll the streets without disguise.

They took two more turns, bringing them off the main thoroughfares of the city, before Devesh led them inside a tinker shop. This was no toy shop, but instead held all manner of large clockwork parts: long steel handles, sheets of raw metal, and gear wheels half the size of Aniri. A row of pamgari stood along one wall, as if lined up for inspection. Their small entourage's entrance drew the attention of two customers, so Aniri ducked her head and held close to Devesh, who was making haste through the shop to the back.

Along the rear wall, racks of small parts—and bins for holding even smaller ones—created narrow canyons of tinker heaven. Buried in one was a woman in overalls with grease-stained hands. It was hard to tell her age with her light brown hair plaited behind her and her face buried nose-first in one of the boxes. She was digging for something. When she found her prize, an irregular bulb of some kind, she held it up with a grin—Aniri guessed she wasn't much over twenty. Only then did the tinker notice the four of them hovering at the end of the row. Her grin quickly morphed into a frown for Devesh, who motioned them to stay back.

"I thought ye went to Dharia." She said it like she wished he had stayed there.

Devesh brushed past that and said, "I need your help."

"Of course ye do." The woman's frown deepened, and she brushed a stray lock out of her face, leaving a faint smudge of grease behind. She scanned them with dark, intelligent eyes. "Whatever trouble yer in, Dev, ye take it right back out of my —" She cut herself off when her gaze landed on Seledri.

Her mouth hung open. "Ye brought the..." She stopped again, then harshly whispered, "Ye brought the *princess?*"

Devesh swooped in with a kiss that was quick,

but nevertheless silenced the woman. Aniri remembered all too well the power of those kisses. The twinge inside her wasn't jealousy, but a sudden heartache for the woman and a spike of anger for Devesh.

"Please, Riva," he said, his hands still cupping her cheeks. "It's for them, not for me."

She pulled out of his hold and slapped him across the cheek.

He bore it easily, as if he expected it. Or perhaps getting slapped was a common occurrence for Devesh. Then he looked in her eyes again. "I know. But I'm begging you."

Riva gave him a look of disgust. "That was for *you*. For *them*, I have a room upstairs." She brushed past him, hesitated in front of Seledri, pressed her hands together for an awkward kind of bow, then quickly slipped past. She motioned them toward a door. Past it was a forest of gleaming clockwork parts, boxes of inventory for the shop, and a set of stairs.

Janak led the way with Seledri, no doubt wanting to be first in case of trouble. Although Aniri doubted they would find any in the back rooms of a tinker shop. It was an excellent hiding place, as she was sure Devesh already knew.

He lingered, letting Riva get well ahead of them.

Aniri shook her head. "Do you manipulate *every* woman you know?"

Devesh gave her a dark look. "Yes." He slipped past her, heading for the door.

Aniri couldn't help it. She laughed under breath.

When they reached the stairs, Devesh shot her an even more menacing look, which only erupted another small laugh from her.

"You find that amusing?" he asked, tightly.

She grinned as they climbed the stairs, still trailing behind Riva, Janak, and Seledri. "The honesty. I find it refreshing."

He blinked, surprised, and then a small smile tugged at his lips.

There were several rooms at the top—from the looks of it, the entire floor served as secondary storage and a laboratory. Riva led them to a small room at the far end. When Aniri and Devesh arrived at the door, she was still scurrying around, picking up spools of wire, wrenches, and a few stray socks in what appeared to be her personal living quarters.

"I'm sorry, yer majesty, I didn't expect..." She

trailed off while she dumped the lot of it into a box on the lone table. She bit her lip. The still-messy room held a single stuffed chair, a miniature kitchen in one corner, and a propped open door to a bedroom. "It's not much to look at, yer majesty, but yer welcome to it as long as ye need." She hesitated, then looked to Devesh. "Should I be knowing why they're here?"

He shook his head. It might not be safe for the tinker to know their plans, she deserved some measure of thanks. Aniri threw back her hood, pressed her hands together, and bowed.

"Arama, Mistress Tinker," she said, opting for the formal name of her trade rather than the personal name that Devesh had used. "We can't thank you enough for your help. We won't bother you long, I promise."

Riva returned the gesture. "Arama. And it's no trouble at all." She glanced at Seledri and said in a whisper, "Is there anything I can get for yer lady?"

Aniri smiled. Being mistaken for her sister's handmaiden was a new experience. And not altogether unpleasant. "I'm sure she'll be fine for the short time she's here. But she's had a bit of a shock today. Perhaps a glass of water and a chance to rest." Aniri gestured to the one chair.

"Yes, of course." Riva hurried to the tiny kitchen, nudging aside a box of spare parts with her boot on the way. She rummaged through the cupboard for a glass.

Aniri tipped her head to the bump of Seledri's belly. "How are you faring?"

Seledri rested her hand there. "Well enough." She looked pale, though.

Riva arrived with the water, offering it to Seledri and guiding her to the chair. "Please rest, my lady. With yer…" She gestured to Seledri's belly with a flail of hands, like she wasn't quite sure what to call the child within. "With the little prince or princess on the way, please sit down."

As Seledri settled into the chair, Riva hesitated, once, twice, then knelt by her side. "Yer majesty, I just wanted ye to know how very glad I am to see ye well. The rumors have been right awful, and I feared the worst. Whatever I can do, my lady, I'm at yer service. Samir needs more people like Prince Pavan and yerself."

Seledri frowned but placed a hand on Riva's, which was clutching the arm of her chair. "That's very kind of you to say."

Riva's face colored a bit with her sister's words. "Don't take my meaning wrong, yer majesty, but kindness has nothing to do with it. It's the plain truth. There's too much hate and fear in the hearts of Samir these days. We need leaders like yerself and the First Son, with open hearts, who understand the value of working for peace." She ducked her head. "I just wanted ye to know we're with ye, my lady."

Seledri's eyes reddened, and she looked like she might cry. This seemed to panic Riva. She jumped to her feet, did that awkward bow again, and hurried to Aniri's side.

"What can I do to assist in yer plans?" Riva asked Aniri, her gaze intense.

Devesh stepped up to them and said gently, "It would probably be best if you remained innocent of our plans, Riva."

It took a moment for her to take his meaning, then she said, "Oh! Yes, of course. I, um… I'll leave ye to yer business, then." But worry was making her pretty face grave. She leaned in to Aniri. "Could I have a word?" She tilted her head to the door they had just come through.

Aniri raised her eyebrows, and Devesh's panicked look almost made her laugh, but she followed Riva to the door. They stepped just outside and closed it behind them.

"Is yer lady truly well?" Riva asked in a quick whisper. "Do I need to fetch a healer?"

"No, she's fine." Aniri smiled at her earnest concern. "And your words truly were a kindness. I'm sure they were a comfort." Given all Seledri had been through, Aniri knew it had affected her. And she wasn't surprised at all that her kind-hearted sister had won over the people.

Riva's shoulders remained hunched, and she fussed with the edge of her overalls pocket, not yet leaving.

"Is there something else that concerns you?" Aniri asked, suddenly worried. They didn't know this tinker, and only had Devesh's word she would keep their secret. Which was to say, virtually no assurance at all.

"It's just…" She bit her lip and looked to her boots, searching for words. "I don't know yer business." She shook her head and looked up. "But I know Devesh. He's got a good heart, but he's always one to get tangled in matters he should be running from, if he had half a brain. He's a bit like an old pamgari—he might get ye where ye need to go, but he's twice as likely to leave ye stranded with a load of rotting fruit."

Aniri held in her laugh. "I know. But we don't always get to choose our allies."

Riva cocked her head, regarding Aniri anew, and for a moment she was afraid the tinker might have guessed who she was. But she only nodded and said, "I'll be in the shop, for after yer done making yer plans."

Her accent reminded Aniri of Karan, and she wondered if all tinkers had it. The Samirian ones, anyway. "Thank you for your help. And for the warning."

Riva ducked her head in acknowledgement and strode purposely down the hall. Aniri took a breath, hoping that Devesh wasn't going to leave them all stranded with much worse than a load of rotting fruit. She pushed open the door to Riva's apartment.

"…the streets aren't safe." That was Devesh, head to head with Janak in her absence. She should have known better than to leave them alone together.

They both looked to her and backed down from whatever argument they were having.

"Your most royal highness," Janak said, stiffly, "will you please instruct your courtesan that we will not be taking up residence in Mahatvak." His tone grew more serious for her. "We've delayed our departure far too long. And we're overdue in getting word to Captain Tarak about our situation."

Aniri frowned and glanced at the aetheroceiver in his hands. Seledri was still in the chair, eyes closed, and she held the glass of water in both hands, like it was holding her up rather than the other way around. The color was drained from her face.

Aniri stepped up to Janak. "I need to discuss a few things with Seledri first." She included Devesh in her words. "Could you give us a moment alone?"

Janak frowned but didn't argue. "I'll check in with Captain Tarak, to ascertain his status. And I'll hold off on revealing our plans." He turned on his heel and took the aetheroceiver into the back bedroom, closing the door behind him.

Devesh hadn't moved from his spot next to her. "You can stay here in Samir. Both of you. I know places you can hide. Safer places, farther from the city. You can wait until all of this is settled, and we can determine Pavan's involvement with certainty. If he is innocent, Seledri can explain she was just being cautious, for the baby's sake. Then she can easily return to the palace, if she wishes."

Aniri had many more questions for Devesh

about what exactly he knew, but first things first. "I need to discuss it with my sister, Dev. Alone."

He swallowed and hesitated, as if he didn't want to leave her side.

"Do I need to ask Janak to escort you out?"

He sighed, giving up. "I'll be right outside the door."

Aniri waited until he had stepped out, then knelt by Seledri's side.

She opened her eyes. "Our father doesn't believe Pavan is involved."

"What do you think?

"I want to believe it, but how did the guards find us? And so quickly after we escaped? Pavan knows where my father's shop is. If he were hunting for me…" Seledri's hands sent trembles through the water in her glass.

"If he were looking for you, would he send the royal guard?" Aniri asked softly. "That seems more like the Second Son than the First. Besides, Pavan visited our father not just once, but multiple times. He wanted to reunite the two of you. That doesn't sound like someone who wants to assassinate you."

"It could have all been a ruse. Perhaps Pavan was simply gaining information. After all, why the delay? Why wouldn't he have simply told me?"

Aniri didn't have a good answer for that.

"Perhaps my husband didn't have a lover after all. But that doesn't mean I'm not a threat to him keeping the crown. I want to think he's not that kind of man, but…" Seledri shook her head.

"What is your heart telling you?" Aniri wasn't sure that was the best compass, but she slowly was starting to believe in it again.

"My heart!" Seledri gave a bitter laugh. "You've always had the freedom to be yourself, Aniri. To follow your heart. No one decided for you what kind of life you would have, who you would marry, whose bed you would share. It's never been that way for me. And Pavan… I didn't think he was the kind who would use me for political purposes, just like everyone else, but with all that's happened… I just can't be sure."

Aniri frowned. "I understand not being certain, believe me. Following my heart has gotten me into more trouble than I care to admit."

Even now, that seemed true. Less than an hour ago, with her long-lost father insisting she remain in Samir, her heart was certain that returning to Jungali and marrying Ash was the right thing to do. Was her heart simply contrary? Or was it spurred on by her disappointment in her father and her anger at Devesh—the only two men she had loved before Ash? And now that her father had sacrificed himself for her, and Devesh was desperate to help her, she was questioning her heart once more. How could one be sure of a compass when it swung so wildly? But she could hardly share her thoughts on this with Seledri, especially when her sister was in the grips of leaving her own husband.

Seledri had fallen silent, the untouched glass of water still sitting in her lap. Aniri hated the sadness that was drawing down her face.

"It seems you've won the hearts of the people, at least," Aniri said softly. "Pavan mentioned it earlier, actually, and now Riva. In fact, she seems convinced he's the kind of man who wants peace, and that you're the kind of Queen Samir needs."

"The people don't know all the royal drama that goes on, Aniri. You know that. Our own mother has apparently been lying to her people about her husband for eight years." She huffed. "Besides, there are plenty of Samirians for whom I am not the ideal Queen."

Aniri shook her head. "I don't understand everything at play here in Samir. All I know is that someone tried to kill my sister and her baby, and I'm here to make sure she's safe."

Tears seemed to threaten Seledri's eyes again. She laid a hand on Aniri's. "You always were the one I could count on. The one who was always there for me."

"And all this time, I thought Nahali was secretly your favorite sister."

Seledri snorted a laugh through her tears.

It made Aniri's heart glad to hear. But she forced a return to seriousness. "It's your choice, Seledri. Do you want to return home? To Pavan?"

Her sister's face twisted, and Aniri feared she might cry. "I want to believe Pavan is innocent of all of this. But I can't be sure. And I need to think of the baby."

Aniri nodded. It was the choice she would make, too.

"I want to go home," Seledri said, her voice shaking. "To Dharia."

Aniri squeezed her hand. "That's it, then."

She quickly rose and summoned Janak and Devesh back into the room. Seledri sat quietly in her chair, head in her hands, shoulders bent.

"Our plan still stands," Aniri said. "Janak, please message Captain Tarak again and arrange for him to meet us outside the city gates."

"Wait!" Devesh held up his hands, eyes wide. "There's another option."

Janak ignored him and strode over to set up the aetheroceiver on the table, shoving aside Riva's box of miscellaneous items to do so. He matched three fingers to the engraved symbols that covered its surface, and the brass box slowly unfolded for him.

"Aniri, your father was right," Devesh said, desperation creeping into his voice. "Soon, it won't be safe to be a royal in Dharia. Or Jungali, for that matter, now that they've moved against Samir."

"The war." Aniri peered into his dark, earnest eyes.

"It's coming, and it's not going to end well for Dharia."

"What do you know, Dev? Tell me. All of it."

He took a breath and gestured helplessly with his hands, like he didn't know where to start. "I'm not privy to battle plans, I just know the ambassador was convinced that Dharia's time was short. She relished the idea of royal blood being spilt just as much as Garesh."

The ambassador. That thought brought back an image of Devesh stumbling from the ambassador's bedroom half dressed. "And she told you this between kisses?"

His look of distaste affirmed Aniri's earlier suspicions that the tryst between them wasn't one he enjoyed. "She let slip more than one secret I was expected to keep."

Aniri's eyes narrowed. "But you're not keeping them. Why? Did she find a new lover?"

"She was never my lover!" Devesh stepped back and ran a hand through his hair.

Aniri took that to mean he had never *loved* the ambassador, not that he had never shared her bed. Then again, he had never shared Aniri's bed, but professed to love her. Devesh clearly suffered a general confusion about the proper order of these things.

The clacking of the aetheroceiver keys filled the silence for a moment.

"Look," Devesh said finally. "I know things that can help you. I know there are other skyships. I don't know how many or what their capabilities are, but I know they're secreted away in the mountains of Samir. The Second Son and the King have to be behind all of it. An operation of this scale requires substantial funds and long-term political strategy. The idea of sending me to Dharia, of keeping the Queen's errant husband under wraps, of partnering with Jungali and leveraging their hopes of rising out of poverty with a new war machine—all of it smacks of a lengthy political strategy to upend the normal ascension order. This isn't just about waging war on Dharia. It's about the Second Son gaining the crown."

Seledri spoke up from the chair. "Do you think Natesh is behind my assassination attempt?" She seemed to be gaining color, which Aniri was very relieved to see.

"Yes," Devesh said, also seeming relieved, although probably because he thought he was winning her over. "A military victory over Dharia would appeal to a great many Samirians." He sent an apologetic look to Aniri. "They are nationalists, but they're unwilling to break with tradition with regards to ascension, especially when the First Son has an heir on the way. But if Seledri and the heir-to-be were removed, the people would easily accept a war hero and his Samirian wife, a lady of the court from a powerful Samirian family, as the next true King and Queen of Samir. An armada of skyships is just what they need to achieve this."

Janak returned from his station at the aethero-ceiver. "What do we *really* know about this supposed armada?"

Devesh bristled under his skeptical look.

Aniri sighed. "We know that the only weapon we have is a lone skyship currently in Samirian territory. Getting the *Prosperity* safely away and ensuring the continuation of the royal line are our top priorities."

Janak gave her an almost approving nod, then handed her a thin, curling strip of paper.

ANIRI: CONCERNED ABOUT DELAY PLEASE MESSAGE EXPECTED RETURN

Aniri crumpled the message and stuffed it in her cloak pocket with the other. Ash's message seemed less angry this time, but no less urgent. And yet she still couldn't reply.

"We need to return to Jungali as quickly as possible," she said. "Ash needs to know about the skyship fleet."

"Agreed," Janak said. "I've suggested to Captain Tarak that he arrange a sightseeing tour via skyship for a few respected nobles in the Samirian court while he awaits the end of your visit. This gives him a plausible reason to leave dock without us. I mentioned that a return before a specific time would not be necessary and to enjoy the view of the city from outside the gates. I believe the Captain is clever enough to take my meaning."

"How much time do we have?" Aniri asked.

"Approximately an hour. But Aniri… Karan still hasn't returned." Janak paused. "We have to consider that he will not be returning at all. That he is, in fact, Samirian, and should by rights be left behind."

Aniri winced. "I trust Karan."

Janak glanced at Devesh. "Perhaps that trust is misplaced."

Her doubts about her judgment surged up again. Karan *was* Samirian: all the best tinkers were. It showed in the marketplace and on the streets, plain for anyone with eyes to see. Devesh's long ago words in Jungali came floating back to her: *How do you think that feels, Aniri? To be more advanced, more proficient in metalwork and clockwork and all manner of steam-driven wonders, but beholden to a backward-looking Queen because she happens to control the food supply?*

Devesh and Janak had fallen into a staring contest. Devesh's glare boiled with anger, and Janak's return look was an open challenge for him to act on it.

Instead, Devesh turned to Aniri. "Your raksaka is ill-informed about Karan, as I'm sure he is about many things. Karan made a name for himself as the youngest tinker ever accepted into the Royal Guild. That won him the chance to prototype the skyship, which already was sufficient to anger many more-experienced tinkers, but now that he's sided with the Jungali, you can count on him being fairly well reviled. I doubt Karan has betrayed you, but he may well be compromised anyway. Any Guild member that happens upon him will take special pleasure in sending him to a royal dungeon."

Aniri drew in a breath. "Which makes me even less enamored with the idea of leaving him behind. But we need to leave, nonetheless. Now."

Devesh returned to being distraught. "Aniri, you can't simply stroll out the city gates. Let me hide you away. At least temporarily." He paused, his eyes turning round and desperate. "What happened before… it doesn't matter now. Please let me help you."

Aniri searched his face. His distress seemed too strenuous to be false. Devesh had brought them to her father's shop, knowing he would attempt to convince her to stay. When the royal guards came for them, he spirited her and her sister away, keeping them safely off the streets. He didn't have to do any of it. Perhaps not everything he said was lies and manipulation.

She stepped closer. "Do you care for me, Dev?" She stared into his deep brown eyes. The ones she used to get lost in. But now she saw merely a boy, and a somewhat lost one at that.

His eyes grew even wider, and he seemed to be holding his breath. "Yes."

She kept her expression stern. "Then get us out of this city."

His shoulders sagged, but after a moment, he nodded. "I know someone who might know how."

Chapter Fifteen

If Aniri had known escaping the city with Devesh's help would involve an overly-intimate ride in a cramped pamgari, she might have considered taking her chances on the streets.

Riva was at the helm, pumping the pamgari lever and standing on the small bridge between the single wheel in front and the cart behind. It was built for two passengers, but they had four crammed into a tight-canopied transport obviously built for short duration trips of minimal comfort. Seledri sat on Janak's lap, clutching the aetheroceiver and looking distraught. Janak steadied her with a hand on her arm, but appeared ready to crawl out of his skin with discomfort—no doubt from the situation, not the ride.

Aniri was perched on Devesh's lap, ruing her decision with every bump of the cobblestones. The intimacy of the ride was nearly unendurable, not least because she once would have enjoyed such a moment far too much. Her only consolation was that Devesh seemed equally ill at ease. His hands kept moving, wavering between holding Aniri's waist, to keep her from bouncing out of his lap, and gripping the wooden seat anywhere but near her body.

She ground out between her teeth. "How much farther can our destination possibly be?"

"We have to travel to the commerce gate." Devesh's voice was equally strained. "The city walls are a holdover from an earlier time, when regular sieges required a stronghold approach. But even now, all pedestrian traffic in and out of the city is through the main gates, or the train station, both of which will be monitored by the Second Son, if he's thought at all about the situation. Which he has, given the royal guards he sent to your father's shop. I know someone who may be willing to smuggle us out of the commerce gate."

"*May*?" If it was possible, Janak's voice was even more strained.

"He's not exactly a friend," Devesh said.

"What does *that* mean?" Aniri asked.

Janak curled his lip. "It means your courtesan consorts with persons of even worse repute than himself."

Aniri wished Janak would stop calling him *her* courtesan.

"It means," Devesh ground out, "that I'm not entirely sure of his allegiances." He took a breath and gripped Aniri's waist again as they bounced with a particular large bump in the road. He immediately let go, much to her relief. "He could be part of the Second Son's network. The prince has a somewhat shadow organization. A lot of shopkeepers involved in illegal activities do so with his implied consent."

"So we could be walking into a trap," Aniri said. "Are you sure this is wise?"

"It's *not* wise at all," Devesh said. "I tried to convince you of that already."

He shifted in his seat, underneath her, trying to keep his balance with the perpetual sway of the pamgari. His hand momentarily grazed her hip, and she tensed, words leaping to her lips to rebuke him, but then, just as quickly, his touch left. Her jolt didn't escape Janak's notice, and his frown made her face light on fire. Surely he didn't think—

Devesh kept talking. "We should exercise caution. All of you should hold back until I can inquire about passage out of the city. We won't reveal your identity at first. Let me handle it."

"And how exactly do you know this person?" Seledri asked. "Won't he wonder why you're smuggling people out of the city?"

"When I returned from Jungali, my mission was over," Devesh said with a sigh. "A rather complete failure, I might add. The ambassador had no more use for me. I was lucky her fondness for me allowed me to walk away with my head still attached. But I still knew some of the people involved in the black market from before I left for Dharia. This particular tradesman deals in large mechanical parts—steam engine boilers, propellers for the Samirian Navy, all very legal. He *also* smuggles used parts and refurbished goods that wouldn't pass Guild inspection but are substantially cheaper than his normal trade. I don't know if he's ever trafficked in people, but his shipment crates are large enough to allow it. I wouldn't be surprised, and neither will he. The trick will be in convincing him to smuggle us out, rather than turning us in."

"That sounds promising." Seledri's sarcasm warmed Aniri's heart. It was good to hear a little of her sister's normal liveliness coming back into her voice.

"I figure your raksaka might come in handy for persuasion purposes," Devesh replied stiffly.

Seledri shook her head.

Janak glared at him.

Devesh ignored him and shifted again.

Aniri was determined to get out and walk if their ride didn't end soon.

Several torturous minutes later, the pamgari came to a stop. Aniri was out of her side of the cart almost before it stopped moving. Riva hopped down and magically produced a small step stool for Seledri to disembark.

They had stopped in an industrial district of the city. Most of the shops seemed to trade in clockwork or metalworks of some kind. The shop before them was large—easily four times the size of Riva's pamgari shop.

Devesh gave Riva a quick hug. "Thank you for your help. I owe you."

She rolled her eyes. "You've owed me since the moment you met me."

He grinned.

Riva climbed aboard the pamgari driver's spot,

then gave a belated bow to Seledri. "Arama, your majesty." She pumped the vehicle away without looking back.

Devesh led the way into the shop, which was indeed crammed with all manner of metalworks. Aniri couldn't identify most of them, but Devesh's description of boilers and other shipbuilding parts seemed accurate. Giant mechanical parts were on display, their weight held up by heavy, mechanical-legged tables. The shopkeeper—a short, gray haired man—stood at the counter in back. Unfortunately, he had a customer already, a large man in a heavy, dark cloak, who towered over him.

"I'm quite busy at the moment," the shopkeeper called to them. "Perhaps you could stop back later?"

"We'll happily wait until you're through," Devesh called, waving Aniri, Janak, and Seledri to the side. They still had their hoods up, so the shopkeeper scarce could recognize them across the span of the shop, but something about the build of the customer tugged at Aniri. She edged forward, trying to get a better look, ignoring Devesh's jittery hand waves shooing her back.

"Pretend you have a heart, Narendra," the

customer said. "Ye know I'm good for the work. I just need something that won't catch the Guild's notice is all."

That voice.

"I'd have to look into it," the shopkeeper, Narendra, replied. "Could take some time."

"Ye don't need to be coy," the customer said, leaning forward across the counter. "Just tell me how much it will take to persuade ye. I'd prefer engines, but I'll take any work they've got. Just tell me who you're shipping parts to, and I can find my own way onto a ship."

The accent. The size. *Engines.* "Karan?" Aniri asked, hoping against hope she was wrong.

The customer turned, and under the dark cloak was a hint of striking blue: the Jungali sailor uniform. Above it, the unmistakable face of Ash's Master Tinker.

His bushy eyebrows flew up. "Fresh! What are ye doing here?" The question was nearly a growl.

"I could ask the same of you." It sounded very much like he was trying to find work in Samir. As if he planned to stay a good long while.

Devesh tugged at her arm, but she shook him off. She glanced back: Janak was keeping Seledri tucked behind a large boiler display. When she turned forward again, Karan had taken a giant step toward her, fully turning his back on the shopkeeper. The smaller man edged to the side, peering around to see who was there.

Karan dropped his voice low and rough. "This is no place for you, fresh."

"This is no place for *you*, Karan." Her heart still didn't want to believe what was plain before her eyes.

"Aye," he said softly. "But things aren't always as they look."

A shuffle from the back drew all their attention. The tail end of the shopkeeper disappeared through a back door.

The tension fled Karan's body. "Well, that's a right mess, now." He shook his head. "Ye could use a few lessons in your spy skills, fresh, so ye don't wander into a den of thieves unawares. Now ye scared him off, just when I was about to find out who's been smuggling propeller blades. The kind that might be useful for a *different* kind of ship, if you take my drift."

Relief coursed through Aniri's body. "So you weren't..."

Karan looked offended. "Do ye think me completely incapable of following orders?"

"I just—"

"Ay!" he cut her off as he peered past her shoulder. "And you! You're that sort from the embassy, aren't ye?" Karan wrinkled up his great brow, like he was trying to conjure whether he knew Devesh's name or just the face.

Devesh's hand was pressed to his head. "I think we're in need of an alternate plan," he said to her while glaring at Karan. "And I suggest we leave. *Now.* Before Narendra pieces it together that, *yes*, we all somewhat know each other here."

Karan's eyes narrowed. "Is this lot bothering you, fresh?"

"No, he's helping me. Well, trying to."

Janak emerged from the shadows with Seledri. "I agree that it's time to leave, especially now that we have Mr. Karan—"

"Leave?" boomed a jovial voice from the back. "But you just arrived."

They all turned. The shopkeeper had reemerged from the rear of his shop, but he wasn't the source of the voice: next to him stood Second Son Natesh, two royal guards, and a tall man dressed entirely in black. The short handles of two swords protruded above his back. *Raksaka.* Aniri's mind grappled with that while taking in the rest: the guards already had their pistols out, pointed at them. Natesh's smile was wide as he sauntered toward them. The front door was just behind them, but there was no chance of them all making it.

They were caught.

"Isn't this a pleasant surprise?" Natesh said, coming to a stop well out of arm's reach and flanked by his guards and raksaka. The shopkeeper lurked in back, like a mouse. Karan had shifted to place his large body between her and them, hand fishing under his cloak for what Aniri assumed would be his pistols. After a moment, Devesh also stepped in front of her, but Aniri knew it was a futile gesture on both their parts.

She slid between Devesh and Karan. "Natesh," she said coolly, scrambling for some plan that wouldn't land them all in the Second Son's grasp. Or dead on an obscure shopkeeper's floor. "Wish I could say this was a surprise. Or pleasant."

"Oh now, don't be that way, Third Daughter of Dharia," he said with a cocky grin. "I was being completely honest when I said your adventures have been quite entertaining. You've given us a run with your antics. And we've been concerned about the

Second Daughter as well. We've looked all over the city for you both, once we discovered the Queen-to-be's bedchamber empty. Well, not quite *empty*." He peered around Aniri, Devesh, and Karan to check out Janak and Seledri hanging back behind them. "Speaking of which, where *is* my brother? I thought sure he had decided to secret his lovely wife out of the city. Imagine my surprise to find you doing his work for him."

"Guess you'll have to work out your family issues on your own."

Natesh's grin turned into a sneer. "I didn't quite anticipate your extreme familial loyalty. But I must say it was considerate of you to deliver your sister out of hiding and directly into our hands."

Aniri's face grew hot. That was exactly what she had managed to do, in spite of all her efforts. She sensed Devesh and Karan shift behind her, drawing closer. She didn't know their plan, but perhaps it was still possible to talk their way out of this.

"You needn't bother with us, really," Aniri said, trying to tamp down the panic making her chest tight. "We'll be on our way and no trouble to you and whatever plans you have for your reign. It matters not to Dharia who wears the crown in Samir."

"Oh, but I think it does matter. A great deal." Natesh smirked again. "Just not in the way you suppose, Aniri." He sighed, as if suddenly bored with the conversation. Tipping his head to his raksaka, he said, "The Second Daughter is to die by poisoning. Please ensure there is no evidence to the contrary. As for the Third Daughter…" He held out a hand to one of his guards, who passed over his gun. "I will take care of that myself."

He pointed the gun at Aniri's head.

Just as he cocked it, Aniri was shoved sideways, a blur flying past her. Natesh's gun cracked, but it must have gone wide, because the bullet found a home somewhere in the metalworks with a biting ping. Aniri was yanked farther to the side and dragged behind one of the boilers. It was Devesh, one hand locked around her arm, a pistol in the other. Across the empty middle aisle, Karan likewise had Seledri tucked behind a giant mechanical tubing display, weapon in hand.

The sing of metal on metal came from the back. Aniri peeked to find Janak fighting Natesh's raksaka, using some metal piping to beat back his two short blades. Their blows were lightning fast, more than she could track, with whirled movements of legs and leaps interspersed between. Natesh and his two guards had retreated to a display, taking refuge and leaving the raksakas clear room to fight.

Aniri faced Devesh in their close hiding spot. "Give me your gun," she whispered harshly.

He squinted but didn't argue, handing it over. She peeked around the edge again, trying to aim at Natesh's raksaka, but she couldn't be sure to hit him. And the pistol was only a single shot.

She growled in frustration, then called out, "Natesh! This is madness. Call back your raksaka."

"It's a little late for that, Aniri," came his casual reply. A shot cracked out, and a fist-sized hole appeared in the boiler behind which she and Devesh stood.

Devesh's eyes were wide. It had missed them by inches.

"Can't exactly let you live now, you see," Natesh called out.

Karan popped briefly from behind his equipment shield and fired at Natesh. The sing of metal and lack of cries told her he missed. Meanwhile, in the raksaka fight, the metallic strikes had been replaced by muscular grunts.

Natesh's first shot wasn't followed immediately by another, even though clearly their protective shield was less than adequate. By her count they had two weapons and had fired twice. They must be reloading. But she still only had the one shot, and far more enemies than that.

She scanned the room for anything else they could use, shield or weapon. Karan was scrambling to reload, her sister shrinking into his shadow, the aetheroceiver held protectively over her belly. Aniri and Devesh had only one weapon between them, with no way to reload.

A groaning that sounded far too much like Janak jolted her: he was still recovering from his gunshot wound from Garesh. Surely he couldn't last long in such a fight.

Aniri peeked out again and jerked back when she saw a guard doing likewise. Another shot rang out and the window at the storefront shattered, spraying glass onto the sidewalk. If there were people on the street, they had long since scattered with the gunfire. Then something Aniri saw in that split second peek registered in her mind. Along the wall behind Natesh and his guards was a row of slim silver tanks. The kind that were pumped full of the gases used for all kinds of welding and metal-works. They were kept secured by hooks and chains because of their explosive potential.

Aniri popped out from her hiding place, took

aim, and fired at the row of canisters. Faster than she could blink, an explosive pop deafened her ears, followed by a blast of hissing gas. Mens' cries pierced the air. Karan peered around his shield, weapon ready. He fired at Natesh and the guards as they fled their cover. Aniri couldn't tell if Karan hit anyone, but they kept running, straight out the back of the shop. In that moment of distraction, Janak landed a blow that stumbled his foe back. Janak pulled something from the back of his ink-black clothing, and one more gunshot cracked the air.

Natesh's raksaka jerked back and lay still on the floor.

Janak's weapon leaked a small trail of smoke. He cast it aside, liberated the twin blades from the fallen raksaka and, holding them like daggers, stalked into the back room.

"Karan!" Aniri said, flashing looks between him and the disappearing back of her raksaka.

Karan nodded and hurried after Janak, although his weapon was discharged, and he hadn't time to reload. But having another in the fight might help, should Natesh and his men decide to make a stand in the shop's back storage rooms.

Aniri went to her sister, still behind the giant tubing display. "Are you all right?"

"Yes." And indeed, her sister looked as if the fight had energized her in some way. "It's a good thing to be sure who your enemies are."

Aniri gave a small smile. She couldn't imagine how relieved her sister must be to hear straight from the Second Son's mouth that her husband wasn't the one seeking her death.

"We really shouldn't remain here," Devesh said.

Aniri peered at the back of the shop. There was no sign or sound of trouble, but she wasn't sure that meant anything.

"How are we going to get out of the city *now*?" Aniri asked Devesh. "Do you have someone else you know that perhaps *doesn't* have a direct line to the Second Son?"

"The shopkeeper can't possibly have wired Natesh and had him arrive so quickly," Devesh said defensively. "The Second Son probably has his people roaming the city, watching for anything unusual. When your tinker showed up here, I suspect that triggered a personal visit."

Aniri grimaced at their apparent bad luck. "What options does that leave us?"

"Aniri, please reconsider. Let me hide you away." Devesh urged both of them to move toward the front door.

"I'm reconsidering how much help you are really providing here." Aniri stared at the shattered window as they approached the front door. She didn't want to leave without Janak and Karan, but she couldn't risk going after them. Before she had to make that decision, they reappeared, Janak stalking in from the back, swords still in hand, and Karan following with the cowardly mouse of a shopkeeper in tow. Karan hauled him past the dead raksaka, pausing briefly to pick up the gun Janak had cast aside, then marched the shopkeeper to stand before Aniri.

"Found him hiding in a barrel," Karan said with a look of disgust.

"It appears the Second Son and his guards have fled for the moment," Janak said, "but I'm sure it is only a temporary retreat. We need to move immediately, then discuss our plans going forward."

"What about him?" Aniri nodded to the shopkeeper. Karan still held him by the scruff of the neck.

Janak moved lightning fast to press the tip of his sword to the shopkeeper's throat. "Which direction to the train depot?"

The man's eyes bugged out. "To the north," he squeaked.

Janak withdrew his sword and somehow stowed both blades in a slip of fabric in the back of his raksaka uniform. Then he knocked the shopkeeper out with a single, effortless blow to the temple.

"We'll head to the pedestrian gate," Janak said, nodding toward the door.

Chapter Sixteen

Devesh led the way out of the shop, followed by Janak and Seledri. Aniri fell into step behind them with Karan. She glanced up at the large man, hoping she was forgiven for assuming he had betrayed them.

He noticed her look and gave her a small smile. "Like I told ye, yer good in a pinch, fresh."

Aniri smiled briefly, then copied Karan as he tucked his weapons away underneath his cloak. The shops were just beginning to leak tentative customers back onto the street. Their group was attracting everyone's notice, but they followed Janak's lead in putting up their hoods anyway. The only chance of staying ahead of Natesh's spies—who must be everywhere by now—was to move away from the scene as quickly as possible.

Devesh led them down an alley that soon blocked them from prying eyes. They weaved past broken crates and piles of sour refuse that reeked of tinker grease and metal. Once out of the industrial district, the stench only worsened, with rotten food and the pests who feasted on it. Devesh finally called them to a halt just before a busy street. News of the gunfight seemed to not have traveled from the industrial sector a dozen blocks away.

"The pedestrian gate is just two streets farther," Devesh said to the group, and specifically to Janak. "But I don't know what you're thinking. The guards will surely be on alert for us, and they're armed as a matter of course."

"We are armed as well," Janak said.

Devesh looked at him like he was crazed and turned to Aniri. "A lone raksaka armed with blades is no match for muskets."

Aniri knew that well enough. She studied Janak: he seemed slightly winded, and a razor-thin cut along his cheek was sending a small river of blood down his neck. He ignored it, but Aniri felt sure the fight with Natesh's raksaka had rekindled his previous injuries. Or worse, he was hiding fresh ones, possibly more serious than a close shave with a raksaka's blade.

Now that they were stopped, Karan was busy reloading his weapons. "We'll have a few shots of our own."

Aniri shook her head. "Janak, I'm not enamored with the idea of another gunfight."

"Nor am I," he said tightly. "But waiting for the Second Son's guards to find us again isn't prudent. And our time grows short."

Aniri pursed her lips. He was right on both counts, but that didn't make storming the pedestrian gate any less risky. "What alternatives do we have?"

She had asked Janak, but Devesh answered instead. "I can still secret you both away—"

Janak cut him off with a glare. "Word will quickly grow of the gunfight, and with a raksaka dead and a princess missing... there are thousands of hostile eyes in this city, my lady, and we cannot be sure of any of them."

Devesh balled up his fists and turned away, shaking his head in disgust.

Janak ignored him. "Hiding is a high-risk option. As long as we reach the pedestrian gate before reinforcements arrive, a couple of armed guards present a much smaller challenge. I will take them myself. Only when the passage is clear, will you and the Second Daughter emerge from a safe location and transit with me."

"Aye," Karan said. "Taking the gate should be less trouble than you think, fresh. Those guards aren't the pick of the crop, usually. And I've a couple of shots to clear the way should they make trouble."

Aniri felt another pang for having ever doubted him. She didn't like the plan, but Janak was right. Time was short and their list of options shorter. "All right. But I want you armed with a pistol as well, Janak." She dug out her gun and handed it to him. He exchanged it with Karan for a loaded one, which then disappeared inside his raksaka wrappings.

"And my lady should have a sword." Janak pulled one of the short blades from its sheath along his back and presented it to her with both hands. It was light, but well-balanced, and it felt better in her hand than the gun. She sheathed her sword through a loop in her belt, under her cloak.

Devesh was still silently cursing and pressing a fist into the cobblestoned wall of the alley. Aniri shook her head and turned to Seledri. She was leaning against the wall, closer to the group, eyes cast down, examining the alley muck at her feet.

Aniri peered at her, catching her eye. "You must be tired."

"And wishing I had trusted Pavan from the start." Seledri's brow was wrinkled, the aethero-ceiver still clutched protectively across her belly.

"That's something you can remedy," Aniri said softly. "But I doubt we would make it to the palace now without being caught. We need to get you to safety first. But are you well enough for this?" She tilted her head toward the pedestrian gate.

Seledri made a face. "If we remain much longer in this alley, I suspect the stench alone will kill me."

Aniri grinned.

Devesh had finally stopped his silent tirade against the wall.

She took a couple slow steps toward him. "You don't have to be part of this, Dev."

He pushed off against the stone wall. "I promised to get you out of the city."

"Your assistance has been underwhelming so far, courtesan," Janak called as he wiped at the blood still pulsing from his face.

Aniri grimaced. That wasn't fair. The fight at the shop wasn't Devesh's fault. She touched his arm. "Thank you for getting us this far, but I think we can manage from here."

"You'll need a distraction," Devesh said, ignoring her words but not her touch. "Someone the guards will not suspect, while your raksaka sneaks up to disable them."

"You don't need to take that risk."

"I promised to get you out of the city," he repeated, darkly. "We're not there yet."

Aniri frowned, not sure why he was so determined. But she nodded her agreement. It *would* help, even though she suspected he was just buying another chance to convince her to stay.

Janak noted her acquiescence. "You'll need to make haste, courtesan, if you want to contribute. But know that I'll not be waiting on you." To Karan, he said, "Stay with the Daughters and find a hiding spot with a view of the gate. Wait for my clear signal." He demonstrated by making two circles in the air with his finger. "Then do not be tardy in joining us."

"Aye," Karan said. "We'll be right on your heels."

Janak jerked his head toward the alley entrance. "After you, courtesan."

Devesh glanced at Aniri, then squared his shoulders and strode past Janak, out of the alley. He took a left, which Aniri assumed was the direction of the gate. Janak went back the way they had come, no doubt looking for another approach.

Karan led them out of the alley, hoods up, onto the busy street. The flow of traffic was even more substantial here at the entrance to the city. The pedestrian gate served, of course, people on foot, but also a small, buzzing fleet of pamgari. The wall surrounding the city was enormous, practically a mountain of rock unto itself. The gates were forged from giant sheets of steel. The massive doors stood open, but two guard houses just inside constricted the entrance, and a thick, mechanical lever arm blocked the cobbled street as it stretched beyond the city gate. Barely visible in the distance sat a small cluster of buildings—a village perhaps that served travelers on their way.

A guard stood at the mechanical arm, turning some pamgari back while others were allowed through, one at a time. There was apparently a limit on how much cargo was allowed to pass, with a lively bartering of excess goods occurring off to the sides of the main traffic flow. Foot traffic was kept separate, transiting under a small arch to the side of the pamgari. One guard waved pedestrians through with only a cursory pause. Devesh must have melted into the crowd, because Aniri couldn't see him anywhere.

Karan stopped at a flower market only three shops from the gate. Heaping baskets of blooms brought color to the relentless grays and browns of the city's landscape. Seledri and Aniri pretended to inspect the offerings, while Karan held the shop-keeper off, saying they were browsing for a wedding, not making a purchase today. It gave Aniri a twinge, thinking of the flower-laden God of Love who was supposed to preside over her wedding to Ash. Somehow discovering Pavan's innocence had settled her heart along with the obvious relief in Seledri's. Aniri wanted nothing more than to return to Jungali and the only man she had loved who was worthy of it.

A commotion at the gate drew her attention. Devesh had commandeered a pamgari from who knew where and was attempting to pass through the gate, but the guard had stopped him. Apparently he was transporting something not allowed, because the guard was waving him out of the line, insisting he turn around, but Devesh was refusing to leave. His arms waved, and Aniri couldn't catch the words, but she was quite certain they weren't civil.

Her body tensed as the guard put a hand to the pistol holstered at his side. They had caught the attention of everyone, including the second guard, who was holding up the line of pedestrians as they quarreled.

"Who is that?" Seledri asked.

"It's just Dev," Aniri answered.

"No *that*." Seledri pointed to a cloaked figure working his way to the front of the pedestrian line.

Aniri squinted. He was too broad shouldered to be Janak. She glanced at Karan, but he was eyeing the figure as well. Then a shadow drifted over the crowd. The skyship sailed over them, a thousand feet in the air and blocking the sun.

"They're here," Aniri whispered.

"Aye," Karan said, just as quiet. "It's time we catch our ride, fresh."

He eased Aniri and Seledri away from the flowers, slowly strolling toward the gate. The cloaked figure had reached Devesh and appeared to be negotiating between Devesh and the guard. Aniri, Seledri, and Karan edged closer to the gate, but they couldn't see the mystery person's face.

Suddenly a cry went up. The guard at the pedestrian gate slumped to the ground, and another cloaked figure—wiry and impossibly fast—whisked from that station to the second guard. He dropped like a stone.

Janak.

Several more cries rose up from the crowd. Karan urged Seledri and Aniri to pick up their pace. As they approached the end of the pedestrian line, the crowd dissolved into chaos: people with goods backing away from the fallen guard, pamgari tipping in their driver's haste to turn around. Aniri strained to see Janak and Devesh and the mysterious figure who stood with them.

Janak made two circles in the air with his finger.

Aniri drew her sword, grabbed her sister's hand, and ran through the stumbling crowd. Karan covered them like a shadow. They nearly collided with a woman clutching her child to her chest. Aniri yanked Seledri back from a driverless pamgari surging away from the gate. Karan's arm at her back steadied them both. A handful of seconds later, they reached Janak and Devesh at the now deserted gate. The cloaked figure turned toward them.

"Pavan!" Seledri cried out.

His eyes were wild; they drank in the sight of her. "Seledri, thank the gods——" He surged toward her, a pistol in one hand, but it was pointed at the ground.

Janak threw an arm in front of him before he had gone two steps. "We're leaving. *Now.*"

Her raksaka dashed to their side, laid hands on both Aniri and Seledri, and practically dragged them toward the gate. Seledri was twisted her head from one side to the other, trying to catch sight of Pavan. Why was he here? And armed? But Aniri had no time for such thoughts as she finally got her feet under her and stumbled toward the gate. Janak, Devesh, Pavan, and Karan crowded around her and Seledri, a human shield intent on ferrying them outside the city. They hurried past the centurion metal gates and mammoth stone walls, emerging into a meadow of color and sunshine, brilliant greens sprinkled with riotous wildflowers.

They had made it outside the city.

THEY RAN hard across the meadow: Aniri with Devesh by her side, Seledri slightly behind with Pavan, Janak and Karan bringing up the rear and glancing over their shoulders for pursuit to spill from the city's gates. The wildflowers were trampled under their boots, while the skyship hovered above the distant village, beckoning them with the promise of escape.

Only now did Aniri realize the jeopardy of the ship in daring such a rescue—they would have to land, and thus be vulnerable to attack from below. Captain Tarak must have spied their fleeing forms, because already the skyship was lowering to the ground, casting off ropes as she went. Several sailors climbed down the ropes, readying for when they would reach the ground, while others threw out thicker ropes—which Aniri realized were actually ladders. The ship's landing spot was near the village, which at the moment, seemed miles away from their entourage.

Aniri's chest labored under the run, and Seledri nearly stumbled, caught only by Pavan's hold on her hand. He took the aetheroceiver she still carried. Aniri slowed to a brisk walk, giving her sister a chance to catch her breath.

"Karan." Aniri panted between words. "Secure the ship."

He nodded and raced ahead.

"Seledri?" Aniri asked.

"I'm fine," her sister said, but she, too, was winded.

Aniri slowed their pace further. They had gained enough distance from the gate that even the sudden appearance of the Second Son's guards wouldn't present an immediate threat. And they could run faster again, if need be.

"Janak," Aniri called back.

He was keeping a close eye behind them. "My lady, I'm concerned about our pace."

"Understood." But Aniri feared pushing her sister any faster. Seledri made an effort, but Aniri could see the toll it was taking. Pavan exchanged a look with her and concern flashed across his face as well.

He tugged Seledri to a stop and cupped her cheek with one hand. "Let me carry you, my love."

"I will only slow you down," Seledri said between pants.

"Perhaps," he said with a smile, then stooped to sweep her into his arms, managing to carry both her and the aetheroceiver. "But it will give you a moment's rest. Should we have to run again."

The caring look Pavan gave her sister was so sweet it made Aniri look away in shame for having thought he was anything other than madly in love with her. Pavan strode forward, carrying her sister at a faster pace than Aniri thought possible, his gaze fixed on the skyship, and determination etched on his face. She and Devesh gave them a dozen feet of privacy then kept pace.

"How did he know where to find us?" Aniri asked Devesh, keeping her voice low.

"He's been looking all over the city for her," Devesh said. "Once he heard the skyship had departed the palace for a supposed tour, he said he knew you must be heading for the gates."

Pavan's strenuous attempt to get his wife and

unborn child to safety was touching Aniri's heart. And it appeared to have affected Seledri as well, with the way she held Pavan's cheek as he ran, carrying them to the skyship.

Aniri nodded her approval. "It's fortunate that he loves her so thoroughly."

"Something that I, for the record, never doubted."

Aniri just lifted an eyebrow. "As if you know anything about love."

"Perhaps not," Devesh said stiffly. "But he's a First Son who took a Dharian wife. Samirians love their traditions, Aniri. Breaking one for love is a Jungali conceit, not a Samirian one."

She decided to ignore the dig. "The prince seemed to recognize you at the gate."

"We met your father's shop, actually. He was in a torment about approaching Pavan and sought me out as a go-between." He paused for a moment. "Your father regrets so much, Aniri."

That made her chest hurt. "Do think he's still alive, Dev?"

"Yes." He hastened to add, "Pavan said your father wasn't in his shop when he arrived." Devesh gave her a soft look. "If your father was dead, Natesh would have simply left his body there. His secrets would have died with him. The guards must have taken him into custody. Probably because that was the more strategic option."

Hope lifted the weight from her chest.

Devesh glanced back, but the gates were still clear. Janak had fallen several yards behind them, and Aniri prayed it was to keep a closer eye on the gate and not because he was suffering injuries he'd failed to disclose. Ahead of them, Pavan put Seledri down, and they now hurried forward together, hands clasped. Aniri was once again struck by the sweetness of it.

"It would appear," Devesh said, watching Seledri and Pavan as well, "that the First Son has finally earned his princess's love."

"You knew?" Aniri wondered how widespread was the knowledge that Seledri had withheld her love.

He shrugged. "It was obvious to anyone watching." His gaze fell to studying the meadow grass in front of them, then rose to the skyship. "I suppose it was foolish to think I could earn your forgiveness as well."

"It's not foolish to believe in someone..." ...*you love.* They were Ash's words. She didn't want to say that last part, but it rang true for Devesh. He had brought her here, risking himself to help her escape. And he helped close the hole in her heart where she had carried her long-lost father's memory, the one promise Devesh made from the beginning. If it was foolish to want to make up for one's mistakes, he was no more a fool than she was.

"Perhaps you were a little naïve," she added.

He grinned, then peeked at her. "From anyone else, I would take that as a terrible insult."

They had finally reached the shadow of the skyship. It floated fifty feet off the ground, fins waving gently in the air, tethered by a dozen ropes and sailors holding her. Bewildered Samirian nobles were debarking from the ship, an awkward train of well-dressed ladies and lords negotiating the rope ladder. Aniri and Devesh caught up to Seledri and Pavan at the base of an unused ladder, kept clear for ascending rather than descending. Pavan held it steady, while Seledri rested her hand on his.

Then Aniri realized: they weren't just escaping Natesh's spies and palace guards any longer. They were fleeing Pavan's capital. And soon, the country.

Seledri was out of breath, looking deeply into her husband's eyes. "Why didn't you tell me about Natesh? And my father? If I had only known…"

He nodded fervently. "I should have. I was

afraid… I feared I might lose the chance to…" He gave her a pained smile. "I was afraid you would leave. Just as you are now."

"I don't want to leave. Not anymore. I want to stay and be your Queen. I want to be *Samir's* Queen."

Pavan looked away from her intense gaze. "I can't keep you safe, Seledri." The words seemed to choke him. "I thought I could, but…" The torment on Pavan's face was almost too much to look upon. "You have to go with your sister. Natesh's plans are far worse than I knew, and I cannot have you here, at risk, and have any hope of stopping him. Because if he ever got hold of you, my love… I would be completely at his mercy."

Tears were flowing down her sister's face now, and Aniri's were close behind. Seledri lifted a hand to Pavan's face. "My love." The whisper of her voice barely carried across the wind.

Pavan's smile broke through the pain holding his expression hostage. He placed his hand on her belly. "Keep our child safe."

Seledri nodded through her tears. Pavan pulled her into his arms, and the passion of their kiss made Aniri duck her head and look away. Devesh was watching them with undisguised jealousy, and it hurt her heart to see it.

"Dev, come with us."

He darted a look to her, caught in the act. Then he frowned. "I'm not exactly fond of torture, Aniri."

"You will *not* be tortured." Although she wasn't at all sure what Ash's reaction would be to Devesh's return. "However, I can't exactly guarantee you won't spend time in prison."

"I'm not fond of prison, either."

"He will be under my protection here," Pavan said, startling Aniri. Her sister was making her way up the ladder, and Pavan's face was still blotched with emotion. He extended a hand to Devesh. "Thank you for keeping watch over Seledri."

Devesh took it, but Aniri could tell it made him uncomfortable. "Of course, your majesty."

Pavan turned to her. "You're the only one I would entrust with her, Aniri."

"She'll be safe with us. And you have Dharia's support, as well as Jungali's. In whatever you need."

He nodded and turned to stride toward Janak, who had kept his distance from the tearful goodbyes while watching the gate.

Aniri turned to Devesh. "I'm sorry, Dev."

He winced like the words caused him physical pain. "That sounds a lot like goodbye." Then he frowned. "Sorry for what?"

"Just *sorry*. For how things turned out."

"Not as sorry as I."

She smiled and against her better judgment, she reached to hug him. It was meant as a simple hug of friendship, of forgiveness, but his hands found her back and held her tight. She feared she would have to pull away, but he slowly eased his hold.

When he released her, he slid his hands up to her cheeks, which flamed with embarrassment at the intimate way he was holding her. Before she could force herself to wrench away, he whispered, "You're everything I've ever wanted, Aniri."

Then he kissed her, lightly, sweetly. It was over before she could protest or push him away. He let her go and stepped back, a sadness in his dark brown eyes tearing at her heart even as she felt a rebuke stall out on her lips.

Before she could muster the words, he gave her a small smile and turned away.

Then she saw them: in the distance, flowing like ants out of a hole, only they were streaming from the gates of the capital.

Royal Samirian guards.

"Aniri!" The gruff voice came from above. Karan leaned over the rail at the top of the rope ladder. His face was stern. "We're leaving, fresh. Are ye comin' with or no?" He asked it as if the answer wasn't obvious, but Aniri had no time to think on that.

She scrambled up the rope ladder like her life depended on it.

Aniri was only halfway up the ladder when the skyship began to ascend.

She swayed underneath the ship, the rope ladder swinging with the sudden uplift, and chanced a look below. The swarm of royal guard was closing in on Pavan and Devesh, but several had already stopped short to aim: and not at the errant First Son and the ex-courtesan he had vowed to protect.

They were shooting at *her*.

A series of pops cracked the air. Aniri twitched so hard she nearly lost her grip on the rope. But after that heart-stopping moment, she seemed to still be intact. A quick scan of the billowing sky-blue gas bag above her didn't show any sudden venting of gas or punctures that would bring the ship right back down again.

"Fresh!" Karan leaned over the rail at the top of the ladder. "Quit yer gawking. I can't pull up the rope with ye on it."

Aniri scrambled up the rest of the ladder, focusing on her handholds and not the rapidly disappearing ground below. When she reached the top, Karan grabbed hold of her cloak and hoisted her over the railing. He quickly disappeared below deck, which was in chaos from sailors hurrying to pull up dangling lines and get below themselves, not least to avoid the gunfire. A second volley cracked the air, and Aniri ducked. She dared a peek over the rim only to find a thin haze from the already fired weapons drifting up. The guards must have decided the skyship was out of range because more stood ready to fire, yet no shots rang out.

Devesh was in handcuffs on the ground, with Pavan and Natesh arguing over him.

Guilt twisted Aniri's heart. She should have insisted that he come with them. At least then, she could have offered some measure of protection. Pavan was in a fight for the crown, and as the First Son said, the casualties in those kinds of battles were often those closest to it. Like her sister.

Keeping below the railing, just in case, Aniri crept to the open bulkhead door and followed the last sailor below deck. Her stomach was unsteady with the constant rising of the ship, but she worked her way forward to the bridge. Captain Tarak was in command, issuing orders to turn downwind, blow their ballast, and generally do everything possible to get aloft and away. Clear blue sky stretched before them, empty of clouds or trouble, and Aniri dared to hope they had actually made their escape.

Karan was bent over his maps and charts. He glanced at her, then went back to studying his papers. "Your raksaka is in the galley," he said gruffly. "I believe he's sending a message to the prince. Ye might think of sending one as well."

His tone was odd. As if suddenly they were no longer friends. It perplexed her.

"I will check with Janak presently." Her voice drew the notice of the rest of the bridge crew, although they tried hard not to show it, pretending to tend to their instruments while peeking at her from the corners of their eyes.

"Karan." She waited for him to look up.

It took several long moments for him to do so. "Aye?"

"Has something gone wrong?" Her chest started to squeeze. Maybe they had seen something she hadn't. Or perhaps something was amiss with Seledri, beyond leaving her husband and fleeing her country with her unborn child. "Is my sister all right? Is there something I need to know?"

Karan heaved a sigh. "No, fresh. Yer sister's fine. I assigned her a cabin so she could rest."

Aniri frowned, waiting for the rest. There must be something more.

He turned to Captain Tarak. "What's our altitude, Mr. Tarak?"

"Closing on two thousand feet, sir."

"I've plotted our initial course. Can ye take the helm for a moment, while I step out?"

"Aye, sir." Tarak came to stand by the maps, to apparently take over the charting of their passage home. He gave Aniri the same odd look the other sailors were trying to hide, like he wasn't sure if he should look her in the eye or not.

Aniri frowned and followed Karan out of the bridge.

They didn't go far before she stopped him. The thin corridor was crowded with tubing vents above and brass rails at midlevel to anchor the sailors during the rough ride through the air.

"What is it, Karan?" she asked, looking up into his face. "Is something wrong back home?"

He gave her an even more odd look, like she was confusing him. "I'm not sure how to say this, fresh."

"Just say it," she said quietly. A shiver climbed up her back.

"We saw ye down there with…" Karan rubbed the back of his neck with one, large, meaty hand. "…with the Samirian."

Aniri blinked. What was he talking about? "Pavan and Devesh helped spirit us from the city. You *know* this."

"I don't mean that." He shifted his weight from one foot to the other. "I mean when ye kissed the boy, fresh."

"I… I didn't kiss him." Aniri's face flushed, because of course she had. At least, she didn't stop Devesh from kissing her. "I mean, it wasn't like that—"

Karan held up his hands. "I'm just sayin' that we all saw it. Everyone. Sailors and passengers alike. They're probably wondering, with the wedding postponed and all, what your intentions are." He peered at her with his dark eyes, normally so filled with humor, but now dead serious. "What *are* your intentions, fresh?"

"I intend to return to Jungali," she said, suddenly angry. "I hope you've laid our course straight there."

He frowned. "Aye, I have. Are you sure that's where you want to go?"

"Karan." Aniri plead with him to understand, hands upturned, mouth gaped. "I'm returning home to marry Ash."

He nodded and stepped back. "Right then." But he didn't look convinced. "We'll be crewing in shifts again to get us back right quick."

"Good."

They stood awkwardly for a moment in the corridor while a sailor edged past them on his way to the bridge. He seemed to shrink inside himself, as if he fervently wished he had taken another route forward.

When he was out of earshot, Aniri asked stiffly, "What did you learn of Samirian capabilities while on the ground?"

Karan fell into a no-nonsense tone as well. "They've certainly the commerce for it. Ye saw it at least a little when ye were down there. Mahatvak is the capital, and inland, very far from the sea, yet they're doing a pretty business moving large clockwork and metal goods. Partly because they're close to the mining—the mountains near the capital are the richest in the land—but partly due to pride. Ye don't know the Samirians like I do, fresh. They've got a bit of head about them when it comes to the trades."

"Perhaps that's warranted," Aniri said. "They certainly seem to have wonders that Dharia hasn't adopted yet. Or that I was even aware of."

"Aye," Karan said. "Don't think there isn't a purpose to that as well. Samir and the tinker's Guild are keen to keep their edge."

"So they have the resources to make more skyships?"

Karan gestured around them. "Much of what ye see on the ship is simply parts adapted from the navy. It wouldn't be hard to divert some from the naval yards to a secret location for building a skyship of their own." He squinted at her. "Aye, did you say *ships*? As in they might be building more than just the one?"

She drew in a breath and blew it out. "Can you keep a secret, Karan?"

"Depends on which secrets you want me to be keepin'." He crossed his arms and cocked his head. "Is this about the boy?"

Aniri balled up her hands then shook them out. "There is *nothing* to that, Karan."

He still looked unconvinced.

Aniri discarded her plan to tell him about her father, and Devesh, and Pavan, and the whole sordid, complicated, and ultimately shameful tale. He would just have to trust that the source was credible, something they needed to take seriously. "This is a secret that... I can't tell you how I know. But I have good reason to believe there isn't just a single skyship the Samirians are attempting to build. That they may, in fact, have an armada."

Karan choked, letting his arms unfold and fall to his sides. When he gained his composure again, he said, "How sure are you of this, fresh?"

"Sure enough that we need to return as quickly as possible to Jungali to warn Ash."

"A whole fleet of them?" Karan rubbed his face, obviously still absorbing what that meant. "How could they have gassed 'em all?"

"That's what I was going to ask *you*. Is it possible they've found another source for the navia gas? Or a way to manufacture it? Did you see any indications in the city of work of that kind?"

He frowned, thinking now. "They'd need the right processors to break it open, crush and heat it until the gas released. That's no standard naval ship equipment." He shook his head. "But I didn't have time to scour the city. They could have a whole manufacturing plant in the industrial district, and I coulda missed it."

Her shoulders drooped. "Then I guess we'll have to assume it's possible."

"The key would be the navia ore itself. Ye can't conjure gas if you don't have the rock. And I've not heard of any special mines of newly discovered ore. But once they knew of the navia, from working with the Jungali, there's no reason they couldn't set some tinkers about to find some in Samir. If only to keep their edge, you see."

"I'm afraid that's precisely what's happened."

"But if they've a fleet, why not deploy it?" Karan asked. "Especially now, with the *Prosperity* afloat and armed?"

"They must not be ready," Aniri said. "Or perhaps they are waiting for the right provocation."

He gave her a sharp look. "Such as?"

"Such as making off with their Queen-to-be and future heir."

He glanced at the bridge. "You think they could be after us even now?"

She held her hands out, palm up. "I don't know what to think."

"The prince needs to know of this."

"And I don't think I can message him. It's too sensitive."

Karan gave her a short nod. "I'll see what we can do to gain some speed as well as altitude, maybe catch a full wind back to Jungali. In case they decide to try to take us in the air."

"Thank you, Karan." The tension in her shoulders stepped down a notch.

He turned to hurry back to the bridge, then stopped. "And fresh."

"Yes?"

"Ye should message the prince. About something, even if not the fleet. He's had a rack of messages coming with no response from ye."

She winced. "I will, Karan. I promise."

He gave her a small smile and retreated in heavy footfalls to the bridge.

The railing was smooth under her hand as she slowly walked the ship, debating what she should or shouldn't say over the aetheroceiver. Finding no good solution, she opted to head to the galley. Janak was there, just as Karan had said, already tapping out and transcribing messages. A pile of curled tapes lay next to the unfolded aetheroceiver. Its clacking and whirring filled the empty room. The crew must be already at their stations or bunked down for the next rotation. Aniri slid into the seat across from him and waited until he was done.

The blood had dried on his face, leaving a jagged red line and deep red smears down to the black of his raksaka uniform. The dark color hid the stain of his blood well. Janak's eyes were pinched and tired, and she wondered again if he had sustained injuries he hadn't told her about. She resolved not to ask, knowing it would only serve to annoy him.

"Messages from the prince?" she asked when he finally looked up.

"And the Queen. They've been rather anxiously awaiting our replies while we were chasing ghosts in Samir."

Aniri peered at him. "Are you going to tell her, Janak?"

Janak shuffled the slips, as if looking for one, but she was sure he was simply avoiding her scrutiny. "There's nothing to tell."

"Janak, my father could be in the Second Son's custody."

He winced, like he was holding back his words.

"Tariq chose sides long ago." He looked up, his coal-black eyes a cold fury. "He chose the wrong one."

She nodded. "He left us. He abandoned his Queen and his three Daughters."

Janak's eyes widened slightly. "He's not worthy of bringing back into her life."

"And I don't want that any more than you," Aniri rushed to say. "But the Queen should know."

Janak pushed back from the table in a motion so quick it ruffled some of the aetheroceiver strips into the air. He stood, feet planted apart, like he wasn't sure if he wanted to leave in a huff of anger or rebuke her some more.

Aniri stood as well. "Janak, she won't go back to him."

"Of course she will, Aniri." He clipped his words, but there was pain underneath that tore into her. "She loves him, and if she had any idea that the Second Son of Samir was holding him prisoner…" He stopped, anger stealing his words.

"Exactly why *we* must be the ones to tell her." Aniri edged toward him, hands out in conciliation. "Don't you see how vulnerable that will make her? The King or the Second Son, whoever is pulling the strings, is undoubtedly involved in the skyship fleet as well. And they will use the knowledge of her long-lost husband to their best advantage. Devesh said my father is likely still alive because he has strategic value to them, and I don't think he's wrong."

Janak curled up a fist and pressed it to the low bulkhead of the galley. "They will use it against her."

"As they have always intended."

Janak squeezed his eyes shut, as if in pain.

Aniri couldn't stop herself. She slid closer and touched his shoulder lightly, bringing his eyes open. "Are you wounded, Janak?"

The sharp angles of his face softened, and his eyes begged her not to ask that of him.

She gave him a small smile. "I meant a wound of the body, not the heart. I've worried for you this entire trip." Aniri glanced to the strips of paper. "I imagine the Queen has as well. For you, for her Daughters." She looked back into his eyes. "My mother is strong, even alone. Now she will have all her Daughters and her most favored companion—*you*—by her side. She can withstand any news then. And far better for her to hear from us. We *have* to, Janak."

He gave a nod so small it was almost imperceptible.

"I will do it with you." Aniri strode over to the aetheroceiver strips. "For now, we'll give her what comfort we can via these messages."

Janak pulled in a breath and joined her at the table.

"I would worry more about what comfort you can give the prince."

Aniri looked sharply at him. "Did *everyone* see that kiss?"

"I imagine the gossip is already flying back to Jungali."

She balled up her fists and pressed them to her forehead. "Janak—"

"I know," he cut her off. "You don't have to convince me it meant less than nothing. But then I've known all along the courtesan wasn't worthy of you."

Aniri's mouth fell open, and she nearly put her arms around Janak. "Perhaps I can threaten to send my raksaka against all who would gossip against me." She was only partially speaking in jest.

At that moment, her handmaiden skittered into the room. "My lady!" Priya cried.

She launched from the entrance of the galley, and Aniri was nearly bowled over by the force of her hug. Her handmaiden pulled back and inspected her, head to foot, as if she expected to find grievous wounds. For once, Aniri was mostly intact.

"I was beside myself with worry." Then her voice turned chastising. "This habit of yours of running off…"

Aniri's eyebrows flew up, and Priya covered her mouth with her hand, as if she couldn't believe the words had escaped her. Aniri very nearly laughed, then she remembered Seledri's handmaiden stone cold on her lady's bed. She exchanged a look with Janak. Priya didn't know what had actually happened to Seledri's handmaiden. Nor did she need to.

Aniri pulled her into a hug. "You are quite the welcome sight, Priya."

When she released her handmaiden, Priya ducked her head shyly. "My lady, Princess Seledri awaits in your room. She hasn't brought a hand-maiden with her, so I've been attending her."

"Thank you for taking care of her," Aniri said, then cast a look at the pile of unreturned messages from Ash. "I will compose a proper reply soon. After I check on Seledri."

Janak frowned but didn't object as Priya towed Aniri from the room.

Chapter Nineteen

"Why can I think of nothing to say?" Aniri asked her sister. Aniri's hands were full with Ash's aethero-ceiver messages.

She and her sister sat on opposite bunks in Aniri's small cabin. The skyship occasionally bumped over some disturbance in the air, but otherwise the ride was smooth. They had many hours of travel yet before they reached Jungali, and nothing but worries to fill them. Not only might Samir be armed with skyships, they were likely to have a fleet of them. The crown was embroiled in a fight between the brothers which seemed destined to spill into a war to settle it. And her beautiful sister had been forced to flee from a country and a man she had finally grown to love.

Aniri's relatively frivolous concern about what response to give her future husband for all his unanswered slips of paper seemed silly by comparison.

But it would distract Seledri, and the crying had been more than Aniri could stand.

Her sister was propped with an abundance of pillows on the too-thin cot, resting with her feet up. Her face was no longer red or streaked with tears, but Aniri knew her good humor covered a heart torn into pieces.

Seledri adjusted one of the pillows. "Perhaps you can take the messages one by one and send him a reply for each."

"There would be no sense to it." Aniri held up one and read it aloud. "*ANIRI: PLEASE VERIFY SISTER'S CONDITION.* And *TARAK: ANXIOUSLY AWAIT WORD ON THE THIRD DAUGHTER.* And this one: *TARAK: ADVICE REGARDING NEED FOR SUPPORT.* He was on the verge of sending troops to Samir in search of me."

"Tell him you were madly coding aetheroceiver messages whilst on the run from assassins and ill-tempered shopkeepers, but that Samir has poor aether and the messages refused to go through."

Aniri was glad her sister's humor was returning.

She encouraged it with a deadpan look. "This is serious, Seledri."

"I agree," Seledri said with a smile. "Demanding husbands are quite serious business."

In truth, Aniri *was* in serious need of advice. Her shoulders drooped for real. "Oh Seledri, this isn't the right time to ask you for advice about husbands. But I'm very much in need of it."

Seledri's smile faded. "I might know a thing or two about them. They're very complicated beasts, and not always forthcoming when they ought to be."

Aniri gave a small smile before dropping her gaze to the messages. She lined them up in a row like soldiers on the cot. "I know you came to love Pavan in a different way. A slower way." She looked up. "But my romance with Ash feels like a whirlwind buried in a storm on top of a hurricane. We're constantly involved in one adventure or another, with war always threatening. Isn't it natural to be hesitant in the face of that? Or is it a sign that, perhaps, I'm making a terrible mistake?"

Seledri frowned and sat up straighter, adjusting her cushions to make a small nest around her. "Is this about Devesh?"

"No!" Aniri scattered the neat row of Ash's

unanswered messages. "That kiss was *nothing*. It was Devesh taking advantage of a moment, as he is wont to do."

Seledri's eyebrows hiked up. "There was a kiss?"

Aniri shook her head in disbelief. "You didn't see? I think you must be the only one in that meadow, on the ground or in the air, who did not." She crossed her arms and slumped against the wall abutting her cot. It was childish, she knew, but she was tired of the effects of rumors and politics tossing her around and controlling her life. She couldn't imagine how Seledri had endured it and still remained as fair-tempered as she was all these years. Her respect for her sister grew even larger.

"So, Devesh kissed you goodbye?" Seledri asked carefully.

"Yes."

"And it meant nothing."

"To *me*," Aniri said, still huffing frustration. "To him, I can't be sure. He's been lying to me from the beginning."

Seledri nodded her head. "What are you going to tell Ash?"

"There's nothing to tell." But Aniri's face flushed at the thought of it.

Seledri sighed.

Aniri ignored the chastising look on her sister's face and picked up the transcripted aetheroceiver messages again, one by one, making a small stack of them in her hand. "I'm tired of the politics. I don't wish for the crown. I never have. But I find myself in love with a prince who is vastly more noble than me, who keenly knows the temper of his people, and who seemingly knows everything about how to run a Queendom. Who, by every natural right, *should* be King even without a Queen by his side. I, on the other hand..." She looked up from her neatly piled notes. "I excel at worrying the people I love, upsetting the political calm, and, apparently, I can't even say goodbye to my ex-lover without causing an international incident."

Seledri chuckled. "You, little sister, do have a talent for stirring up things."

"I have a talent for foolishness." She tossed the notes onto her cot again. They fell like withered leaves from a dying plant. "And now, when we arrive back to Jungali, there will be war on the horizon and ever more reason for Jungali and Dharia to be allied. Ever more reason for the marriage to cement that alliance. And all I can think is how part of me wants to run away, just as our father did. Even knowing about his cowardice and how he abandoned us for his lover. Ash, on the other hand, is always steadfast. Loyal. He tends to his country and prepares for war while I'm off stoking the engines of it." She paused, then looked up. "He's a better man than I deserve, Seledri. Perhaps I *should* have run off with Dev. Not because I love him—I did once, although now I see he's really just a boy trapped in a web of lies and politics—but because Dev's foolish. Just like our father." Aniri dropped her gaze to her hands, which were now busy with slowly rolling the strips into tiny rings. "Just like me."

Seledri didn't say anything, and when Aniri looked up again, she saw her sister gingerly walking across the floor, toting a pillow with her. She settled onto Aniri's cot and clasped Aniri's hand in hers. "Now you listen to me, little sister. You are just as noble as any prince from Jungali, not because you are a Daughter of Dharia, or even because you are my sister, and therefore automatically imbued with great royal character."

A small smile forced its way onto Aniri's lips.

"But because," Seledri said, "you do bravely foolish things like rescue your sister from a country bent on killing her. And foolishly brave things like running off to the barbarian mountains to discover their secrets only to win their prince's heart. And, not least of all, you are the only one who can put First Daughter Nahali in her place, and for that, you should rule any Queendom you choose."

Aniri's smile grew, and she squeezed her sister's hand. "You should have seen her at the rehearsal. She was in rare form."

"You should consider sending her on a skyship tour during the wedding."

Aniri chuckled. "That could possibly be a treaty-breaking offense."

"There will be treaties, and wars, and all manner of politics and other calamities." Seledri waved her hands around as if conjuring these things out of thin air. "Devkasera herself cannot prevent it. But you, my dear, sweet, sister, have a man who loves you. A *worthy* man. And now that I can be in attendance, I insist that you forget about everything and anything else, and marry the man you love before fate leaves you on a ship, carrying his child and sailing away into the sky without him."

Aniri nodded through tears beginning to torment her eyes.

Seledri glanced at the notes lying scattered on the bed. "And perhaps you should send him a note telling him your intent to do so."

Aniri scooped up the notes, kissed her sister on the cheek, and hurried from the room in search of Janak and the aetheroceiver. Her heart had finally found just the words she needed to send through that cold device to tell her prince she was coming home.

WAS HORRIBLY DELAYED SORRY FOR WORRIES BE HOME SOON

She hoped the message would tell Ash everything she couldn't with prying eyes and the awkward too-long delay in aetheroceiver transmissions. As soon as she arrived, she vowed to tell him everything, including her worries, the reasons for her silence, and all the contents of her heart.

Meanwhile, Priya had made do with the limited supplies on board to make Aniri presentable again. She was still in adventuring clothes, but she thought Ash might even prefer those. She gave as little thought to such matters as possible, so she hadn't really noticed if he had a preference before, but given that most of the time they had truly spent together had been in one adventure or another, it seemed a natural choice.

The skyship slowly descended, sinking through clouds tinged pink with the morning sun. The sky was calm and clear on their way down to the highest tower of Ash's palace. *Her* palace. She needed to stop thinking of herself as an outsider. A guest. This was going to be her home. And she had fallen in love with more than just its prince—the mountainscape was breathtaking from the air, snow-tipped mountains rosy with a kiss of sun. The domed towers and white-granite walls of the estate perched on the very edge of a thousand-foot cliff. It was an exotic mix of beauty and danger that beat through all the mountain cities and hearts of Jungali. Including hers.

"It's lovely, isn't it, my lady?" Priya stood on the deck with her, a cloak pulled tight against the chill air.

"Indeed, it is." Aniri spied a flurry of figures on the tower, but she couldn't hear any of their shouts over the pulse of the skyship's propellers and the whipping of the breeze. "Now that we've returned, have you plans for a wedding as well?"

"Only yours for now, my lady." But Priya had a secret smile.

"Don't tell me you've eloped, Priya. I won't forgive you." The horror on Priya's face made Aniri laugh. "What, then? Do you not have *any* plans?" She couldn't imagine that Priya had done anything less than laid out the entire ceremony, celebration, and probably a few extra parties as well.

Priya held her head high. "First I have my duty, and Mr. Karan has his."

"Mr. Karan's duty may carry him away again soon," Aniri said softly. "Perhaps you should attend to more important matters first."

Priya's eyes sparkled. "As soon as my duty is done."

"And what is that?" Aniri smiled.

"To see my lady properly wed." Priya gave a sharp nod as if this was obvious. Aniri supposed it was, and she wouldn't deny that pleasure to her handmaiden for all the wealth in the three Queendoms.

Sailors now buzzed around the deck, readying the cast off lines. Aniri peered over the railing. She searched the parapet for a lone, tall, dark-haired figure, finding none but those busy in helping the skyship in its final descent. A small ache pierced her chest, but it was silly to expect him to be awaiting her at the moment of their arrival. It was not as if they were constantly messaging their expected flight times. Janak had relayed the essentials of their flight and plans to Ash, at least the information that was already known to the public: that they had Seledri on board, that she and the baby were well, and that they were expected early this morning. The rest of the debriefing would have to wait until they arrived in person.

Ash had sent word that the Queen and First Daughter had returned to Dharia, after extensive treaty negotiations, which Aniri took to mean preparations for war with Samir. The Queen would have to implement those personally back in Dharia, rather than message them by aetheroceiver, to ensure those plans did not leak out—Aniri had come to believe Devesh when he said that Samirian spies were everywhere, including her mother's court. Although now that the Second Son had Devesh, surely he would know all that they knew: about the skyships, about Natesh's plans, about everything.

Aniri pulled in the crisp morning air and let it out slow. When she was finally reunited with Ash, she wanted nothing more than to throw her arms around him. But she would have to keep the kissing to a minimum in order to leave room for all the things he should be briefed on.

"My lady," Priya said. "I believe we should go below decks to debark."

Aniri swept a last look across the tower, now so close that it was quickly being obscured by the bottom of the ship. Still no sign of Ash. She lingered a moment more, then followed Priya through the bulkhead door. They quickly filed down the stairs and across the metal-floored corridors to the walkplank, then waited for the docking to be complete.

Priya muttered something about missing parcels and scurried off into the bowels of the ship to retrieve them, leaving Aniri alone. Once the walk-plank was secure and the sailor on the parapet gave her the signal, she strode across. She had hoped Ash would have heard of the arrival of the skyship by now, but the terrace was occupied only by sailors in their brilliant blue uniforms. Aniri wandered the stone tower roof for a moment, then strode purposely toward the stairwell. If Ash was detained on some business, she would come to him, perhaps surprise him, if he was not yet expecting her or couldn't tear himself away from the business at hand.

The stone staircase echoed her boot steps as she spiraled down deeper into the palace. The regular staff of the estate bustled through the hallways, paying her no mind. She would only seek help if she couldn't find Ash on her own. Her first thought was the receiving room, but when she arrived, it was empty, except for a stoic guard at the door who let her through and a maid at work on the tea set. Ash's adjacent private office had the door closed.

The last time she had been inside was when she still was spying on him, pawing through his things while an assassin set her bed on fire. Ash had rushed into that burning room to save her—and that was before they were in love and betrothed for real. The juxtaposition—her spying, his heroics—made her falter once again. Then she straightened her shoulders and crossed the room to knock on his door.

There was no answer. She almost knocked again, but then she heard a scuffle of footsteps inside.

After a moment, the door opened. "I told you, I don't—" Ash cut himself off when his gaze reached her face. "Aniri." He seemed flummoxed by the fact that she was standing before him.

"I'm back." She smiled, but the moment was painful. Did he somehow not expect her?

He glanced over her shoulder, as if looking for

something, but there was no one in the receiving room. Even the maid had finished her duties and vanished. He stepped back, opening the door wide, and welcoming her in with a sweep of his hand.

"Please come in."

She hesitated, crossed the threshold, and waited for him to close the door. "Must we be secretive about meeting now?" Something was very wrong, and it was sending tremors through her heart.

"No, of course not." Ash crossed and uncrossed his arms, holding onto the door frame, then letting go. He seemed unable to decide where to stand. Finally, he stepped closer to his large desk and leaned against it. The rosy morning sun filtered in through the balcony door and gave a cheerful look to the room that was at odds with the discomfort screaming from Ash's rigid perch on the edge of his desk.

"You're angry with me." Aniri felt all her doubts rush back in a haze that clouded her mind.

"No." But he dropped his gaze to his boots and gripped the edge of the desk on either side of where he leaned against it. "Captain Tarak says your sister is well in spite of your harrowing escape from the city."

"I… yes, she and the baby are both fine." How

much did Captain Tarak message to Ash? Aniri had assumed it was too risky to share too much. "Pavan insisted that she leave in the end—that it wasn't safe for her there anymore."

Ash looked up and peered into her eyes, but it was cool, like he was merely seeking information from her. Nothing more. It made her heart seize up. "So the plot against Seledri's life was from within the royal household? Tarak said he suspected as much through his coded messages, and Janak confirmed it once you were back on board."

"Yes." Aniri frowned. What coded messages? And what else did Tarak say? "The Second Son sought to remove Pavan's Dharian wife. I believe it is part of his plan to make war on Dharia."

"But not Jungali?" Ash's voice was even cooler.

She frowned. "Jungali too." Her heart pounded. He knew. Tarak must have told him about the kiss, and he was angry because of it. She took a tentative step toward him, but he leaned back and folded his arms, so she stopped and clung to the side of his desk for support. He was *very* angry. "Ash, please, I don't know what you've heard…"

"I haven't heard much at all. From you." His voice was hard.

Aniri winced. "I was being foolish."

"*Foolish?*" Ash gave a bitter kind of laugh. "Is that what you call it?"

"I only meant that it was foolish for me not to message you more frequently. Or perhaps more thoroughly." She floundered for the right words. How could she explain? "I was so absorbed in trying to spirit Seledri away from danger, that I didn't think—"

"No, you didn't think!" The anger finally broke through the restraining hold he had put on it. Ash shoved away from the desk and paced to the door, hesitating there. For a moment, she feared he would simply order her away. Instead, he ran his hand through his hair and turned back to her.

"I thought perhaps Jungali wouldn't be enough to hold a Daughter of Dharia. That maybe you regretted your decision because, once the adventure had passed, you realized we were too... *backward* for you. But apparently a courtesan is more than sufficient to hold your interest." The words seemed wrenched from somewhere deep inside him. "If that is what you want, Aniri, then you may have him. But don't embarrass me by kissing him in front of a skip full of Jungali sailors."

Her heart suspended its beating while he spoke, the word *no* echoing through her mind with every word. When he finally stopped, she surged toward him, but he backed away, hands up. She balled her fists and brought them back close her sides.

"I *do not* want Devesh." Her voice cracked. "The kiss was just... just... I didn't even know he would..." Her words tangled with the lump in her throat. "It doesn't *mean* anything, Ash, I promise you."

He just shook his head, like he couldn't believe the words from her mouth. "It means something to me."

"That's not what I meant." Tears were threatening to burst forth. Nothing she said was coming out right. Her words were only making him angrier. "Please, Ash. Please trust me when I tell you there is nothing between me and Devesh."

He took a deep breath, but just shook his head slowly. "Aniri, I trust you to leap to the defense of your sister in need. I trust you to be recklessly brave in protecting the people you love." He gave her a pained look. "I just don't trust you to know who exactly that is."

"I do *not* love him, Ash. I swear it." She reached tentatively for his arm, but he leaned away.

"The treaty still stands," he said coolly, all business again, "especially now that war seems even more likely. Your mother and I have fashioned plans to fortify our countries against attack from Samir, and now that you've returned with the Second Daughter, the Queen is returning to Jungali to retrieve her. In accordance with our treaty and our plans, I will use the skyship to defend Dharia if it's within my power to do so." He took a breath, paused, then let it out. "But I will not hold you to the marriage, Aniri. You may return to Dharia with your mother when she arrives."

Aniri wanted to speak, but her throat had completely closed up. She ducked her head so the tears in her eyes wouldn't show.

"I would like—" Ash's voice cracked.

Aniri looked up, hopeful, but he simply cleared his throat and pressed on.

"I would like to debrief your raksaka, if that is acceptable to you." His voice was formal, but not cold. Not harsh. Because, even in this, he was a better man than she deserved. "It won't be necessary for you to attend. But it would benefit both our countries to have as much information shared as possible about the capabilities of the Samirian fleet, whether on the sea or in the air."

She nodded, mutely. She still couldn't force words past her lips. And even if she could, she feared they would reduce to sobs and spoil Ash's noble attempt to release her from their marriage with some measure of dignity. She forced her legs to shuffle to the door, taking care to give him wide berth along the way. She gave him one last nod before turning the knob and pulling it open.

"Aniri."

His voice jerked her to a stop, and she turned to him, her heart in her throat. At any moment, the tears were going to crest her eyelids and course down her face.

He opened his mouth to say something, stopped, then finally said, "Safe journey home."

She pressed her hands together, bowed quickly, then fled as fast as her feet would carry her from his office without breaking into an actual run.

Chapter Twenty

TEARS BLURRED ANIRI'S VISION, so it was fortunate she knew the palace layout well enough to find her way. She passed a few household staff, but she ignored them, keeping her head ducked. When she arrived at her room, she threw open the door, and let it bang against the solid granite of the walls.

The sound startled Priya, who stood amongst a pile of teetering parcels. "My lady?"

Aniri didn't answer. She stalked to her cases and pushed aside one after another until she found the one with her swords. Heaving it out of the pile, she turned to march toward the door.

"My lady, what's wrong?" Priya's soft slippers pattered on the stone floor after her.

Aniri picked up her pace, nearly breaking out

into a run, out the door, down the hall, dashing the long length of the top palace floor until she arrived —breathless, tears streaming down her face, barely holding in the sobs—at the door to the fencing hall. She wrenched the door open and heaved a desperate exhale of relief when she found it empty. Closing the door behind her, she threw open the case, yanked out a blade, and stalked to the automaton at the far end.

It was larger than her automaton at home, with more brass and obvious clockwork. It looked Samirian, but didn't appear to be steam-driven, and Aniri had no idea how to activate it.

She cared not at all.

With a guttural scream, she raised the sword above her head and slashed down upon the automaton's shoulder. The blade bounced off and sent a wincing ache through her arm with its reverberations. She brought it around for a sideways hack at the mechanized creature's neck, and the resounding clash of metal on metal pierced the air. The automaton didn't respond. Whatever mechanism it had inside lay as still and silent as death. She hacked and slashed and stabbed at it, blinking free the tears that surged out of her. Her growls and the clang of her metal-on-metal strikes echoed off the solid walls of the large, empty fencing hall. The one refurbished for her by Ash, her future husband who now wasn't. Who finally discovered the truth about her foolishness in time to save himself from the mistake of marrying her. And who would go on to be a good and righteous King and probably save her homeland of Dharia again in the process. All without her help.

He had no need of a princess who would embarrass him with her fecklessness.

She held the sword aloft with two hands, driving it with a final scream into the heart of the Samirian clockwork beast. The blade stuck, finding purchase between two mechanical plates, and remained there. She yanked and yanked, trying to free it, but got nowhere. Her arms aching, she finally released the hilt, and only then, did she see the saber for what it was: the blade Ash had fashioned from his dead brother's dagger especially for her. A saber meant as a promise for their future together. *I want to give you that future, Aniri, if you'll let me.* Ash's words haunted her now. *If you'll let me.*

She had made it impossible for him.

Aniri dropped her hands to her sides, hung her head, and quietly let the tears fall to the polished wooden floor by her boots. Her sobs ghosted through the hall, returning to her in whispered breaths. The soft sound of footfalls followed behind and made her frown. She looked up, seeking the source of it: Priya had followed her to the hall.

The pain on her handmaiden's face was more than Aniri could bear. She quickly faced the automaton again, wiping her face and sucking in air to regain her composure. Priya came to stand quietly beside her.

"What can I do for you, my lady?" Priya asked softly.

Aniri avoided looking at her and gestured to the saber still lodged in the automaton. "I've stabbed it in the heart, and now it refuses to return my blade."

Priya hesitated, then asked, "Did you mean to hurt it, my lady?"

Aniri turned sharply to her. The torment on her handmaiden's face had turned to the sweet earnestness that Aniri loved so much. "No, Priya. I didn't." The ache in her heart forced her to turn back to the automaton. It was as strong as the mountain it was forged from. Resolute. Implacable. But even it could be pierced with a strike in the right place.

Priya edged closer, crossing her arms.

Aniri was surprised to find herself already in the same pose.

"Is it a thing worth having?" Priya asked, eyeing the saber sticking out of the automaton.

"It was a gift. Forged from the past. A promise for the future." Aniri paused. She knew they weren't talking about the blade. "Yes, Priya. It's very much worth having."

"Then you must fight for it, my lady." Priya stepped up to the automaton. Placing one silk-slippered foot on the solid mechanical leg of the thing and grabbing the saber's grip with both hands, she made a valiant effort at pulling it free. After a moment, she gave up. "I'm afraid I'm no help here. My lady will have to do this herself." Priya's dark eyes were filled with challenge.

Aniri held her gaze a long moment, then gave her a small smile. "You're wrong, Priya." She reached to take hold of the sword. It required considerable twisting and yanking and wrenching, but finally, the blade came free. Aniri held it up like a hard-won trophy, then flipped it down and planted the tip firmly in the wooden floor. "You are considerable help."

Priya beamed. "I will assist you in any way I can, my lady. You've but to ask."

Aniri examined the blade that Ash had given her, forged from the pain of his past. He had taken that pain and turned it into something good. Something *better*. Earning the trust of someone that noble at heart would take more than words and apologies and declarations. "I may need help from more than just you, Priya." She looked up. "And it's possible that, in the end, it may be too late."

"No prize worth having is so easily won." Priya stood taller. "And I've yet to see my lady not win any battle that she's engaged."

The tears threatened to make a return, so Aniri hugged her handmaiden fiercely to ward them off. When she released her, Aniri managed a grin.

"Where would I be without you, Priya?"

"In a much worse state, I am sure. Less well dressed, to be certain."

That forced a laugh from her. She grabbed Priya's hand and led her to gathering her swords. She had no idea if winning Ash's trust again was even possible. And she had little time in which to do it, before he would send her packing back to Dharia. But even if she failed in that, she was determined to repair the damage she had already wrought.

That alone was something worth doing.

Chapter Twenty-One

ANIRI FOLLOWED Priya across the walkplank onto the skyship.

She had stopped to change out of her adventuring clothes, wash her face of her self-pitying tears, and put on royal garb befitting a Daughter of Dharia. That was all she could lay claim to now, and it was in that capacity that she tremulously set foot back on the ship to fix some of the damage for which she was responsible.

The corridors were busy with sailors hurrying down to the lower levels where the engine room lay or bringing fresh supplies and crates of coal on board. Aniri imagined they were readying themselves for duty, should it be called upon them.

Which was precisely why she needed to make her amends now, and quickly.

"Do you think Karan is most likely on the bridge or in the engine room?" Aniri asked Priya.

"No telling, my lady. He prefers engines, to be sure, but Captain Tarak is still new in his job."

"The bridge, then," Aniri said. "But I'd like Karan to gather the crew, if possible. I have a few words to share. After I speak to Captain Tarak."

Priya nodded, and Aniri was glad she didn't press for what those words might be. She wasn't at all sure herself. She only knew she needed to right things before they flew into battle over Jungali or were faced with risking their lives to defend Dharia. Aniri and Priya weaved past the sailors hurrying to their duties, garnering a few backward looks, but mostly undeterred until they reached the bridge.

Karan and Captain Tarak were both there, standing next to a giant brass horn.

"What do ye mean?" Karan's voice boomed into the horn, each word slow and well pronounced. "The starboard turbine's brand new out of Sik province."

He waited a moment, then a tinny voice came from the depths of it. "Aye, sir! But it's not starting all the same."

"Perhaps we took some damage during the extended flights to Samir," Captain Tarak reasoned. "We never shut them down in Samir while waiting to hear from you. I don't think you designed them to run and run like that, aye?"

Karan sighed. "Aye." He finally caught sight of Aniri and Priya standing at the threshold of the bulkhead door to the bridge. His smile was warm for Priya, less so for Aniri.

She would have to apologize to him as well. "Is this a bad time, Karan?"

"Well, I suppose that depends on how ye mean it, fresh." He sighed. "It's a right miserable time for the starboard turbine to be having a bellyache. We're doing our best to get the ship ready for any orders that might be coming down from the prince."

She nodded. "I understand. I just need a quick word with Captain Tarak, if that's all right."

Captain Tarak stiffened as she said his name. His gaze darted between Karan and Aniri, and she felt sure she was terrorizing him with the threat of a royal inquisition.

Karan arched his eyebrows and glanced at Tarak. "I need to make a run to engines anyway, Captain."

"Of course, Mr. Karan." Tarak swallowed, clearly wishing that Karan wouldn't leave at all. "You are relieved."

Karan sighed and strode across the width of the bridge. As he passed Aniri and Priya, he said quietly, "Go easy on him, fresh."

That they both thought she was here to chastise Tarak made her chest tight. She needed to do better than inspire fear in the people serving Prince Malik and Jungali. Aniri tilted her head to Priya to have her follow after her betrothed and explain that Aniri wanted to have a word with the crew as well. Her handmaiden stepped lightly after Karan, who waited for her once he knew she was following. They disappeared down the corridor, but Aniri could already hear Priya's whispered explanations.

Aniri faced Tarak, who stood clutching the rim of the bell horn like he might fall down without it. "Your majesty." His voice wavered slightly. The light glinted off the two, small brass bars on his collar that signified his rank.

She stepped closer, and his body grew even more rigid. "I've come to understand that you've been sending coded messages to the prince."

"Those were my orders, my lady." His words were as strung tight as his body.

"Can I assume you've told him everything that happened in Samir, at least the parts you had knowledge of?" She needed to make sure she understood exactly what had happened.

"Yes, my lady." A muscle started twitching in Tarak's cheek.

She gave him a small smile. "Thank you for doing that, Captain Tarak."

The tension in his body released in a gush. "My lady?"

She pressed her hands together and made a small bow to him. "Thank you for keeping the prince informed as he should be. I have to apologize for putting you in the position of having to deliver such uncomfortable news to him. And doubly so for carrying the burden of apprising him of my whereabouts when you were left to tend the skyship on your own. I should have been more forthright with the prince all along the way, but especially on the return home."

Captain Tarak's eyebrows were fixed high on his forehead. "You're apologizing? To me?" He clearly thought the reverse would be required to keep his position. Or possibly his head.

"Yes. It's a belated apology, and somewhat embarrassing, but yes." Aniri sighed. "I made a mistake, Captain Tarak. Several mistakes, truth be told, but the worst among them was allowing a Samirian courtesan to kiss me in front of a Jungali crew who were risking their lives to rescue two Daughters of Dharia. Especially when one was betrothed to their prince."

Captain Tarak frowned. She suspected he noticed her use of the past tense.

"Have you ever made a mistake, Captain Tarak?"

"Aye, my lady." His look softened. "Mr. Karan is always telling us what matters is what we make of them."

Aniri smiled. "Mr. Karan is a very wise man."

"I tend to agree, my lady." He looked less terrified now, more calm and confident, the way he did during their trip to Samir, when he was instructing her in the use of the star navigator. Aniri decided he would make a fine captain after all. In spite of his youth.

"The crew needs to be confident in their prince and their cause," she said. "And they need it before they're called into a duty more harrowing and dangerous than flying into a field to rescue some wayward Daughters. Captain Tarak, can I count on your help with setting this right?"

He gave a small bow. "It would be my honor, your majesty."

"I had hoped to have a word with your crew. Where would be best place to do so?"

"The galley is probably fit, at least for the crew on hand," he said. "Some are already on leave, but set to return on the morrow."

"Well, they will miss all the fun, then," she said ruefully. "Hopefully their crewmates will pass along the word about the Third Daughter of Dharia and her mistakes."

"I think it will have just that effect, my lady." He regarded her anew. "That is your intent, isn't it?"

"Yes." She swept out a hand. "If you would, Captain Tarak. I don't wish to keep you from your duties any longer than necessary."

He gave her a short nod then led her from the bridge.

They didn't speak along the way to the galley. Tarak stopped each sailor they passed and told them to gather the others. Aniri's heart started to pound with the nervousness—not of admitting her errors, but of finding the right words to bolster the crew. She didn't want rumors of her to distract them from their duties, which would no doubt be critical in the days ahead, for both Jungali and Dharia.

When they arrived in the galley, Karan and Priya were already there, along with a contingent of blue-uniformed crew who had filled the few tables and started to line the walls. Karan's face was alight with curiosity, although Priya must have already told him Aniri's intent.

She swept a look around the room. It was a tight space, growing tighter as more crew filtered in. And her slight stature wasn't a help in ensuring she would be seen and heard. She made straight for a table in the center, sturdy with wooden legs and benches around it. The sailors there immediately stood, clearing a path for her to sit. Instead, she lifted her formal skirts to avoid tripping and, with a bit of balancing, managed to climb on top of the table.

There were maybe twenty sailors all told surrounding her, eyes large and questioning.

She waited a moment longer, as a few more stumbled in, before she began. "You have important duties to attend, so I won't keep you long." She took a breath to steady her nerves. "First, I want to thank you for your service in helping to bring my sister, the Second Daughter, out of Samir. As you saw by the muskets they trained on us as we departed, there was grave danger to her life all along. Indeed a plot within the royal house of Samir is, at this very moment, posing a threat to the stability of all our countries."

She paused to let that sink in and hoped she wasn't revealing state secrets that would haunt her. But she felt they had a right to know the stakes for which they might be called to fight.

"Second, I want to apologize for the unseemly gratitude I showed to one of our Samirian rescuers. I realize now how that might be misunderstood to be something more than it was, and I regret putting you in the position of bearing that unfortunate news back to Jungali."

The sailors shifted in place, some sharing knowing glances, others staring at their feet. Captain Tarak was the one who brought the news directly to Ash, but only because he knew, as she could see now, that once they arrived, the rumors would fly through the city faster than a skyship. And perhaps they already had, even within the short time they had been on the ground. Murmurs began to swell up in her silence, so she began again.

"My greatest regret, however, isn't the unfortunate

kiss of a Samirian courtesan. It's that I didn't keep Prince Malik as well advised of our mission as I could have. I failed to give him my full confidence when I had every reason to. Your prince is an extraordinary man. He is selfless and noble. The people of Dharia, as I know well, have long held biases against the mountain peoples, but I can tell you with assurance— there is no man I know more honorable than Prince Malik. He would give his life for any one of you. I should know—he ran into a burning room to save me, a Dharian not even yet his wife. He would do no less for the people of the country he loves."

She paused this time because she felt the tears working their way back, and she couldn't afford that in front of Ash's people. His skyship crew. The people upon which they may all depend.

"So, I beg of you to not let any of my mistakes distract you from your purpose: defending Jungali and a prince who has earned your trust and your loyalty. There may be difficult days ahead." She swept a slow look around the room, trying to meet each of their gazes, to impress upon them the gravity of her words. "And in those days, your service to Jungali will make all the difference in bringing about the peace your prince has long worked for. Please show him that he can count on you."

She hesitated a moment, but there were no more words she could think to say. Taking hold of her skirts, she attempted to make a graceful exit from the table. A half-dozen hands suddenly held her by the arms and steadied her back. A snapping of fingers rose up and filled the galley with an applause she certainly didn't deserve. Shame flushed her face, but she managed a smile of gratitude to her helpers as well as the rest when they settled her to the floor. She pressed her hands together for a quick bow before striding from the room. From the corners of her eyes, she caught several sailors bowing in response.

Before she got far down the corridor, and just as she was pulling in a deep breath of relief, she felt Karan's large presence at her side, catching up.

"That was a fine speech, fresh." For once, his tone wasn't mocking her.

"I only hope it effects its purpose and allays the impact of my mistakes," she said. "Your skyship crew can ill afford them going forward."

"Aye." Karan stopped in the hall, and Aniri halted with him. "And here I thought you were come to take the captain's chair from Tarak for your own."

She looked at him like he was crazed, and then realized he was speaking in jest. A breathless huff of laughter escaped her. "Not hardly, Mr. Karan." But her smile banished the tears that had been threatening before.

He smirked, then ducked his head. "I've a turbine that needs tending to."

"And I've other apologies yet to make."

She turned to go, but his hand at her elbow brought her back.

"It's going to be fine, fresh." His small smile was meant to be reassuring, but it only pained her heart. Priya must have told him the truth about Ash, even though Aniri herself hadn't yet said anything direct about it to anyone. Nor would she, until forced.

"Only as long as you get your ship in the air and ready, Mr. Karan."

"Aye, my lady." He gave a short nod and turned to head toward the engine room.

Aniri smiled at his retreating back.

She was quite certain he had never called her *my lady* before.

Chapter Twenty-Two

Aniri waited for Priya outside the skyship. Her handmaiden had some short business to discuss with Karan, probably making plans for their own wedding, now that Aniri's no longer presented any danger of happening.

Aniri closed her eyes, drew in a breath, and forced her thoughts elsewhere.

The sailors would spread the word of her apology, but it might not be enough. Rumors had a way of running faster than the truth that followed behind them. Especially when the truth was less tantalizing than misplaced kisses and broken promises. She would have to do more to counter it. How exactly, she had no idea.

"My lady, are you well?" Priya's voice came from her side.

Aniri's eyes snapped open. "Just thinking, Priya. It takes all my effort sometimes."

Priya smirked, looped her arm around Aniri's, and tugged her across the stone terrace of the skyship's makeshift dock. "My lady is far more clever than she believes. She has single-handedly squashed the most powerful rumor engine known to all three Queendoms."

"Handmaidens?"

Priya gave her an offended look. "Jungali sailors."

"Of course." Aniri grinned, and it calmed her heart in a way only her handmaiden seemed to manage.

They reached the stairs and pattered down the one flight to the top level of the estate. Hers and Priya's room was close, around the first bend in the slowly curving hallway.

"What are my lady's plans now? If she's willing to share—" Priya cut herself off as they rounded the bend. Aniri looked to see what had caused it.

Ash stood in front of her door, hand raised to knock. He hesitated, went to knock again, then stopped. He caught sight of them and dropped his hand. He pressed his two hands together as they approached.

"Arama, Aniri." He bowed as well. "Priya."

Aniri simply stared.

Priya squeaked, then quickly said, "I've much unpacking to do." She practically slammed into the door in her haste to get past it and leave them alone.

Aniri found her breath, but still had no words. "Ash." She couldn't help looking over her shoulder, wondering if he somehow had divined what she had been doing on the skyship. It didn't appear so, with the deeply scowled look on his face. At least, she hoped she hadn't unknowingly done something to anger him further.

"Aniri, you rushed out—" He stopped. "I didn't have a chance… that is…"

It tormented her to see him so uncertain.

He cleared his throat. "I wanted to tell you that I would wait to make any announcements until you're on your way to Dharia. I don't want you to…" He struggled again, dropping his gaze to his boots. "I don't mean for you to suffer any discomfort. I thought it would be easier for you if we waited." He looked up again. "But I neglected to say anything—" This time he stopped because he spied something over her shoulder.

She glanced back to see Ash's sister-in-law Nisha hurrying down the hallway, her royal Jungali blue gown sweeping the floor. She looked dressed for tea but her pretty face was marred with fury. Aniri's heart seized. She hadn't even thought of telling Nisha, who had welcomed her to the family like a sister from the start.

Aniri turned back to Ash, eyes wide.

If it was possible, he seemed even more panicked than she felt. "Is that agreeable to you, Aniri?" he said in a hush, quickly flicking looks to the fast approaching Nisha.

"Yes, of course," Aniri said, just as fast and low.

Ash hastily pressed his hands together, bowed, and fled in the opposite direction.

Aniri forced a smile onto her face that must look a horror, then turned to face Nisha.

She scowled disapproval at Ash's retreating back. "What is this I hear?" Nisha demanded. "These ridiculous rumors about a kiss? What is going on?"

The urge to deny it welled up in Aniri. To retreat into saying that it meant nothing, that it was just Devesh taking advantage of her, but she knew

Nisha would understand even better than her that none of that mattered. She was far too sensitive to the temper of her people, and it was no surprise that the rumors reached her first.

Aniri took a deep breath. "My ex-lover was one of the Samirians who helped us escape. He kissed me just before we left. In full view of everyone on the ground and in the air."

The anger dropped off Nisha's face, and she blinked. "You're saying the kiss actually happened? I thought… I was sure someone else had spitefully started that awful rumor." Her disbelief was quickly turning to disgust, and Aniri didn't want her to get too far down that path.

"It was a mistake, Nisha. I shouldn't have allowed it. Or I should have explained right away that it meant nothing. To me, at least. I should have messaged Ash. He should have heard it from me first. That mistake has already cost—" She stopped herself. Ash didn't want to make any announcements until after she left, which she could understand. She believed him when he said he wanted to spare her. But it also would be hard on him. It was impossibly awkward already, and no one yet knew, except Priya. And possibly Karan.

But Nisha wasn't just anyone. More importantly, she might help Aniri fix some of the damage.

Nisha was peering at her. "What has it cost you?"

"It cost me Ash." She pulled in a breath, fighting back the surge in emotions that came with that.

"What?" Nisha was horrified.

Aniri didn't think she could say it again. So she pressed on. "I should have known it would spread like a fire rushing down the mountain, Nisha, but I didn't. And now I would just like to stop the rumors, maybe repair some of the damage, make sure the people have their confidence in their prince, before I have to leave."

"*Leave?*" Nisha became even more aghast. She squeezed her eyes shut, shaking her head and apparently trying to sort the mess, then opened them again. "You're telling me that one kiss has put off your wedding?"

"Rather permanently, yes. And it wasn't just one kiss."

"There were *more* kisses?"

"No! I just… it's difficult to explain."

Nisha gave her a knowing look, then reached for the lever on Aniri's door. "I have time," she said resolutely, pushing the door open and dragging Aniri inside.

Priya looked up from her unpacking and frowned when she saw Nisha come through the door. Perhaps she expected Ash. Nisha closed the door and let Aniri go no farther.

Nisha eyed Priya. "Do we need to be alone for this conversation?"

Aniri sighed. "Priya knows everything. Pretty much at all times, actually."

Priya hurried over, but stayed quiet, watching them.

Nisha frowned. "Then tell me. What is really going on?"

"While I was in Samir, I failed to return a lot of Ash's messages. We were on the run a lot, I wasn't sure who to trust, and I never had the right words." She shook her head. "Anyway, I know now that I was just uncertain. And preoccupied by the threats to my sister's life. And there was more that I found in Samir…" She couldn't talk about her father, at least not to Nisha. Soon enough she would have to bring it to the one person it would hurt most: her mother.

"You found this Samirian." Nisha scowled. "The one you kissed."

"No!" Aniri said. "I mean yes, I found him there, but *he* kissed *me*. And it wasn't like that, Nisha. I used to love him, but I don't anymore."

Nisha's eyebrows hiked up. "I see."

"Devesh is the one who betrayed my lady," Priya threw in with a nod. "If you knew half the things he's done—"

Aniri held a hand up to quiet her handmaiden. Priya ducked her head but not without a *but it's true* look.

"This isn't Devesh's fault," Aniri said. "It's mine. I take full responsibility for all of it spinning out of control like it has. It wasn't just a single kiss that made Ash not trust me, Nisha. I did that all by myself, with my worries and hesitations and—"

"And the thought that you're rushing things?" Nisha asked.

"Yes."

"And a nagging feeling that you've made a mistake?"

"Yes." Aniri folded up her arms, hugging them close.

"And the desire to run off to places unknown and escape it all?"

"Yes, all right. All of those." She hadn't

expected Nisha to see her foolishness quite so clearly. She squirmed underneath her steady gaze.

"You mean, all the normal things a bride-to-be feels before her wedding day?" Nisha shook her head. "Aniri, I wish you had come to me sooner."

"The circumstances weren't exactly in support of that." But a warm glow spread through her. Maybe it wasn't entirely her foolishness at work. Maybe it was a normal thing, as Nisha said, to have doubts. Second thoughts. She wished she had known that sooner. Perhaps all this could have been avoided, if she hadn't been wrapped in the adventure and the drama. Which was ironic, given her worry that drama alone had drawn her and Ash together. Now that she had possibly lost him, she knew there was so much more that bound them together in the first place. Or at least, her to him. For him, perhaps not.

"This entire thing is ridiculous and must come to an end." Nisha said it as if she could simply wave it away with her words.

"I completely agree," Priya spoke up again, then peeked at Aniri to see if her words were out of turn.

Aniri just shook her head. "I'd simply like to assure Ash's people that, whatever they think of me, they should have faith in their prince. They're going to need that faith, Nisha, and I need to fix this before Ash sends me away. Or the Samirians decide they're done with waiting and declare war on us."

Nisha slowly nodded her head. "The faith of the people."

"Ash has earned it." The more Aniri said it, the stronger it felt. "No matter what happens between the prince and me, I can't be the thing that brings him down. I'll do anything to keep that from happening. Please tell me you'll help me with this. I know you have the people's favor. Perhaps you can help counter the rumors?"

Nisha smiled. "I have an even better idea."

Priya's eyes sparkled even though she couldn't possibly know what Nisha was thinking any more than Aniri did. But it didn't matter. Aniri had already embarrassed herself on a ship full of Jungali sailors. She would do whatever was necessary to fix this.

"Let's hear it, then."

Chapter Twenty-Three

Nisha's idea apparently involved a festival on the streets of Jungali later in the day. In fact, it was nearly into the night. Nisha had scoured her wardrobes for a proper costume for Aniri, coming back with a traditional Jungali dress that had four different swaths of color. There was no corset, and a surprising amount of bare skin: her shoulders and midriff were exposed, along with bare feet underneath the full, sweeping skirts. The sleeves were comprised of thin, draping strips that fluttered with each small movement. It was entirely exotic, and the ink swirls Priya was applying to each of her feet and hands made it doubly so.

She looked thoroughly Jungali.

It made her heart ache.

But Nisha was convinced that participating in the festival would be just the thing to counter the rumors about her that had swirled throughout the city all day long. And for that, she would wear what was customary and do as she was told.

Nisha and Priya donned similar costumes, and Nisha had even fashioned one for Seledri that accommodated her baby. Her sister seemed delighted by the entire affair, and that Seledri's tears had been banished was justification alone for any attire.

When the four of them emerged into the twilight of the courtyard outside the palace, Aniri saw why Nisha had insisted they all dress this way: every female, from grandmothers to tiny, tottering girl babies, were wearing the same thing. It was a dizzying feast of colors, made deeper and more lush by the flickering of the lamps, which were, quite literally, *everywhere*.

From tiny clay pots to enormous trays festooned with flowers, thousands of oil lamps burned throughout the courtyard, giving it a warm, flickering light that fought against the waning sun. The street's gaslamps had all been turned down. Small children climbed the poles as if they were trees, extinguishing the brighter, more modern gaslight and leaving behind the soft romance of a million, brilliant, tiny flames.

"Nisha," Aniri said with awe. "It's beautiful."

Seledri and Priya were likewise struck, but Nisha just smiled. "Oh, it's only getting started."

"You said this was a celebration of an ancient King's return home to his Queen, after being thought lost to the mountains," Aniri said. "But what is the purpose of the lamps? And the costumes?"

"The costumes are the Queen's dress of the time," Nisha said. "It's from hundreds of years ago, when the provinces were barely formed, and there were as many people roaming nomadic through the mountains outside the walls as there were within them. The four colors are the four provinces, first brought together under Queen Kazmi's rule."

A small girl carrying a basket of miniature earthen pots interrupted Nisha. Each of the four of them received one tiny lamp, so small it fit in the palm of Aniri's hand. Another girl followed behind with a fistful of sticks in one hand, and a flame-topped one in the other. She lit their lamps, one by one, then scampered off into the crowds.

"Do we carry them?" asked Seledri, seeming as entranced by the whole thing as Aniri was, and her tentative smile made Aniri's heart glad. They edged forward into the crowd.

"Yes," Nisha said. "This is the Festival of Lights, and these are the lamps Queen Kazmi kept lit in the highest tower of the palace, through four winters and four summers, so her King could see them from anywhere in the mountains and find his way home. The legend says that Devpahar herself manifested as a shashee and found the King buried in a landslide. She used her great tusks to move the mountain and unearth him again, then she followed the lights. We use them now to remember that, even in dark times, there is always a light to guide us home."

Aniri's lamp was cool in her palm, the flame winking and throwing shadows across the curling ink designs on her hand. She tried to put on a smile, pushing away thoughts of how this wouldn't be her home for much longer. They slowly worked their way past knots of dancing girls, some no bigger than toddlers. Clusters of women arranged more lamps and flowers along the walk, making some kind of pattern that seemed meant to be viewed from above. Aniri imagined flying the skyship over the city and admiring the beauty below as she left

Jungali forever. She had to push that thought away, too.

"But where are all the men?" Priya asked as she tiptoed around a spiraling design of lamps, taking care to lift her skirts and keep them from catching fire.

"They will be along soon enough," Nisha said with a grin.

As they progressed, Aniri realized they were heading toward a stage of some kind: it was a simple elevated platform, a few feet off the ground, but it was heavily decorated with baskets of flowers. In the center, small lamps were arranged in a pattern that looked like a star, with tiny lights radiating out from an empty circle in the middle. The scent of so many flowers and flames made the air heady. The cool cobblestones on her bare feet and the light breeze fluttering her gossamer sleeves added to the light-hearted effect.

We're a romantic people, Ash had once told her. Even as those words pricked tears to her eyes, the beauty of this festival couldn't do anything but warm her heart.

Seledri bent her head to Aniri's. "Are you all right?"

"I'll be fine."

"Why do you think they're lining up?" Seledri pointed to a line of young women who had started to form at one end of the platform.

"This is where you come in, Aniri." Nisha took her by the shoulders and steered her to a place at the end of the line.

"What do I do?" Aniri was already garnering glances and raised eyebrows and whispered conversations. The girls in front of her in line were all about the same age as her: young enough to not yet be wed, but old enough to want to.

"Just watch the others. You'll be perfect." Then Nisha urged Priya and Seledri away from the line, although they could all just as easily have joined her. Priya at least. Seledri and Nisha were a little older and married. And, now that she thought about it, Priya was betrothed. She sighed when she realized she actually *was* the only one without a husband, present or future.

The line started to shift, and she craned around the other girls to see why. The first girl in line had stepped up on the platform. She stood in the center of the pattern of lamps and raised her tiny lamp in the air.

In a loud voice, she called, "Devpahar, I pray you bring my King home."

A hush fell over the courtyard as all the women, young and old, stopped their preparations and turned to watch the girl on the stage. She held her lamp aloft a moment longer then stooped to place it at the edge of the circle. Then she lifted her skirts clear of the ring of fire and quickly leaped over it. Another girl took her place, skirts hiked to bridge the circle, then holding her lamp high above.

The quiet of the courtyard carried her voice to the walls of the palace and nearby taverns and shops, echoing it back to her. "Devpahar, I pray you bring my King home."

Aniri swallowed. What in the three Queendoms what Nisha thinking? That Aniri would stand up and say those words in front of Ash's people?

The girls in front of her were whispering behind their hands and sending her furtive looks. Behind her, there was no one. Apparently she had scared off whoever else might have been interested in giving their supplications to Devpahar to bring home their own lovers, their personal Kings, whoever that might be.

The line edged forward. Aniri had a sinking feeling in her stomach. She gritted her teeth and remembered her purpose: this was to negate the rumors. To ease the prince's embarrassment at having his future-Queen run off to another country and kiss a Samarian. And above all, to bolster the people's faith in their prince, in the event that those same Samarians decided to wage war.

The two girls in front of her had reached the platform. Their giggles threatened to keep them from performing the ritual, but they sobered just in time. Aniri felt impossibly old compared to them, even though she couldn't be more than a year or two their senior. It wasn't that long ago when she could safely indulge in the giggles of childhood.

Not anymore.

Nor, strangely, did she want to. As they cleared the stage, and she was the only one left in line, she solemnly ascended the two short, wooden steps and carefully gathered her skirts so she could step into the ring of tiny lamps. There were so many of them now. They pulsed heat toward her bare feet, their growing flames threatening to lick far enough to catch the edges of her colorful skirts. It flushed heat up to her face as she remembered the night Ash saved her from a cloak on fire. It was in a dingy inn buried in the province of Mahet, where they had taken refuge on the way to the skyship.

Trying to save you from fire is becoming a habit of mine. Ash's words rung in her mind, but he wouldn't be saving her from this fire. This was a problem of her own making, and one she would have to solve alone.

The crowd before her had grown silent. Expectant. The ones who were close enough to see their faces in the waning, flickering light wore expressions of surprise and amazement. Clearly, they didn't expect the Third Daughter of Dharia to step up to the platform in the middle of the Festival of Lights.

Aniri raised her lamp over her head. "Devpahar, you don't need to return our King, because he is already here." She held her light aloft a moment longer and briefly considered saying no more. Setting her burden down and fleeing. She shoved that thought straight out of her mind and lowered her arms, holding the light before her so that it would shine on her face. Even those at the far reaches of the crowd should be able to see her now.

"You already have a prince who, in any sensible world, would be King. He doesn't need a Queen from Dharia to prove his worth. He doesn't need a Queen at all. He puts to shame any royal from the plains, proving his nobility time and again in acts of bravery and wisdom. In leading you constantly toward peace. In negotiating with countries five times Jungali's size to bring prosperity to the country he loves. In risking his very life to stop a war. People of Jungali, your King is already *here*—" She swept one hand up to gesture to the balcony where Ash usually addressed his people. She stuttered to a stop when she saw a lone figure there. A dark outline of a man who could only be Ash, standing on his balcony, watching her.

She swallowed and dropped her gaze back to the crowd. Her heart pounded. "Your King is already here," she said again, weakly. Her mouth had run dry, her voice had fled, and her mind had gone blank. She should exit the stage now, before she embarrassed herself. But before she could set down her lamp, two small girls skittered to the front of the platform and smiled up at her. They looked at each other and exchanged a mischievous grin.

Then the one on the left started dancing.

She held small hand aloft as if an imaginary lamp were perched there. Her other hand swept up to tap it, as though lighting the lamp. Her wrists slowly circled, as both hands spiraled back down to her sides. Then, throwing one arm crooked over her head, she stamped her bare little foot on the cobblestones as she turned in a circle.

Once she had completed the turn, she looked to her friend. Together, but not quite exactly matching, they repeated the moves. *Hand up, lamp tap, circle down, circle around.* When they finished, two more girls, slightly older, hurried out from the crowd to join them. A drum beat started up from somewhere, followed by a flute and some kind of horn Aniri didn't recognize. Two women joined the girls, and then two more, still older, all dressed in the same costume, flicking the air with their hands and beating the cobblestones with their bare feet.

It was a simple routine, but beautiful, and somehow hypnotic.

Aniri watched as more and more women joined them. She shook herself out of the trance and finally set down her lamp. Careful to lift her skirts, she stepped over the flames to leave the platform. Everywhere was movement, as women pressed in and filled the square with twirling skirts. She couldn't find Nisha's face, or Priya's or Seledri's.

A chanting rose up.

At first, Aniri thought it was the women, but the sound was too deep and muscular. Down the main street, she spied a massive shashee—it was painted in the colors of Queen Kazmi's costume and possessed a lone rider. On either side, men danced, stamping their feet and singing as they went. It was a similar routine to the women's, but rougher, more masculine. They repeated their spinning and jumping movements again and again as they marched to meet the women in the courtyard.

They were the King returning home to his Queen.

The male and female dancers met and blended, seamlessly filtering together. Boys with grandmothers, tiny girls with giant burly men, shy embraces of women and men of courting age, and knowing ones of those a little older. It was love and reunion put in motion.

Aniri was glad her speech was done, because her throat had closed up once more.

Nisha appeared at her side. "I knew you would be perfect in this," Nisha shouted into her ear, to be heard over the stamping feet and music.

Aniri just shook her head and didn't try to speak.

Seledri and Priya danced with one another. Nisha dragged Aniri past them, deeper into the courtyard, then started the dance routine again in front of her. Nisha's graceful movements spoke of a dozen Festivals of Light before—surely she had been performing it since she was a girl. Aniri's arms were leaden, but she made a grand effort to follow along. Nisha laughed and corrected her flicking wrist movement, then laughed again when Aniri's efforts were more flailing than before. The two little girls who started the celebration joined them, and Aniri finally recognized them as Nisha's daughters. A genuine smile grew on her face as they instructed her in the proper way to dance the Festival of Lights.

She hoped the smile and the low flickering lights of the lamps hid the tears that slowly leaked from her eyes.

Chapter Twenty-Four

THE FESTIVAL of Lights was slowly growing dimmer.

Children had long gone to bed, taking many of the smaller lamps with them. Nisha had retired with her two girls, escorting Seledri to her room as well. Given all the trauma of leaving Samir, their long flight and early arrival, not to mention being with child, Aniri was surprised her sister lasted as long as she had. Aniri sent Priya along to attend to her, figuring she could share a handmaiden until they returned to Dharia.

Return to Dharia.

It wasn't what she wished or planned, but it seemed imminent nonetheless. She stared up at the twin moons rising over the palace, wondering what in the name of the gods she would do when she returned to her country. Perhaps help her mother prepare for war. Maybe she could travel the countryside and speak to her mother's people, bolster them to have faith in the Queen, just as she had been doing with Ash's people.

And who were her people? The question felt hollow, like it didn't really want to be asked. Or answered.

The air sweeping across her bare midriff and shoulders now felt cold. The granite steps to the palace had lost the day's heat and chilled her bare feet. Her footfalls were heavy. She managed a nod to the guards at the estate's entrance, but she felt the fatigue all at once as she contemplated the climb to her room.

The steps grew warmer as she ascended, but her head was heavy. She watched each step of her artfully inked feet, afraid the fatigue might take her completely before she reached the top. Boots clattered down the steps from the floor above. She didn't look up until they slowed and stopped before her.

Aniri blinked twice before she realized it was Ash staring back at her.

He frowned.

She didn't have the energy to wonder why.

"Aniri." His voice was chastising. "What are you doing?"

"I'm trying to summit the stairs." Her temper rose a little. All her tears had dried in the summer air, and she merely wanted this day to end. Not that tomorrow would bring better, but then she might have the mettle to withstand it.

Ash took another step down, closing the space between them, so she didn't have to strain quite so much to peer up at him.

"I meant…" He hesitated, as if he wasn't sure what he meant.

If he was looking to Aniri for answers, she was certain she had none.

"First you talked to the skyship crew." His frown grew more stern. "And now, the Festival." He shook his head a little. "What are you attempting?"

Aniri couldn't tell if he was chastising her for speaking out of turn or simply confused about why she would be trying to right what had gone wrong. And maybe he was right. She was tired enough to admit the possibility of it having no effect at all on his people.

As she worked up a response that was coherent, more footfalls whispered on the steps above. These weren't the heavy clumping of boots, and when Janak rounded the corner of the stairwell, she should have guessed it would be him. Or possibly Priya back to retrieve her.

"There you are!" Janak exclaimed, as if he had been scouring the palace for her.

She looked to Ash, but he had already retreated a step up the stairs, avoiding her gaze. Instead, she said to Janak, "It's true. I was trying to deceive you by hiding on the stairwell, but you found me out, Janak."

He scowled, not at all amused. "Your mother arrived some time ago. I assumed you would return to the royal guest rooms with your handmaiden, but when she brought your sister instead..."

Aniri shook her head, trying to clear the fatigue from it so she could decipher his meaning. "Are you saying my mother wishes to see me before she retires?"

"That might be best." Janak's scowl faltered, and that look of uncertainty was enough to jar her fully awake.

"She *should* be debriefed as soon as possible,"

Aniri said with a small nod. Janak had agreed to tell the Queen about her father, and Aniri had promised to help. But she couldn't broach that subject in front of Ash: he already knew her father wasn't dead, but he didn't know they had found him, and that he was possibly in the Second Son's custody. Janak had insisted her mother know before anyone else. That included the Prince of Jungali, especially now that he was no longer her betrothed.

She turned to Ash, and for a moment, his concerned looks were too soft. They wrenched her heart. But she steeled herself against it. "I assume, Prince Malik, that you have had a chance to discuss the events in Samir with my raksaka?"

Ash nodded, lips pressed into a line.

"Naturally we need to do the same for my mother. And sooner is better." Whatever explanations he wanted to demand from her would have to wait until tomorrow.

"Of course." Ash stepped aside to let her pass.

Aniri took a deep breath and marched past him in her bare-shouldered, bare-footed costume with as much royal presence as she could manage. The ancient Jungali dress was an unfortunate choice for addressing her mother as well, but it couldn't be helped. The night was already wearing on, and her with it.

Aniri followed Janak up the steps, her fatigue flying away in front of the prospect of telling her mother that her father lived, had been unfaithful, and now lay in the hands of the murderous Second Son of Samir. The twisting in Aniri's stomach was matched only by the torment that showed through in flashes on Janak's face.

Her mother had been assigned one of the royal guest rooms on the top floor. Janak knocked. Her mother's handmaiden answered and held the door for them. Aniri exchanged a quick look with Janak, and he took the handmaiden aside to ask her to leave, while Aniri crossed the room to greet her mother.

"Aniri!" Her mother dropped the corset she had been unpacking and hurried to meet her. She hugged Aniri tight, which only made Aniri's stomach clench more. "I can't tell you how relieved I am to see you in the flesh." She pulled back and held Aniri by the shoulders, giving a quick, curious glance to her costume. "Janak has told me all about your escape from Samir."

Aniri dashed a look to Janak, who was closing

the door on her mother's befuddled handmaiden. He gave Aniri a small shake of his head *no*.

So, not exactly *all* about the escape.

"I saw Seledri before she retired," her mother continued, brushing at Aniri's costume as if it held some kind of dust she could liberate. "She seems well enough. Astonishing, given the circumstances. Please tell me you've recovered as well."

"It may take some time." The honesty slipped out without Aniri's permission. But there would be more of that to come, soon enough.

Her mother frowned. "Is this about that dreadful boy, Devesh, kissing you? Janak explained that it has caused some friction between you and the prince."

That was one way to put it. But that wasn't her primary concern at the moment. "Mother, there's something I need to discuss with you."

Her mother stopped her fussing and gave Aniri a more critical look. Then she glanced at Janak. "Is this something we need to discuss in private?"

Aniri almost smiled. She didn't know what her mother imagined she might need to keep secret from Janak—she probably thought it was some sordid affair having to do with Devesh, like everyone else—but she simply shook her head. "No,

I would very much like Janak to participate in this discussion." Aniri beckoned him closer.

He dragged his raksaka feet as though they were made of stone.

"While we were in Samir…" Aniri took a breath for courage, but it was probably best to simply get it all out at once. "I found my father. He's been keeping a climbing shop in the capital."

Her mother released Aniri's shoulders and stepped back, head shaking back and forth in tiny movements. Then she sent a scathing look to Janak. "You promised!"

Aniri had never seen Janak shrink the way he did before that accusation.

"No!" Aniri held her hands up. "It wasn't Janak's doing. I'm entirely to blame, Mother."

The Queen ignored her. "I told you she would find him." Then she turned away from them both, hands balled at her sides.

Aniri hesitated, uncertain what to say next. Janak stared at the floor, failing miserably in keeping his composure. This was *not* how she wanted this conversation to unfold.

"Mother." Aniri waited, but she didn't turn. "I know this is painful, but you need to know."

"He found someone else, didn't he?" Her mother's voice was so weak, trembling. Aniri rushed to her side, stopping just short of putting a hand on her mother's shoulder.

"Yes." That single word felt like it wrenched out an entire section of Aniri's heart.

Her mother turned enough for Aniri to see tears forming at the corners of her eyes. "How did you find him?"

"He sought me out."

Her mother's face twisted.

Aniri said the rest in a rush. "He was trying to protect Seledri. And me. He knew how dangerous the Second Son and the King could be. And when they came for us..." She didn't want her mother to think her father a hero, but she should know: when his daughter's lives were threatened, he did everything he could to save them. It should count for something. "When the Second Son's guard tried to take Seledri and me, he fought them. He won us a chance to escape."

A single tear broke free. "Is he... did he die?"

"I don't think so. I'm not sure, but I think he paid for our freedom by being taken prisoner himself."

She nodded, eyes cast down.

"Mother." Aniri reached for her mother's hand

and gently urged her to turn. "The Second Son will try to use this against you. I'm not sure when or how, but I couldn't let him be the one to tell you." Aniri glanced to Janak. "Neither of us wanted that."

Her mother looked to Janak, who had managed to regain his stoic face. He faced her as if ready to take whatever punishment she might mete out for failing her orders. Which wasn't fair at all.

"Janak warned me against going to him." Aniri stood straighter. "But I don't regret doing so. He had valuable information we needed."

Her mother's eyes unfocused. "Now that they have your father, they will hurt him."

Aniri sucked in a breath. "They've been planning all along to use him against you, Mother."

Her mother blinked, her eyes focusing on Aniri again. "All along?"

"They've always known where he was hiding. They've held the threat of exposure over him from the start. He *chose* to stay hidden. He chose to abandon us. And he's paying the price for that. I don't wish it upon him, Mother, truly I don't, but if Samir moves against us in war, there will be many more lives at stake."

"Dharia will not be brought down by an errant

King." The soft creases of pain left her face, driven out by the commanding presence that Aniri had always known.

Relief washed through Aniri. "I know. Dharia's Queen is far too strong for that."

Her mother frowned, then put her hands to Aniri's cheeks. "You were right to bring this to me. And I am so sorry, child. For not telling you sooner." She gave a small smile. "You don't need my protections anymore, do you?"

Aniri sighed and placed her hand over her mother's. "Perhaps not. But I do have two requests." She glanced at Janak. "Possibly three."

Her mother dropped her hands. "What do you mean?"

Aniri kept her tone light, in case she might be trespassing too far. "First, I would like you to forgive any and all grievances you may have against my raksaka."

The Queen frowned at him. "Are there other grievances of which I should be aware?"

His eyes were wide with heightened attention.

"No unforgiveable ones," Aniri said quickly, to draw her back. "And I need him to be in top form for any dangers that lay ahead."

The Queen tore her questioning glare from Janak. "And the second?"

"I need you to support First Son Pavan in any way that you can. He's in a fight for the crown, and it's not just the fate of the father of Seledri's baby hanging in that balance: the winner could determine whether Samir will wage war against us. I assume Janak has told you about the means?"

She nodded. "We'll be hard pressed to prevail against a skyship armada. I'll see what I can do on the political front for Pavan. What's the third?"

Aniri swallowed and stared at her bare feet peeking from below the flamboyant Jungali dress. The heaviness stole back into her heart. "I may soon be returning to Dharia."

"This strife between you and the prince? It's that serious?"

"Yes." Another single word that ravaged her heart. "I need more time. To set things right before I leave."

The Queen studied her, but was quiet for a moment. "Anything you need, my Third Daughter, you may have it. Especially in this."

Aniri gave her a weak smile. "Then please think of a sufficiently plausible reason as to why you cannot return to Dharia, taking me with you, on the morrow."

She gave a small smile and tapped a finger to her lips. "I believe I may be in need of a skyship tour. I hear they are the rage for nobles these days."

Aniri grinned and threw her arms around her mother. It was the first time, in far too long, that Aniri remembered doing so without the slightest discomfort for either one of them.

Chapter Twenty-Five

ANIRI SLEPT HARD, falling into bed nearly the moment she returned to her room. When she awoke, the sun blazed in her face, blinding her as it streamed in from her balcony window. It startled her so badly, she nearly jerked out of the bed, saved only by the fact that all her limbs were still so heavy with sleep, she could scarcely move.

Slowly, she sat up. The Jungali costume from the night before was tangled all around her, which only brought back all the drama and heartache of that day. A yawn overtook her. She fought against the urge to lie back down, forcing herself to ease off the deep softness of the bed.

"Are you alive, my lady?" Priya asked from across the room, where she was busy unpacking and repacking some of their cases. "I feared you had survived Samirian guards only to succumb to Jungali dancing."

"It's too early for your wit, Priya." Aniri fought another yawn.

Priya brought over a deep purple dress with far too many layers and held it up to Aniri. "That's where you're wrong, my lady. It's nearly midday." Then she shook her head at the dress, as if it had offended her and whirled to go seek another.

"Midday?" Aniri said, disbelieving. But the sun high in the sky outside her window spoke the truth of it. She had bought an extra day from her mother and already wasted half of it.

Her body was stiff, but eventually obeyed her commands as she quickly washed up, dragged a brush through her hair, and shucked off the Jungali costume of the night before.

"Priya, I need something suitable to any task." She wasn't sure what she intended for the day. "Have you seen Nisha?" That was as good a place to start as any. Ash's sister-in-law had certainly been right about the Festival last night—she may have annoyed the prince, but Ash's people seemed to have forgiven her. At least somewhat.

"No, my lady. I've been attending to you and

Princess Seledri this morning. Perhaps Princess Malik escorted the Queen on that tour of Bhakti by skyship that she wished for? Your sister was still too fatigued to accompany her."

"Is she not well?" Aniri scowled, not only for Seledri's health but Nisha's possible absence.

"She is fine, my lady. Just with child and recovering from the excitement of recent events. I instructed her to take to her bed and found a Jungali handmaiden to attend to her for the day."

"You're a wonder, Priya."

"It is about time my lady realized as much."

Aniri grinned.

Priya held up a pair of lightweight breeches and a soft linen shirt. "These should suit any purpose, my lady, even dancing."

Aniri quickly pulled on the breeches. "And what of the prince? Have you heard of his plans for the day?"

Priya gave her a serious look. "There is much activity in the palace today. Karan told me there are plans afoot to fortify the city for a possible attack from the air. I would imagine the prince would be engaged in such efforts."

"Then so must I." Aniri tugged the shirt over

her head and tied the laced strings that held it closed in front.

Priya's eyes sparkled. "May I accompany you, my lady?"

"That would be most welcome." Aniri wanted to do something *real*—some actual thing beyond speeches and dancing, that would show her solidarity and support for the Jungali people. And their prince. Then she could head home to Dharia knowing she had done all she could. From there, she would help her mother prepare for a war that felt like it was creeping up on her in inches, a stealthy black cat hidden in shadows just waiting to pounce when she wasn't looking. Or when she overslept.

She and Priya traveled the length of the top floor, but all the royal guest rooms, except Seledri's, were vacant. The meeting rooms on the next level down were likewise unused. But at the ground level, there was much moving of furniture and crates and goods of all kinds. Dozens of people carted items out of the palace and into the courtyard, then returned empty-handed for more.

"My lady?" Priya asked, puzzled. "Perhaps they are making room for more festivities?"

"I don't think so, Priya." Whatever was happening, the people carrying out the contents of the royal household wore grim expressions in their work.

While Aniri and Priya watched, a single-file line of bedraggled prisoners emerged from the stairwell to the levels below. Heavily armed guards, two for every shackled inmate, accompanied them in a slow procession that took them outside. Priya and Aniri edged toward the large doors of the palace, which were thrown open. Outside, a shashee-drawn cart awaited the prisoners. The cart looked to be used for hauling coal, now repurposed to carry human cargo.

"Prisoners?" Aniri asked, wondering why they were being moved.

"From the prince's dungeons, it would appear." Priya pulled back from an especially massive and smelly man shuffling past them, shackled both hand and foot. Only then did Aniri recognize them as the Samirian crew from aboard the skyship—from before Aniri, Ash, Karan, and Priya led a mutiny against them and claimed it for the prince. Ash was moving them out of the underground dungeons. But why?

The last of the prisoners filed up from the depths of the palace. At the end of the line came

Ash, dressed in adventuring clothes and dark boots that appeared to have already seen rough usage. He was dusty from head to foot and walked along with the final guard, head bent close, talking quietly. He didn't notice Aniri and Priya, buried in his discussion as he followed the prisoners.

He paused at the door to the palace and said to the guard, "The Samirians destroyed much of the embassy property before we arrested them. There may be doors which you cannot yet adequately secure. Check every one, and in the meantime, keep the prisoners shackled."

"Our tinkers are at work on it, your majesty," the guard said. "Last I heard, they should have the entire embassy building secure soon."

"Good. Still… be on your guard. Some of these traitors are Garesh's men, but many were employed at the embassy. They know the building better than you do."

"Yes, your majesty." The guard strode after the line of prisoners.

Ash watched them go, running a hand through his hair and looking more harried than Aniri had ever seen. She hesitated to interrupt his thoughts, but before she could decide whether to bother him or retreat, a woman emerged from the same stairwell and strode toward him. Her dark hair was bound back, and she was dressed in dust-covered work clothes like Ash, but Aniri recognized Nisha immediately. She was intent on a parchment clutched in her hand, looking up only when she reached Ash.

Nisha's eyebrows flew up when she saw Aniri, stalling out whatever urgent message she had for the prince.

But Ash noticed his sister-in-law's approach and turned to her. "Nisha, tell me we'll have enough room." Then he startled when he recognized Aniri and Priya standing nearby. The shock quickly morphed into a scowl and a short nod. "Aniri." He seemed torn whether to say anything more, finally settling on, "I thought you had taken the tour with your mother."

Nisha jumped in. "Actually, I'm glad Aniri is here," she said, a shade too cheerily. "I could use her help in preparing the rooms below."

"What rooms?" Aniri asked.

The scowl Ash had for Aniri had nothing on the ground-burning glare he sent to Nisha. "You do *not* need additional help. And if you do, there is no need to burden the princess with it. I will obtain more assistants for you." He signaled one of the many keepers moving the royal household contents out of the palace.

"I don't need assistants," Nisha said archly. "I need someone to consult on the rigors of our plans."

"I'll help in any way I can," Aniri said. "Waiting for my mother to finish her royal duties can be excessively tedious."

"Very well," Ash said, now glaring equally at both of them. The staff he had just signaled arrived at his side, but he waved him away. Confused, the man glanced at them, seemed to realize they were all royalty except for Priya, and beat a hasty retreat. "Come with us, then," Ash said to Aniri. He strode toward the stairwell without waiting for a response.

Aniri gave Nisha a wide-eyed shake of her head. "Are you sure this is wise?" she whispered as they fell in behind Ash's retreating back.

"Absolutely," she said, smiling broadly.

Priya looked delighted as well. Aniri's stomach, meanwhile, was twisting itself into knots. The last thing she wanted was to anger Ash even further. That would only add a burden on top of the ones he was already carrying. She wanted to *help*, not hinder. But she trusted Nisha, so they descended the stairs after Ash.

He had already disappeared down the darkened stairwell.

The palace was built farther into the mountain than she ever suspected. Three levels down, they came to a dank series of cells that must have been previously occupied by the prisoners. The walls were carved from the bare granite of the mountain, and the floors were no more than dirt. Iron bars had been driven into the rock ceiling and walls to create a series of cages. It was far from hospitable, and smelled of unwashed bodies and mildew, but Aniri was glad to see no instruments of torture or any other dark devices. Although she should have known that a prince who went to great lengths to house even his enemies safely wouldn't resort to such measures.

"As you can see," Ash said, gesturing to the cells with a both arms out, his voice still tinged with bitterness, "we've emptied the cells and are working on reclaiming this space."

"For what purpose?" Aniri asked, although she was beginning to guess already.

"Bunkers," Ash replied, the sarcasm fading. "In the event of aerial attack, we need a place for the people to go for protection."

Aniri glanced around. The cells were probably

at capacity with just the two dozen or so prisoners Ash had just relocated. "There isn't much room."

Ash sighed. "No. Not nearly enough. But these lowest levels could hold many children, at least temporarily. And the two levels above can hold more. The entire palace is a fortress of stone, but each level down from the top will be successively more impervious to attack."

"You plan to bring children here?" Aniri asked carefully. Priya was lifting her skirts to keep them out of the dust, but it seemed a pointless gesture. The air itself carried the fine grit everywhere.

A dark look crossed Ash's face.

"Just temporarily," Nisha said brightly. "I was tallying how many would fit."

"Perhaps you could bring a few down here to acclimate first?" Aniri suggested. "Maybe allow them to bring their paints and decorate? Make it less frightening for the others."

The clouds vanished from Ash's face, and even in the flickering gaslamps that dimly lit the dungeon, she could see her idea had affected him. He turned to Nisha, "Is that something you could arrange?"

"Of course," Nisha said, giving Aniri a smile.

"Is there more room on the levels above?" Aniri asked Ash, but he had already turned away.

"Once we clear them out, yes," he said over his shoulder, not looking at her. "Would you like to visit them as well?"

He was inviting her. She hoped that was a positive thing, and not him dragging her off to chastise her for meddling.

Nisha chirped, "Priya, dear. Can you give me a hand with sweeping this cell? I want to see if we've anything below all this dust that can decently be made into a floor."

Priya immediately said, "Yes, of course, my lady." She grabbed a whisk broom that was leaned against one of the open cells and quickly tiptoed after Nisha toward the far side of the cells.

Ash gave her a look that made her think there was definitely a chastisement in her future, but she followed him back up the stairs anyway. They passed several more staff headed down to assist in the dungeon. The next level up was larger, but still nowhere near the size of the other floors above ground. It was sectioned into rooms, some by low walls, some by complete walls with doors, all of which were open as more staff circulated in and out, clearing the last of the contents. At least this level had painted walls and a smoothed stone floor, but it still appeared to be carved out of the mountain.

To forestall Ash's complaints, whatever they were, Aniri broke the silence first. "You are most fortunate to have such bunker-like accommodations already built, right here in the palace. Dharia will not be so similarly equipped."

"It won't be enough." His eyes bored into hers.

"No," she said, chastened. "I suppose not."

They stepped aside to allow a pair of household keepers to pass. They were carrying a crate—a quite heavy one from the way their muscles strained.

When the workers had disappeared into the stairwell, Ash dropped his voice even further. "Aniri."

She ignored his bid to start whatever argument he wished to have and gestured to the workers emerging from the stairwell carrying jugs. "Are you storing supplies down here as well?"

He gritted his teeth, then said, "Yes. In the event we suffer a sustained attack."

She casually strolled down the hallway.

He hesitated then followed.

She dropped her voice so the other milling staff

wouldn't overhear. "Have you told the people of the full threat?"

He sighed, clearly impatient with her stalling. "Only a few trusted staff members. But word will spread quickly enough. I will have to address the people soon, as will your mother when she returns."

Aniri nodded. "I honestly wish we had been able to confirm the extent of the Samirians' capabilities whilst still in country. But, Ash—" She stopped him with a touch on his elbow that she instantly regretted, even if he didn't pull away. "They are much more advanced than we are, technologically. You probably already knew that, but it was a shock to me to see all the mechanicks their tinkers have conjured. I have no doubt that they're capable of building an armada, if not now, then soon."

"I know."

"Is there any hope of building a counter-fleet?"

He gave a frustrated sigh. "Yes, but it would take months. Or longer. And we haven't the resources the Samirians have, Aniri. We need time, and I'm afraid we have precious little of it."

She ignored the flush of warmth that her name on his lips surged up. "Dharia can help with that.

The Queen has tinkers with experience with ship-building."

"I know. Your mother and I have discussed it. But the Samirian infrastructure is so much larger than ours and even more extensive than your mother's. The Samirians have a head start that may be insurmountable."

They had reached the far end of the hallway, which dead-ended into a wall of rock. Aniri placed her hand on it—not as cold as she expected, for being underground. "You have so many resources in the mountains: the navia. The mines. And the love of your people, Ash. You can do much with that."

Ash closed his eyes briefly and sucked in a breath. "Aniri."

"What?"

He glanced down the hall. The closest staff member was two dozen feet away. Still, Ash lowered his voice. "What are you doing?"

"What do you mean?" Aniri asked, although she suspected they had reached the chastisement portion of their conversation. She wanted to steer it away again, but she had avoided it long enough. Whatever he had to say, she could endure it, just as she had mustered the courage to speak to his skyship crew and his people in the square.

Instead of rebuking her, he took her by the elbow and pulled her inside an empty room next to them. Shiny spots on the floor spoke of furniture recently moved, but the mustiness of the room implied it had been used infrequently in its time before being designated a bunker.

Ash closed the door, then pressed a fist against the frame. When he turned to her, an intense look had taken hold of his face.

"Aniri, just… *stop*."

"Stop what?" She crossed her arms over her linen blouse and tried hard not to shrink under his demanding glare.

He stepped closer, eyes pleading her to make this easier. "Stop trying to… *fix* this."

She gave him a half-hearted smile. "Is it working?"

"Aniri."

Her shoulders sagged, and she bit her lip. "You want me to stop talking to your people?"

He frowned, but said, "Yes."

"And stop trying to help?"

Frustration twisted his face. "It's not that—"

"And stop dancing in the streets and

proclaiming how you're the best King that Jungali could ever hope to have?"

"Aniri, please."

She unfolded her arms and stepped closer. She was nearly toe-to-toe with him, peering defiantly up into his face. "Well, I'm *not* going to stop. Not until I've fixed the damage I've done. Or run out of ways to try. Because some things are worth fighting for, Ash. Things like your sister when the Samirians are threatening her life. Things like your country when a fleet of ships could sweep out of the sky at any moment and destroy it. Things like a prince who dares to give everything he has to his people."

His eyes went wide with her speech and her intensity.

She hesitated, but only for a moment, her temper rising to full steam. "You're a noble man, Ash. The most noble I've ever known. You're good and decent and righteous, and believe me, I know exactly how rare that is—in anyone, but especially in a royal. You fight for peace and for your country and for everyone else. And someone like that, someone like *you*, is worth fighting for." Somewhere in the middle she had started to stab him in the chest with her finger.

His pale amber eyes blazed. "Say that again."

"Which part?" She pressed her lips tight, her face burning with having laid her heart so bare.

"All of it," he demanded.

She would say it as many times as he liked. "I'm not going to stop—"

He cut her off with a kiss so intense she would have stumbled back into the wall had he not captured her in his arms. He kissed her again and again, then deepened the kiss and pressed her backward until she was finally flush against the wall. It was cool on her back, but the heat of Ash's lips and hands set her body on fire. Her hands dug through his hair and bunched his shirt. His body was pressed against every part of her, and still, she couldn't get enough.

His kisses traveled across her cheek and down her neck, and she gasped, needing air and feeling as if her chest might explode with the surges in her heart.

"Gods, Aniri, what you do to me," he whispered in her ear, his voice hoarse.

She brought his lips back to hers. There were no words she wanted more than his kisses. He smothered her with them, and her heart soared. Then she suddenly had to know. Had to hear it. She pulled away from the kiss, tucked her face into the crook of his shoulder, and held him tight with her arms around his neck.

"Am I forgiven?" she whispered into his collar, barely letting the words escape her lips.

He slowly tugged her hands from around his neck and held them close to his chest. "*Now.*" His voice was husky. "We need to be married *right now.*"

Her smile was hesitant, afraid if she let it show on her face, her heart might burst. "But… what about…?"

He pulled her away from the wall and dipped his head to capture her with that intense stare again. "Now."

Her nods were tiny but frantic. "Now," she whispered. Then her smile broke loose.

He captured her in another kiss, then clasped her hand in his and towed her to the door.

Chapter Twenty-Six

ASH AND ANIRI wove around the contents of the royal household—which were now littered across the courtyard—holding hands and nearly running in their haste. They were well disguised in adventuring clothes, and if anyone noticed Prince Malik and the Third Daughter of Dharia fleeing the palace, hand-in-hand, as if on a mad caper, they certainly didn't try to stop them.

After they left the courtyard and wound down one street, and then another, Aniri tugged on Ash's hand to slow his pace. She couldn't tame her smile, and the intense look on his face was starting to give way to one as well.

"Where are we going?" she asked, breathless.

"To find a priestess, of course." His tentative

smile broke into a grin, and he curled their clasped hands closer to his body. They rounded another corner to a street less busy than the main ones which branched out from the palace.

"You're not worried about what the people will think?" Aniri asked, catching her breath a little as they slowed down. "I thought eloping would make them wonder about the legitimacy of the marriage." She was teasing him, mostly. There was nothing that could keep her from marrying Ash as soon as they could find a priestess to perform the ritual.

Ash tugged her to a stop and kissed her quickly. "The people already love you. I'm mostly concerned that your mother will flay us both alive." His smile said he did not, in fact, care at all.

She stood on her toes and dropped a quick kiss on his lips in return. "She's been ready to adopt you from the start. I'm fairly certain you could do no wrong in her eyes."

His smile tempered. "And in yours?"

"If I had a Daughter, I'd want her to marry you, too."

He laughed outright, then cupped her cheeks and kissed her more thoroughly. She didn't mind in the slightest, but she playfully nudged him away. "Time for that after we visit the temple."

His eyes flashed, his gaze drifting to her lips. He ran his thumb over her bottom lip, and his touch warmed every part of her. Suddenly, the idea of consummating their marriage seemed an urgent task. Ash took her hand in his again and strode even faster down the winding Jungali street.

They passed tinker shops and vegetable stands. Beast-drawn carriages rumbled past, along with human-drawn carts filled with lighter goods. The people were dressed in a rainbow of colors, and their goods were just as vibrant. Bhakti was smaller, less busy, less advanced, more colorful, and different in a thousand other ways from the Samirian capital of Mahatvak. And she couldn't be happier that it would soon become her home for good.

Ash stopped at a flower vendor and tried to purchase two garlands of white. The stunned shop-keeper refused to take the yakles from him and thrust the garlands into Ash's hands. The man kept bowing, saying, *Arama, your highness, Arama*, over and over. Ash gave up, returned the gesture, then handed Aniri a garland.

For a moment, he stood before her, saying noth-ing. Right when she remembered that she—the bride—was supposed to go first, he reached forward to place his garland over her head. She grabbed hold of the collar of his open-necked shirt to keep him close so she could do the same. He grinned, stole a kiss while bent, then pulled her by the hand farther along the street.

They were gathering stares now. Maybe it was the wedding garlands. Perhaps it was the mile-wide grins on their faces. After a while, Aniri started waving to the gawkers as they strolled past. Ash joined her, and soon the shopkeepers and tinkers and artisans waved back. Which only made her grin all the wider.

A shadow passed over the street, and her heart seized as she searched the sky. But it was only the *Prosperity* passing over on her mother's tour of the city, now heading back to the palace. Aniri waved vigorously to the ship. Ash did as well, giving her a mischievous smile. She doubted her mother would recognize them at that height, even if she chanced to look down, but it brought the grin back to Aniri's face anyway.

The streets grew quieter and even less populated as they wound their way through. Just as Aniri wondered if they would ever reach their destination, they came upon the city's gate, a behemoth of wood strapped with metal. It was so massive, thick chains on wheels were necessary to open it. Next to the gate stood a red stone building that Aniri recognized all too well.

"Does Sage Padma reside at the Samirian embassy now?" Aniri asked, frowning. The embassy was where she went looking for Devesh and stumbled into being captured and drugged by Garesh. Then she remembered Ash transferred his prisoners —Garesh's men as well as the Samirians he conspired with—out of his dungeons and into the embassy building. Several of Ash's guards stood around the entrance.

"No," Ash said with a chuckle. "Our destination is next door."

He pointed to a blue-domed temple that sat on the opposite side of the gate. The ornately carved granite walls were inlaid with glistening blue stones. Perfectly pointed arches framed a pair of towering entrance doors that were made from the richest of dark woods. A half-dozen steps led up to the entranceway, which was framed on either side with lush, flowering bushes. Their perfume reached the street, and the temple's beauty rivaled anything found in Samir or Dharia. Hand-in-hand, Aniri and Ash climbed the steps and stood before the imposing doors. Ash pulled on a thick, gnarled rope that dangled to the side. A solemn gong sounded within the temple.

Aniri couldn't help smiling. "I hope I don't have to ring that as part of some deeply significant Jungali wedding ritual. I'm not sure I could keep from laughing."

"I think you're safe." Merriment shone in Ash's eyes. He tugged her close again with their clasped hands and bent down to kiss her. Aniri slipped her hand around the back of his neck and showed him with her kiss how she never wanted to stop. Never wanted to quarrel. Never wanted anything to come between them again.

The door creaked open with a low groan.

Aniri and Ash broke apart quickly, caught in a moment a bit too passionate for the doorstep of a holy place. Sage Padma stood in the threshold, dressed in her plain robes, with a young acolyte lurking behind her.

The priestess raised a single eyebrow as she took in the two of them, standing at her door with wedding garlands around their necks. "Impatient, are we?"

"I know it's irregular, Sage Padma—" Ash started, but she held up a single hand to stop him.

"It's highly irregular." Her dark eyes held his gaze. "You should pledge yourselves before your people, your families, and your gods. However…" She let a small smile tug at the corner of her mouth. "If you're going to choose one, at least you chose wisely."

Ash smiled wide.

Sage Padma stepped back into the darkened interior of the temple, and Ash gestured for Aniri to go first.

Before she could step inside, an earthshaking explosion ripped sound out of the world. Something as powerful as a god picked Aniri up and threw her into the air. She landed on a thousand daggered fingers that scraped across her face. Her head rammed something solid, a wall of rock buried in the prickled arms that held her.

Blackness shut down her world.

Pain leaked into Aniri's consciousness first. As if a thousand ants were feasting upon her flesh. But the biting was nothing compared to the forging anvil banging repeatedly on the back of her head. She struggled to open her eyes, only to find a cross-hatch of shapes blurred in front of her. She moved, but that only angered the ants, and they bit harder.

Holding still, she swallowed the dryness in her throat and tried to reason out what had happened. She had been at the temple door with Ash. Something exploded. She was now in a world of tiny pains. But alive. Something had cushioned her fall.

The bush around her came into focus. She had been thrown into the flowering plant to the side of the temple door. One that apparently hid thorns of great sharpness. She tried to gingerly work herself loose, but that only dug the thorns deeper. With a growl, and teeth gritted against the pain, she flailed her way free and fell to her knees on the cold stone floor of the temple entranceway. Her hands were bloodied with red streaks, and her clothes suffered a myriad of small tears, but she would live.

Ash.

She looked to the temple door, but it was closed. Smoke drifted up the steps from the street. Ash was nowhere to be seen. As she struggled to her feet and stumbled forward, the carnage at the base of the temple steps and beyond stalled out her search.

The street was littered with rubble. The giant gate of the city had been blown clean away. Chunks of it, both large and small, wood and metal, had been thrown everywhere, even to the temple steps. A piece of jagged wooden beam lay against the closed door where Ash had been just moments before. Or was it minutes? She had been unconscious, with no way to tell how much time had passed. But it couldn't have been too long. Where could he have gone?

Her head pounded and the whole scene seemed a nightmare. She slowly descended the steps. A sizeable portion of the embassy across the street was gone, leaving gaping holes beyond which she could see paintings of Samirian Queens. Bodies lay in the debris—bodies wearing Jungali blue uniforms. There were more dead around the perimeter of the building, but none were dressed in the adventuring clothes Ash had worn.

Aniri slowly realized there were also *live* people in the street, moving through the rubble. But they weren't Ash's guards: they were the prisoners, liberated by the blast. Their movements were coordinated, with a tall one directing some to help the wounded prisoners, while others fled toward the gaping hole in the city wall.

Before Aniri could think of what to do about that, another explosion sent tremors through her boots. She twisted to look: the sound had come from farther inside the city. As she watched, a plume of dust and smoke arose a block or two away, closer to the heart Bhakti. Anguished cries tore through the air, and that's when she saw it, drifting high in the sky.

The *Dagger*.

It had to be the ship from the schematics—it had the same general design as the *Prosperity*—only it sported a black-tar-coated ship below and a Samirian-red gas bag above. And it seemed larger than the *Prosperity* when it had passed over the city not long ago, although she couldn't be sure with the distance. The *Dagger* was probably a thousand feet above the city, and the *Prosperity* was nowhere to be seen. Something tiny dropped from the *Dagger*, hurtling straight down onto the city she loved. Another explosion rocked the ground, and another plume rose up with screams into the air.

Gods, they're bombing the city.

Her stomach hollowed out, and her limbs felt numb with it. What could she do? How could she stop them? Out of the corner of her eye, she saw four figures in black moving through the street. They were raksaka. *Raksaka.* In the streets. Talking to the prisoners and gesturing to the gate. Then two of the raksaka peeled away and fanned out the width of the cobblestone street. They stole with light raksaka steps deeper into the city. *Toward* the bombings. They had swords crossed on their backs, pistols holstered at their sides, and one carried a small aetheroceiver strapped to the middle of his back.

They're headed to the palace.

She moved without thinking, following the two raksaka. She heard a shout and a scuffle of feet behind her, but she ignored it. At the edge of the temple property, she stumbled into the street to see where the raksaka had gone, but they'd already disappeared around a corner. She did another sweep of the street behind her, looking for someone in dark boots and adventuring clothes, praying to whatever gods would listen that she would find Ash among those still moving and not the fallen. Where could he have gone? Why hadn't he taken her with him? Did he not see her thrown into the bushes?

A burly man stalked toward her. "Ay! You there. Where you running off to?" Broken chains dangled from his wrists and hands. He peered at her as he got closer. "Wait now, you're that—"

She turned and ran.

His boots pounded behind her. She made it across the street, but he was gaining too fast. She grabbed hold of a cart full of tinker toys and heaved it over. It spilled a thousand small mechanicks that bounced and skittered into the street, creating a hazard that might buy her a couple of seconds.

She bolted away from the shop.

Curses rang out behind her, but she didn't look back to see if the now-liberated prisoner was still pursuing her. Instead, she ran with all her strength, crossing over the street, taking one turn, and then another. A third explosion blasted the air, and Aniri ran toward it. The *Dagger* was bombing their way to the palace, with their raksaka following close behind. They could only have one purpose: to assassinate the royals within. And the people she loved had no warning.

She didn't know what she could possibly do to stop them.

But she had to try.

Chapter Twenty-Seven

THE CARNAGE WAS ALMOST TOO much for Aniri to bear.

As she ran toward the palace, she had to climb over rubbled streets, avoid sobbing children and wailing mothers, and pass men and women of all ages trying to dig victims out from the ruins. Most of the streets were clear, and through those she could run like she was on fire. But where the bombs hit, it was like the goddess of war herself had taken a bite out of the city and spit back death and horror. By the third cratered-out blast, she had to stop looking. Had to ignore the misery and climb right over it, or she would be immobilized by the crushing grief that threatened to drown her.

She focused on one thing and one thing only: reaching the palace.

Through the smoke-filled haze that lay on the streets she could see the palace had been hit already. Black plumes rose from it, obscuring the tallest tower where the *Prosperity* should have been docked. Her scans of the sky showed neither skyship aloft. Of course, that didn't mean anything. Either could be tucked away, out of her sight, beyond the city walls or simply hidden behind the teetering buildings and the growing haze surrounding them. The smoke and the running made her wheeze, but she pressed on. When she reached the courtyard of the palace, her lungs burned with the need for air.

A big section of the top floor was now open to the sky. Aniri stood staring at it, stunned into motionlessness. People streamed into the palace, directed by soot-faced guards who were sending them down into the bowels of the mountain where they might have some semblance of safety. The people buffeted Aniri on either side as she stood there, mouth hanging open, unable to move.

A child ran up and grabbed hold of her legs, burying her face in Aniri's breeches. That was what finally shook her loose. She picked up the girl, who couldn't be more than five, and looked around for her mother or father, but there was no one with her. The child buried her face in Aniri's shoulder. She didn't trust herself to speak, so she just carried the girl up the steps and into the relative safety of the building. She took one last look over her shoulder, scanning for the *Dagger*, to see if it was coming around for another pass, but there was nothing but trails of smoke tarnishing the sky.

Inside, the palace was darkened with people blocking the doors and windows. They pressed close as they worked their way down the stairs, the entrance of which was clogged like a drain hole stuffed with too many leaves. Nisha was there, directing people into the stairwell and chastising them in a soft but firm voice not to push, not to shove, to make room for the children. Aniri let out a small sound, a whimper of relief, and nearly tripped on her way to Nisha's side.

She didn't realize who Aniri was and tried to clear room for her to go down the stairs, but that wasn't where Aniri needed to go.

"Nisha!" Aniri wheezed. "It's me."

She looked up. "Gods, Aniri, you're alive." She threw her arms around her and the child, hugging them both. Aniri could feel her shake.

"Please take the girl," Aniri said, her voice

growing stronger. "Have you seen…" She looked back over her shoulder. There was no way Nisha could have seen anything in this crowd and the chaos, much less raksaka intent on *not* being seen. "I have to go check on the others."

Nisha took the girl from her arms, and thankfully, the child went willingly. "Where is Ash?"

Aniri just shook her head, unable to speak for a moment.

Nisha must have thought something even worse. "No!" She clutched the girl harder.

"No, Nisha." Aniri clamped a hand on her shoulder. "He's alive. I know he is. I just don't know where he is at the moment. We *will* find him. But first…" Aniri dropped her voice. "There are raksaka here. Samirian. Any royal is in danger. You need to find somewhere safe below and stay there."

She nodded shakily.

Aniri suddenly remembered she had left her handmaiden with Nisha. "Where is Priya?"

"She's downstairs. I made her stay. To help keep the calm."

"Good. Go be with her. And be safe."

Nisha nodded again, a little stronger now, and started down the stairs with the girl. Aniri watched them go until they turned the corner, then tore herself away and fought the crowd to reach the center stairwell—the one that would take her to the top, bombed-out floor. And where she prayed she wouldn't find any bodies like those in the streets. Before she went, she stopped one of Ash's guards.

Staring up in his face, she said with as much command as she could, "I need your weapon."

He frowned down at her with a glazed kind of look. Suddenly he recognized her. "Yes, my lady." He fumbled to pull his pistol from his side holster. She thanked him and tucked it into the back of her breeches. It was only one shot. Against a raksaka, she probably had little hope, but at least it was something. What she really wanted was a blade, but that would be even more pointless.

She took to the steps, and each one lodged her heart further into her throat. The acrid stench of bomb residue grew thicker as she went. The number of people quickly thinned out with everyone headed *down*, not *up*. When she reached the top of the stairwell, the roof was gone, and she had to climb over rubble to summit the last of the stairs. The bomb had blasted away the roof to her right—Ash's bedroom, the refurbished fencing hall, what had been a few empty rooms. It sent weakness to her knees with relief, and she dared to hope that no one had actually been killed.

Yet.

Aniri pulled out the guard's pistol and held it in front of her. She couldn't see anyone in her stretch of the gently curving hallway, but she was fairly certain she wouldn't see a raksaka until they were upon her. She lifted her gaze above the jagged edge of the ruined ceiling to the sky. Still no sign of the *Dagger*, but she could just barely see the top of the blue, rippling gas bag of the *Prosperity*. It was docked. She wasn't sure if she was glad to see that or not. It was good to see it still intact, but docking only made their skyship, their one real weapon against the Samirians, a target for the *Dagger's* bombs as much as anything else. And if it was docked, that meant her mother had likely debarked and was now somewhere in the palace.

With the raksaka.

As Aniri advanced down the hall, she tried to quiet her breathing. But once she was beyond the bombed out portion of the hall, it echoed off the hard marble as if she were a legion of guards wheezing across the floor. At least some of her noise was covered by the wind whipping around the jagged debris behind her. When she reached her mother's room, she cringed to see the door slightly open. She pushed it wide, holding her breath.

Inside, her mother was on the floor in Janak's arms. Her eyes were closed.

No, no, no. Aniri stumbled forward. As she got closer, she saw another raksaka lying on the floor behind them. He was unmistakably dead, his head no longer quite attached to his body. Aniri reached her mother's side and dropped to the floor next to her.

Aniri could hardly breathe with the vise gripping her chest. "Janak, is she…"

Janak didn't respond, didn't even acknowledge her presence. His eyes were glazed as he held his Queen cradled in his lap. He had one hand pressed against her side, but her blood had already seeped into a bloom of red under it. Where his other hand held her head, his fingers moved slightly, gently stroking her hair.

Aniri's hand shook as she reached to press her fingers to her mother's neck. She fully expected to find nothing but the coldness of death, but her mother's skin was warm, and Aniri found a slight beat. She sucked in a shaky breath.

Then her mother stirred under her touch.

"Mother?" A gush of relief coursed through her.

The corners of her mother's eyes crinkled, but she didn't open them. "Aniri." Her voice was a tiny, pained whisper, but it jerked Janak's attention to it.

His hand on her head shifted slightly to hold her better. "Hush, Amala. You need to rest."

The corners of her mother's eyes relaxed. Aniri watched her chest move, slowly drawing in one tremulous breath after another, then swiped at the tears that had leapt to her eyes. Her mother was alive, at least for the moment, but she would almost certainly die if she didn't get a healer soon.

"Janak!" Aniri said harshly, trying to break him out of his shock. "We need to move my mother. She needs a healer."

He gasped a short kind of breath, like he had forgotten to breathe in a while. Then he slowly seemed to recognize Aniri.

"I killed him," he said, staring at her with dead eyes.

Aniri frowned and glanced at the raksaka behind him.

"I killed the man who shot her," he elaborated.

Frustration hitched a ride on her voice. "I know,

Janak. But we need to get the Queen to a healer. *Now.*"

He peered down and adjusted the pressure against her mother's wound. "Yes, that would be prudent. You should fetch a healer for your mother, Aniri." But he said it like it was an unimportant task. Like he thought finding a healer was the same as bringing her flowers.

He thinks she's going to die.

Aniri had to bite back her whimper. She needed Janak to snap out of it, but she had no idea how to accomplish it. "Janak, there's another raksaka in the building," she tried.

His eyes flitted momentarily to Aniri's. Then he shook his head minutely and focused on his blood-covered hand. He nodded to himself. "It's all right, Aniri. I killed him."

"No, there are *two*." She kept her voice as calm as she could, even though a black panic was crawling up the back of her neck. If this wouldn't rouse him, nothing would.

But he didn't seem to hear. He simply repeated that small petting motion again and again, gently cradling her mother's head to his chest. "It's all right, Amala. I killed him for you."

Aniri let out a breath that almost pulled the life out of her. What could she do?

She forced herself to think: if Janak were coherent, he would gather weapons and hunt the other raksaka until he was sure every royal in the household was safe. Then, he would scour the city to find a healer for his Queen.

Aniri turned to the slain raksaka behind them. His back was arched up unnaturally, with the aetheroceiver still trapped underneath him. He had a blade in one hand, and a pistol near the other, with a second sword fallen to the ground next to him. The second blade must belong to Janak—the grip carried a Dharian crest, and it was smeared with the dead raksaka's blood. Aniri stumbled over to snatch Janak's blade from the floor, then wrenched the raksaka's blade from his grip. The pistol had already been fired, so it was of no use. She slid the dead raksaka's blade into a loop at her waist—a clumsy sheath, but it would do for the moment—then she returned to kneel next to Janak and her mother.

She laid Janak's sword next to him. "If anyone comes for the Queen, *use this*."

Janak nodded several times, but it wasn't really in response to her.

A muffled scream sounded from the hall. Aniri bolted upright, holding her gun toward the open door. She slowly crept forward, but the screaming came again, and it propelled her from the room. Down the hall, two figures slipped from view around the bend before she could properly see them, but the cries traveled back to Aniri.

She ran.

As her boot steps pounded through hallway, she forced herself to slow and hug the wall. The raksaka was almost certainly still armed. But he apparently wasn't out to kill her sister: he was *kidnapping* her. But for what purpose? And how could he possibly think he could haul Seledri the length of the city and somehow escape? It didn't make sense, but Aniri didn't want to do something foolish and force the raksaka into killing Seledri instead.

Aniri crept down the hall, her heart ripping with each muffled sound of struggle. Finally the sounds faded, and Aniri shuffled ahead faster, afraid she had somehow lost them. But they had merely reached the end of the hall, where the stairwell led to the roof.

What? Then she figured it out: he was going to

take the skyship. Possibly her sister as well, but most definitely the ship: it was his ticket out, and it was the only weapon the Jungali had left that might have a chance of fighting back.

Aniri ran up the stairs as fast as she could without making a ridiculous amount of noise. She hoped the raksaka might be distracted by Seledri, or other things, once he was on the terrace. All she needed was to be there during that moment of distraction and use her one shot on him.

She reached the top, and the sun momentarily blinded her. She shaded her eyes and blinked fast while she scanned the stone terrace. He was already a third of the way across the expanse, but he wasn't heading for the skyship.

And no wonder—the *Prosperity* was blown half to bits.

An entire chunk of the ship was missing, the bridge window blown out as well as the cargo hold below. A good piece of the terrace was gone as well, its ragged edges burnt to blackness. Crew members scrambled up the side of the gas bag, working to repair a scattering of holes that had pierced it. Aniri had no idea how it stayed inflated at all with so much damage.

A muffled scream carried across the terrace, riveting Aniri back to the raksaka and her sister. It drew the attention of several of the crew as well, who shouted their alarm, a commotion that in turn drew the raksaka's notice. He stopped trying to cover Seledri's mouth, instead grabbing her wrist and twisting it awkwardly. She cried out, but she didn't struggle against him anymore.

Aniri let out an animal sound and raised her gun. But she was too far to be sure of her aim, and besides, her sister was in the way. Aniri realized belatedly that he was using Seledri as *cover*. Aniri lowered the gun and stalked closer. He wasn't watching her, instead keeping his eye on the skyship crew who were starting to spill out along the walkplank, armed and ready to rescue Seledri. And he kept flicking looks to the sky.

To the sky?

The *Dagger* hovered a couple hundred feet above them, poised like red death. Aniri's mouth fell open and she froze. They could bomb the entire terrace *right now*. And likely kill them all. Or at least a good portion, depending on just where the bomb fell. But instead of dropping bombs, there was a snake made of rope winding its way down.

The raksaka was trying to strap something on her sister—it looked like a climbing vest—but she was fighting him, screaming and trying to twist away. She was in no danger of escaping, but she was definitely impeding his ability to strap her in. Aniri aimed her gun at the raksaka's head and crept steadily toward him. If Seledri broke loose for even a moment, she would kill him. And she wasn't the only one—sailors from the ship were closing on him as well.

In one quick motion, he hit Seledri, then caught her as she slumped, unconscious, into his arms.

Aniri almost pulled the trigger, but Seledri was too tight against him. And now he was able to strap her in. The rope kept unwinding and lowering. It was nearly there. Aniri growled her frustration, then swung her pistol to aim at the skyship. She fired, but she couldn't see any effect. She tossed the gun to the ground, drew her sword, and rushed at the raksaka. He had Seledri not only strapped into the harness but to him as well, leaving his hands free to grab the rapidly descending rope.

He missed it on the first swing, but before Aniri could reach him, he caught it on the way back. Grabbing the hook at the end and snagging it onto the harness, he swung out over the edge. Aniri raced to the precipice, stopping just before tumbling over the parapet. She waited for him to swing back, but by the time he did, he was already a dozen feet above her and ascending fast. Something was pulling up the rope with a speed that had to be mechanical. She stared at the raksaka quickly rising and realized it wasn't just the rope that was hauling him upward—the *Dagger* had also started to rise.

Her mouth dropped as she realized what that meant.

"Get back on the ship," she shouted at all the gawking sailors, who were likewise hoping to either shoot the raksaka or otherwise stop him. She ran past them. "Back on board! Now!"

She flew across the walkplank, tore into the ship, and raced to the bridge. It was half missing, but Aniri knew most of the instrumentation and controls were along the back. Karan would either be there or on engines, and she only had time for one guess.

Thank the gods, he was there.

The wind whistled past the gaping hole that had been blown out of the ship. "Karan!" Aniri shouted to be heard over it. "Get us in the air. *Now.*"

"Aye," he said tightly, flipping a series of toggles

on the panel in front of him. "Mr. Tarak!" he shouted into the brass bell at his side. "I need yer full steam."

A tinny response came squeaking through that Aniri couldn't understand.

"I don't care if she's primed or not," Karan shouted back. "We'll all be cinders if ye don't."

A second later, the ship surged underneath them. But it didn't rise up, simply rocked back into place.

"Queen's breath, we're still lashed, Aniri," Karan said in a hushed voice. Aniri followed his gaze out the front, where thick ropes still held the *Prosperity* to what was left of the terrace.

Aniri's eyes went wide. She spun and raced back out of the bridge, along the corridors and then out of the ship itself, nearly crashing into two sailors along the way. "Clear the ropes!" she shouted as she emerged on deck, but the crew was already on it. Only now the lines had grown taut as the ship surged, foiling their attempt to unwrap them from the cleats. Aniri still had the dead raksaka's sword in her hand. She swung it at the nearest rope, but it just bounced off. She changed her grip and started sawing. The other sailors followed her lead, finding whatever they could—axes, knives, daggers—to spring them free. Aniri only got through a few of the twisted strands before the rope snapped. She craned up to see where the *Dagger* had gone.

She didn't have to look far—it was right on top of them.

"Take cover!" she shouted into the wind, never tearing her eyes from the pitch black underbelly of the ship. A door in the bottom opened, and what looked like a giant bullet rolled out and plummeted toward them. Someone grabbed her by the arm and hauled her inside the nearby bulkhead door. She dropped the sword and fell into the sailor as someone else closed the door behind her. Once she righted herself, she ran from the door, like the rest of them. She didn't get ten feet before a tremendous crack ripped the air and threw her from her feet. Another of the sailors broke her fall. They all had been tossed to the floor and piled up against the wall. The door to the deck had become twisted metal hanging loose on its hinges, and the side of the ship was bowed in, but both had saved them from the blast. Only now the ship was listing badly. Then it swung back the other way, rolling them all around like dolls.

She had to get up front. Aniri grabbed hold of a wall railing and climbed over and around the sailors who were likewise picking themselves up. She worked toward the bridge. The ship heaved under her feet, keeping her off balance, but when she reached it, she gasped at what she saw.

They were aloft.

"What?" Aniri said, to no one in particular.

But Karan answered. "Something broke us free, fresh."

Aniri peered around the edges of the broken bridge. They were a hundred feet above the terrace already, and she could see how: the bomb had blasted away another chunk of the tower, including the anchors where the ship had been lashed.

She looked above them. "Where's the *Dagger?*"

"Still above us." His voice was strung as tight as the ropes that had tied the ship.

"We need to get above her."

"Aye," he snapped. He banged a serious of switches, flipping them back and forth, again and again. "I've vented all our ballast. There's something else weighing us down. Or we've just lost too much gas."

Aniri frowned then held the edge of the broken bridge and leaned as far into the wind as she could, looking for the Samirian skyship. They were heading away to the east. Aniri's heart skipped a beat, a moment filled with hope… but then the *Dagger* started a slow, sweeping turn.

"They're coming around, again," she shouted over the wind.

Karan swore, then jumped over to the brass bell horn again. "Tarak! Dump her! Dump her now!"

The tinny response squeaked, but Aniri couldn't understand it at all.

"Every last bit. Do it *now!*" Karan's voice boomed so loud they could probably hear him in engines without the horn.

Nothing happened.

The *Dagger* kept turning: a slow, graceful arc of blood-red gasbag billowing against the Jungali-blue sky. The ship was Devkalaka herself, her black fins caressing the air and gliding her through the heavens. She was coming with an aching but inexorable slowness to spill her fiery destruction straight down upon them.

Aniri pulled her head back in from the wind, eyes glued to the *Dagger* as it approached, still a hundred feet above them. "We need more altitude, Karan," she said quietly, even though she knew he had already done everything he could. And they were still far too far below the *Dagger*. They were a target, sitting in the air, waiting for it.

"Aye, fresh." The way he said it… he knew it, too.

She turned to him, a numbness taking hold of her. "The Queen still lives. She will avenge us all."

He glanced over her shoulder at the *Dagger*. "She can't fight 'em without a ship, fresh."

The bottom dropped out of Aniri's stomach, but not because of Karan's words: *they moved.*

The *Prosperity* shot up and up and up. Aniri grabbed the edge of the bridge to keep from tumbling to her death. They ascended so fast, her stomach hadn't yet rebounded when suddenly they were face-to-face with the *Dagger* and flying past her… straight *up*.

"Well done, Mr. Tarak!" Karan shouted into the bell horn, his face split into a wide grin.

Aniri stared in amazement at the *Dagger*, now below them. They had passed by so close she had seen the startled faces of the bridge crew. They were no more surprised than she, although probably a lot less pleased. Aniri grabbed hand holds around the edges of the bridge, all the way back to Karan's station by the panels. He was busy checking dials.

"Can we take them, Karan?" she asked, giddy with the rush. Their ascent had slowed, but her stomach was still hollowed. "Can we force them down or use the butterfly…" She stalled out. They couldn't destroy the ship. Her sister was on board.

Karan frowned. "Fresh, I can keep us alive. Maybe. And I might land again without killing the lot of us. But I can't do much else. Tarak dumped all our fuel to get us aloft." He rubbed his face with one meaty hand and turned to face her. "And we better pray the Samirians turn tail and leave. We've got five minutes, maybe ten, before we start to lose steam. We'll lose heat in the bag… then we won't so much land as *fall*."

"We can't go after them." Aniri stared into his eyes, hoping she misunderstood.

"No, fresh. We can't."

She shuffled back to where the wind whipped, cold and gusty, past the broken edge of her skyship. Her limping, bleeding skyship was the only thing standing between her country and a militarized enemy bent on destroying them. She watched the *Dagger*, now several hundred feet below them, point toward the east in a much sharper turn than before. Once they made the turn, they kept going, plotting a straight line for the distant horizon.

They were heading home. With her sister. And she couldn't stop them.

"Keep us aloft as long as you can, Mr. Karan," she said quietly. "Then land us wherever is safe."

"Aye, Captain."

Aniri frowned, but she didn't look back. Her eyes were fixed on the *Dagger*, and she watched as it grew smaller and smaller into the hazy distance.

Chapter Twenty-Eight

A NIRI WALKED AMONG THE WOUNDED, gently touching shoulders and heads and hands—wherever wasn't covered in blood or bruises. The people were battered, taking refuge in the bunker-like safety of the palace, at every level except the bombed-out top. They needed her reassurance, her quiet presence, and she gave it—but she needed something more.

She searched every face, but Ash wasn't among them. Her mother lay in her room upstairs, closer to death than Aniri could bear to think upon. And she was far from the only person who had lost, or nearly so, a loved one today.

A fog pushed against her mind—the same haze she had seen cloud Janak's eyes as he held her mother, bleeding in his lap. Aniri couldn't afford that kind of retreat, so she blasted the fog away with a righteous anger at the carnage and destruction the Samirians had wrought. They had taken a beautiful, peaceful, loving city and beaten it bloody. They had terrorized the people, kidnapped her sister, attempted to kill her mother. *And Ash.* She knew he was alive. He wasn't thrown to the bushes like her. He wasn't among the wounded.

He walked away.

Not that she believed for a moment that he had abandoned her. Or his people. But he had somehow walked away from that first bombing of the gate. The one that had brought the raksaka in and allowed the prisoners to escape. Because escape they had: there was no sign of them now. Nor any sightings of Ash. It was possible they took him. Or he was hiding somewhere. But wherever he was, she knew he would have a purpose. A plan.

It fell to her to carry on until he returned.

In the chaos after they finally landed the ship, she had issued a slew of orders. Search for the prisoners, inside and outside the city walls. Search every cubby hole for the prince. Bring a healer for her mother, even though there were none to be spared. Repair the *Prosperity* immediately, in case of another round of attacks. Keep the wounded and children protected in the palace. Rebuild the gate at the entrance to the city. And finally, start the cleanup. And the burials.

Aniri would attend—she already had called upon Sage Padma to begin the preparations—but she wouldn't mourn. She couldn't let the possibility that she might have a funeral of her own to prepare —for Ash, for her mother, possibly even for her sister—enter her heart. She would lead her people, but she couldn't let herself join them in their tears. Not and still keep the pretense of carrying on.

Aniri found Priya sitting with a little girl. The child's face had been bloodied, and Priya tended to her wounds while telling her an outrageous story about Devpahar digging crystals the size of the girl's head out of the ground, just so she could wear them for earrings on her massive shaggy ears during the Festival dance in her honor. Priya smiled up at Aniri without breaking her story, and Aniri tried hard to call a smile to her face. But she couldn't. She laid a hand on the girl's head, gently and briefly, and moved on.

When she'd finished with the ground level, she moved up to the next floor. Nisha was there, directing the healers to the most critical amongst the wounded. Aniri drifted past, feeling more like a ghost with each touch, each empty wave. But she kept going. Finally, when she'd walked every room in the palace, she returned to the top level.

It was half gone and nearly empty. A couple of sailors padded down the stairs, in search of supplies for Karan as he scrambled to patch up the ship, but the sailors didn't stop at the level that housed the royal family. Or had, until half of it was bombed.

For once, Aniri was glad for First Daughter Nahali's stubbornness. She had refused to come with their mother, unwilling to reunite with Seledri. If Nahali had come to Jungali, she might well be dead. As it was, she was safely in Dharia, in command. Aniri had messaged her, using their mother's aetheroceiver, immediately after the attack.

SAMARIANS SKYSHIP ATTACK MOTHER INJURED SELEDRI KIDNAPPED

Aniri had left out that Ash was missing and the extent of the carnage within the city and deep within her heart. She had to trust that any Samirian spies that might intercept the message would already know what had happened that day in the Jungali capital of Bhakti.

Nahali had messaged back right away.

WILL SEND HEALERS SUPPLIES MUNITIONS PRAYERS

It was terse. But it was exactly what they needed. Nahali would make a fine Queen someday. Perhaps even *this* day. A shudder ran through Aniri once again at the thought of how gravely injured her mother was. Janak had refused to leave her side, and now that the immediate danger had passed, there was no force on earth that would make Aniri tell him he needed to.

Aniri's slow steps led eventually to her mother's guest room. The healer had gone, and her mother's handmaiden flitted about the room, keeping at the ready. Her mother lay on the bed. When Aniri had last visited, her mother had been asleep, and Janak had been in a chair, a hand laid upon hers. A startled flush of warmth filled Aniri to see her mother was now awake.

Janak kneeled next to her mother on the bed, propping pillows behind her and helping her into a more comfortable sitting position. She winced from the pain that caused, but the healer must have given her some vapors, because the tiny lines of pain that radiated from her mother's eyes before had been mostly erased. Seeing her mother move at all warmed the deathly chill that had taken hold of Aniri's heart.

She hurried to her mother's side of the bed, looking for some way to help, but Janak had already settled her into place. Rather than rising from the bed, he eased into it, sitting next to her and draping his arm behind her, like a protective embrace that enclosed all of the space around her. His gaze never left her face, and she gave him a small smile of gratitude in return. It was a tiny but surprisingly intimate moment that made Aniri falter in her greeting. That, and she wasn't sure what her mother knew about the state of things. Nor did Aniri want to alarm her while she was so gravely injured.

After a moment, Aniri said quietly, "How are you faring, Mother?"

"Better." But her voice was weak. "I'm sure I'll be up and about soon enough."

"The healer says you'll do no such thing." Janak's normally stoic face was a torment of half-lidded guilt, concern, and a sternness born of worry. Aniri could only imagine the internal pain he must be enduring, having failed to keep the assassin from lodging a bullet in the woman he loved. "You were extremely lucky," he chastised her, then turned to Aniri to explain.

"The healer says the bullet passed through without damaging anything tremendously serious. But she needs her rest. I've already lost two arguments in favor of more sleeping and heavier vapors. Perhaps you can impress upon your mother the importance of the Queen taking proper care of her health." Without giving Aniri a chance to say anything, he turned back to her mother. "I do not approve of you tempting the patience of the gods with insufficient rest. The world will carry on without you for a spell."

"You worry too much." Her mother put a hand to his cheek. Janak leaned ever so slightly into it and closed his eyes momentarily.

It was so gentle that it made Aniri's heart melt a little. The way Janak looked into her mother's eyes, Aniri was certain it had melted him all the way through.

"I already have a handmaiden to fuss over me," her mother said, quietly, "and now a healer too. I don't need you to worry about me any further."

"Are you firing me, Queen Amala?" His voice was soft, his face close to hers. And he was using her *name*. No one ever did that anymore, not even her Daughters. Aniri had noticed it before, but now her mother was awake to hear it as well.

"Can you fire a raksaka?" her mother mused in

a teasing voice. "They seem awfully difficult to get rid of."

"I assure you, my Queen, we have our weaknesses."

Aniri glanced at the handmaiden, who was quickly fleeing the room. Perhaps Aniri should leave them alone as well. Then her mother's aethero-ceiver, sitting on the table at her bedside, caught Aniri's eye. She should take it with her and message Nahali again, to see when they might expect those supplies to arrive. Especially the healers with their medicines and tinctures.

She tried to catch Janak's eye, but his attention was absorbed by his Queen.

"You have your own habit of catching bullets," she said, a small smile on her face. "I don't recall you being willing to take an appropriate rest when duty called."

"The last thing you should do is take lessons from me." The anguished look was back on Janak's face. "With regards to almost anything."

Aniri backed away from the bed. "I'll return when you're better rested, Mother."

But her mother didn't let her get two steps. "Aniri, wait." Her voice gained a bit of her normal command. "Janak told me about the

Samirians kidnapping Seledri. Have they contacted you yet?"

"No." Aniri rushed to soften that word and reduce the worry on her mother's face. "But I can't imagine they would hurt her, Mother. Else they would have done worse than steal her away."

Her mother nodded, but the worry didn't diminish. "Any word about Ash?"

Aniri's mouth opened to answer but nothing came out. She closed it again, then forced out another, "No." This time, she couldn't find any reassurances to offer, her heart iced over with the fear that had eaten at the edges of her mind. Her mother's sympathetic look just carved deeper into Aniri's frozen heart.

"Prince Malik sought my opinion on the security at the embassy, in order to move the prisoners there," Janak said. "And I hear they are missing as well. Is it possible he was at the embassy when the bombing started?"

"Yes. Well, not exactly."

Her mother's eyebrows had hiked up.

"Ash and I had…" *Pledged our hearts. Promised ourselves. Tried to make our vows.* "We had reconciled," she said stiffly. "We were at the temple next to the embassy."

Even Janak raised his eyebrows at that. He snuck a look to her mother, but she wasn't angry. More like trying to hide her smile. If Aniri's heart wasn't frozen, she would have smiled in return.

She forced herself to continue. "The blasts began at the gate. I was thrown. And unconscious for a few moments, possibly longer. When I roused, Ash was already gone. It's possible the prisoners found him first and took him after the blast. Janak, there were more than just two raksaka who entered through the gate."

Janak's eyes narrowed. "How many?"

"Four." A chill shuddered through her. If the prisoners had Ash, it was possible they would kill him. Probable even. For revenge. For spite. Or simply because he was a royal, and they were fleeing his city. With raksaka in their company, ones obviously bent on killing the royals in the capital, Aniri couldn't imagine why they would keep him alive, even as her heart desperately protested that thought.

"And the raksaka entered through the gate," Janak said.

"Well, there wasn't exactly a gate left after the Samirians dropped their bomb upon it. Or much of the street or the embassy entrance for that matter."

"That does not make sense." Janak's normal scowling face returned.

"I took a knock to the head, Janak. But I know what I saw."

"I'm not questioning you, Aniri," he said softly. "But raksaka would hardly need to bomb the gate to gain entrance to the city."

It was Aniri's turn to lift her eyebrows. Of course. Raksaka could steal in any way they wished. "So the bombings. They were simply to terrorize us. Perhaps provide a distraction."

"Or provide a way back out."

"But they never intended to leave the way they came. Seledri's kidnapping wasn't by opportunity, it was planned. The raksaka who stole her from the roof was prepared with a harness, and..." Aniri stalled out. *The aetheroceiver.* "And they had a means for messaging the skyship when they were ready."

Janak nodded. "The one who attacked your mother had an aetheroceiver strapped to his back."

Aniri glanced around the room. The raksaka's body had long been removed, and the handmaiden had taken away the floor coverings soaked with his blood, but the aetheroceiver still lay tucked in the corner of the room. Aniri hurried over to retrieve it and bring it back to the bed.

"They must have had a plan for escape from the beginning." She set it down next to her mother's aetheroceiver. They were twins in shape and function, but the Samirian was steel-colored and smaller. "They had four raksaka originally, more than enough to effect an attack on the palace. But then why the bombings?"

"Perhaps they intended to liberate the prisoners as well," Janak said. "A line of bombings to clear a path from the palace to the gate would facilitate the escape of a large group of non-raksaka individuals."

Aniri nodded. "And when they found the prisoners at the gate, they changed their plans. Two remained behind to shepherd out the prisoners, while two went ahead to take the palace."

"They likely intended to use the aetheroceiver to let the *Dagger* know of their success at the palace. Or failure," Janak said. "Battle has a way of shifting plans."

Aniri frowned as she studied the Samirian aetheroceiver. Could she unlock this one, like she had Devesh's? Aniri picked up the box, examining all the small, intricately carved symbols. "The code has a pattern. One that the Jungali have copied."

"Our tinkers designed the code into the box as well," her mother said.

Janak scowled. "It has always struck me as rather poor security."

"But simple," Aniri said. "And easy to remember under duress. Besides, the enemy may break open the aetheroceiver, regardless, once it is in their hands. Which I will have our tinkers do in short order, should this not work." Aniri ran her fingers across the box. It took three symbols to unlock—a tinker, a crown, and a ship—the three symbols of Samirian prowess. She quickly found the tinker, plus a sleek Samirian trade ship with sails turned sideways that was clearly the skyship in disguise. That left at least a dozen crowns—she would have to try them all. By the fifth one, it unfolded, revealing the cranks and the code wheel of the aetheroceiver within.

Aniri dug through the box, but there were no messages left waiting to be discovered. She glanced to the spot where the fallen raksaka had been. "What if they never had time to message the *Dagger?*"

"They had to have messaged at least once to arrange transport," Janak said.

"But they may not know their raksaka is now dead."

"You think they're still expecting another message?" Janak asked skeptically.

Aniri gestured to the empty spot where the raksaka had been. "If this raksaka had survived, but missed the rendezvous with the *Dagger*…"

Janak frowned. "…he would be working his way out of the city. And trying to meet the rendezvous point with the prisoners."

"And, perhaps, sending them another message."

Janak straightened in his place next to the Queen, although obviously not intending to leave her side. "It's worth a try, my lady."

Aniri cranked the wind-up of the aetheroceiver. It whirred and clacked its tiny metal gears.

"Janak, what if they have the prince with them?" She didn't want to speak her fears that he was already dead, but now that they might actually find where they had taken him…

"Determine the location for the rendezvous first," Janak said, softly. "Then we'll find a way to retrieve the prince." Of course, Janak could help, if he was willing to leave the Queen's side. Even if he wasn't, she had an entire capital filled with Jungali who would give their lives for their prince. And, with any luck, soon the *Prosperity* would be flight-worthy again to help as well.

Aniri took the tiny pencil and paper tucked in the back of the aetheroceiver and wrote her first message.

CALLING DAGGER

It was vague enough. Hopefully someone on the other end would be waiting. A long minute stretched into two.

Aniri tapped her foot. "When we were above the *Dagger* in the *Prosperity*, the Samirians sailed east and kept going."

"They could easily have crossed the horizon and circled back."

Aniri nodded and wound the aetheroceiver once more. "Maybe they've already—"

The aetheroceiver started clacking, spitting out a response. Aniri's heart thudded in her chest as she took the symbols one by one and transcribed them. She gritted her teeth halfway through, but finished it before straightening and reading it aloud.

THE DASHING THIRD DAUGHTER I PRESUME

Janak let out a low breath. "It's Natesh."

Her mother said, "Aniri, that doesn't mean—"

The aetheroceiver started clacking again,

making Aniri jump. A new message was coming through. She transcribed it again, her hand gripping the pencil so tight her bones ached. A shiver ran the full length of her body as she read it aloud.

HAVE YOUR PRINCE AND SISTER

She picked up the aetheroceiver and clutched it. She wanted to throw it across the room. No—out the window and down the thousand foot ravine outside. Her hands shook as she slowly set it down.

"What does he want?" her mother asked, her voice tight.

"He wants what he's wanted all along." Janak's voice had gone grave as well.

"He wants the crown of Samir," Aniri said. "And of Dharia and Jungali, too."

"Does he seriously expect we will surrender our countries?" Her mother's voice grew stronger, indignant, but it didn't matter. Aniri knew it didn't matter. "And how can he expect to threaten royalty like that? If he harms them, he has to know there will be a price."

"He's not concerned about any price we can exact," Janak said.

"They have an *armada*, Mother," Aniri said dully, the fog threatening to press in on her mind once more. *They have Ash.* They would kill him if she didn't surrender his country to them. And Ash, should he live, would never forgive her for that. But Aniri had already seen the destruction that one ship could do.

One.

The aetheroceiver clacked again. It was like the bones of a skeleton rattling against her back. Her stomach clenched as she watched the symbols spit from the device in a long, thin parchment of demands. When it stopped, she just looked at it for a moment, unwilling to render the black printed lines into something with meaning. Because she knew all too well what it would say. Her hands shook as she forced her eyes to compare symbol-to-letter and etch each transcribed letter, one by one, onto the strip.

She held it up, but she couldn't force her lips to say the words.

SURRENDER NOW AND I WILL SPARE EVERYONE

"What does it say?" Her mother's voice was strained.

Aniri crumpled up the thin piece of aethero-ceiver paper she had just transcribed and threw it on the floor.

"It says we're at war."

About the Author

Susan Kaye Quinn is a rocket scientist turned speculative fiction author who now uses her PhD to invent cool stuff in books. Currently writing hopepunk climate fiction, but her works include SciFi, YA, gritty future-noir, steampunk romance, and that one middle grade fantasy. Her bestselling novels and short stories have been optioned for Virtual Reality, translated into German and French, and featured in several anthologies.

www.susankayequinn.com